PRAISE FOR *EMBERS ON THE WIND*

"A vital stop along the Underground Railroad, the historic Whittaker House should be a symbol of freedom and hope. Instead, it cries and whispers into the modern era, telling stories of all that was risked and lost by those who sought refuge there. Throughout this spellbinding, heartbreaking novel, Lisa Williamson Rosenberg weaves a tapestry from the lives that are bound to one another through a singular event. As this shared history comes into focus, readers come to understand the poignant and devastating impact of one word: *almost*."

—Bobi Conn, author of *In the Shadow of the Valley*

"Lisa Williamson Rosenberg's *Embers on the Wind* is a delight that will keep you turning pages to the very end. Her lyrical writing transports us from the nineteenth-century Underground Railroad to the Brooklyn of today, and in Rosenberg's hands, the history is as vibrant as present-day life. The women in this book are searching for freedom, and luckily for us readers, they bring us along for the magical ride."

—Cary Barbor, host of NPR's Gulf Coast Life Book Club

"*Embers* is a story that pulls you in with richly drawn characters and a skillfully intertwined plot twist that you'll never see coming. It's a perfect and delightful read, entertaining from beginning to shocking end."

—Dawn Porter, award-winning film producer
and director of *John Lewis: Good Trouble*

"A gorgeously layered novel, cinematic in scope and yet hauntingly intimate. *Embers on the Wind* crosses the barriers between the living and the dead, illuminating how intergenerational trauma reverberates through history. An incandescent debut, luminous and mesmerizing."

-Marco Rafalà, author of *How Fires End*

"Ambitious and enthralling, *Embers on the Wind* is a richly told story of women bound by generations past and by spirits struggling to uncover truths and gain some semblance of freedom. Gripping and harrowing, start to finish."

—Susan Bernhard, author of *Winter Loon*

"An intricate, magical, suspenseful, and expertly crafted tale of how the devastating collective trauma experienced by Black American mothers and daughters is woven through time and connects generations. The force of this powerful story held me in an ever-tightening grip until the very end. It blew me away."

—William Dameron, author of *The Lie:*
A Memoir of Two Marriages, Catfishing & Coming Out

"Centering on a Berkshires home that was part of the Underground Railroad, *Embers on the Wind* bends time to bring together a kaleidoscope of Black and white lives that seek, shatter, and rise in a stunning conclusion. Lisa Williamson Rosenberg has written a powerful, haunting tale of the modern African American diaspora."

—Laurie Lico Albanese, author of *Stolen Beauty* and *Hester*

"Lisa Williamson Rosenberg captures both the conflagration of slavery and its ignited sprawl through time in this stirring novel of linked stories surrounding Whittaker House—a location imbued with Morrison's 'site of memory' connecting people by time, circumstance, and of course, place. Whittaker House is as impressively rendered on the page as it is in our collective literary imagination of places with long memories and the people who comprise and/or curate the histories and stories of them. *Embers on the Wind* speaks of our connections—temporal, relative, corporeal, and spiritual—in ways that reckon with an ever-present past."

—M Shelly Conner, author of *everyman*

EMBERS

on the

WIND

EMBERS

on the

WIND

A Novel

Lisa Williamson Rosenberg

Text copyright © 2022 by Lisa Williamson Rosenberg
All rights reserved.

No part of this book may be reproduced, or stored in a retrieval system, or transmitted in any form or by any means, electronic, mechanical, photocopying, recording, or otherwise, without express written permission of the publisher.

Published by Little A, New York

www.apub.com

Amazon, the Amazon logo, and Little A are trademarks of Amazon.com, Inc., or its affiliates.

ISBN-13: 9781542036863 (hardcover)
ISBN-10: 1542036860 (hardcover)

ISBN-13: 9781542036887 (paperback)
ISBN-10: 1542036887 (paperback)

Cover design by Micaela Alcaino

Printed in the United States of America

First edition

For Jon

If a house burns down, it's gone, but the place—the picture of it—stays, and not just in my rememory, but out there, in the world.

—Beloved, Toni Morrison

Contents

1

MIDNIGHT

Little Annie

Whittaker House, Monterey, Massachusetts, October 2019

It's like being awakened from a dream, a real-feeling dream where you didn't know you were sleeping. Like being pulled from a thick, muddy river bottom into cold, clear water. Though last I checked, rivers don't have candles, and this place is full of them. Voices murmur around me: a prayer I've never heard. I can't see any people at first, just feel heat from their bodies and breath. Something in me quickens, and I get a notion that one of my children is nearby, like God opened the world just a crack to show me my boy. Louis, baby? Are you here?

I do know this place. The first time I came, my companion was a pregnant girl by the name of Clementine. When the pattyrollers came, I got free but had to leave her behind. I can feel her here too, my sweet friend and the child she called Birdie.

Now the candle lights dance, showing me parts of people: a sleeve, a shoulder, hands, and fingers intertwined all around the table. But where am I? Where is my body? The mangled hands I'm known by?

This massive figure is not my own, which was light and compact, no bigger than a young boy. I look down to see heavy white hands holding the brown ones on either side of me. Thick white fingers—five on each hand, making a full ten, which proves my hunch. From Craven County all the way to Wilkes, anyone who ever heard of Little Annie Durham knew I hadn't but eight.

Dominique

In the glimmering light, shadows dance and faces become glowing masks of themselves—each participant hoping for the miracle of a reunion. Lady Leanna, holding hands with two of the Seekers who took their seats early, lifts her chin, beginning to rock. Dominique is just as determined to make contact as the rest of the group members, but the mindset eludes her as she checks on her little boy, who's sitting on the floor in the corner, playing on his iPad. If she had childcare, Dominique would have been here in time to secure the spot she's entitled to, by Lady Leanna's side.

The Seekers—named after their freedom-seeking ancestors—wouldn't even be here at Whittaker House if not for Dominique. It was she who found the aged seer's business card on the bulletin board at the Red Lion Inn in Stockbridge: *Lady Leanna, Mistress of the Occult*—curling font full of promise and potency. From a Google search, Dominique learned that Lady Leanna's real name is Leigh-Ann Whittaker—of the Tyringham-Monterey Whittakers, the abolitionist family who built this house 225 years ago, one of many Underground Railroad safehouses in Berkshire County. Some fugitives got no farther than this house, perishing within these very walls or elsewhere on the grounds.

Lady Leanna has led a few séances for the Seekers before this, but tonight is the first time she's invited them to Whittaker House. And

Dominique has a feeling in her gut that this is the place where he passed through: the ancestor of Grand-mère's stories.

She sensed it the moment she stepped out of the car. Gazing up at the sprawling farmhouse, whose chipped red paint looked iridescent in the moonlight, her pulse quickened. Dominique woke Sidney, which wasn't easy, then pulled the drowsy child up the gravel walk.

Lady Leanna stood in the doorway, disapproving. "You've brought your baby again."

Sidney is three, not a baby. Under normal circumstances he would have corrected the mischaracterization, but Lady Leanna's grand proportions, pallor, severe gaze, and towering, silver-white hair intimidated him.

"There was no one to watch him," Dominique explained. "But he'll be good, I promise."

When Lady Leanna ushered them inside, Dominique could smell the package-fresh autumnal potpourri mingling with old wood—as if someone had taken pains to cover up the odor of something sinister. All these old safehouses have stories to tell, some less savory than others. The floorboards creaked, echoing the deep, metallic ticking of a grandfather clock whose face lit up as Lady Leanna's candle sailed by. Sidney squeezed Dominique's hand but didn't complain about the scary darkness as another child might. He's used to being dragged along, to observing these meetings in murky alcoves, the candles, the grown-ups' excited whispers, the chants aimed at reaching the dead.

While the group members took turns kissing Lady Leanna's hand, Dominique imagined how this would look to Michelle, her nonbelieving ex-girlfriend. Eight young Black people groveling before an old white lady dressed in beads and lace. But Lady Leanna says touching a seer with your lips as well as your fingers quickens communication with the spirits. Besides, Michelle is not here.

Sidney is fine now, calm with his iPad. He's so good. Dominique glances at him once more in the middle of the initial incantation and sees he's not alone. A little girl about his age, with fluffy coils of hair, is sitting beside him, delicate chin on his shoulder, eyes appearing to take in the images on his device, just as natural as can be. Sidney either doesn't notice her or doesn't mind the company. *I should worry,* Dominique thinks, since she doesn't know who the other child is or where she came from. But a worrying sort of mother wouldn't bring Sidney to a midnight séance at all.

Dominique exhales and adds her voice to the last lines of the chant as Lady Leanna shudders, rocking more violently. The whites of the old woman's eyes shine in the candlelight. The deep and scratchy voice that comes from her throat is not her own.

Little Annie

"Who's here?" I say aloud. Ha! The voice—that's mine, hoarse and craggy. Clementine used to say I sounded like an old man with a throat full of ash.

Someone whispers, "Holy shit, it worked!"

"Welcome, spirit." A woman's voice comes at me through the dark. "To whom are we speaking?"

I identify myself, thinking he'd recognize his mama's name. "Annie. Little Annie's what I was called on account of my size."

"Hello, Annie, thank you for—"

"What do you want?" I've never had patience for niceties. Is he here or not?

Oh, Louis. How I've searched for that boy. Followed him all the way to Canada. At first, wherever I asked, people shook their heads. No one had heard of him. Then I came across a young girl who said she'd known a Louis in Queen's Bush. She was a pretty brown skinned girl whose eyes filled with tears when she talked about my boy. I noticed that—along with the fact that she was big with child. Louis was on the run, this young girl said. A man who looked like him had killed a white man just south of the Canadian border. It wasn't Louis, the girl said, she swore it wasn't, but witnesses said it was. Last she heard he'd escaped aboard a ship bound for England.

"When he gets there, he'll send for me," the girl said, words sure, but voice full of doubt. I understood her meaning. If that baby inside her was kin to me, I might have ended my journey right there. But why, if I didn't hear it from my own son, should I believe that girl was anything to me or my Louis? I put her and her baby right out of my mind.

Louis was gone. Taken from me a second time. It ripped open the scar that had grown thick over my heart, turning my thoughts to the other children, lost or sold years before. They were always in my dreams, along with Clementine, the young friend I'd left here in Massachusetts. On the darkest nights, my mind returned to North Carolina, to the day they cut me and fed my fingers to the hogs. I was stealing bread for my children, just a bit that no one would miss. Those nights in Canada, I'd feel the spaces where the fingers used to be and know that only part of me made it north.

The woman who spoke before says, "I'm trying to find someone who knew an ancestor of mine. A man."

"What name?"

"I don't know his name. But mine is Dominique. Dominique Sowande."

Sowande means nothing to me. As far as I can see, she's a big, high yellow girl with dark, undone hair falling over her shoulders. No sign of my children in her.

"What'd he look like, your ancestor?"

"Black," Dominique Sowande says. "Midnight black."

Midnight black sounds about right for all six of my lost boys, but I keep hope to myself for now. I don't know who she is, this Dominique Sowande with long, loose hair, asking after her kin. I'll give her something—just not an answer. Not yet.

"*Hmph*. Your 'midnight-black' ancestor wouldn't have come in the house," I tell her. "He would have hidden out back in the root cellar. You know about the root cellar? About the fire and the ones who died?"

I take her silence for a no. I look at all their faces, at the candles and these big white hands I've got. Thinking on what I know from my own journey, my own stay in the root cellar of this house. By the time Clementine and I came to hide down in that old cellar, the ashes had been swept away, but the spirits of those who'd burned alive remained. I listened to their stifled cries, their story of the one who made it out.

What will I tell this yellow girl?

This is true: There wasn't enough space for more than three down in the cellar—not enough space, food, air, or hope—but there were ten when it happened. The kerosene lamp tipped over and started it. The terror inside spread as fast as the flames. The door that swung open let in the gust of wind that fed the fire, which spread quickly throughout the root cellar. The walls were dry from a recent drought. The floor was dust. The howling from within was heard too late. The one who heard the howling first—she froze for too long before running for help.

Those parts are true. So is this. The three who should have moved on and finished their journey into Canada, making room for the next three, had stayed put. It was not safe to go. There were catchers, patty-rollers, active in the vicinity. A message got lost. Confusion had messed the plans of the helpers, the station masters, the conductors. More of those who sought freedom moved in before the others could move out. The root cellar filled beyond what it could safely hold.

This next is the part I guessed.

One seeker of freedom was a beautiful black-skinned boy named Louis, who had loved a mangy spotted dog back in North Carolina. He had always loved dogs, but loved this one most. Once upon a time, Louis had a family—an eight-fingered mama and five younger brothers—but they were a distant memory along with the day he was sold away. The spotted dog was all he loved. And now, packed tight in the cellar with the others, Louis dozed and dreamed of his dog back home. His lids opened halfway and, in his half state of half sleep, he saw a shadow dance on the wall and imagined it was his dog. When Louis reached for the friend he longed for, he tipped the lamp, whose flame caught the dust and the dry and led to calamity.

It did not take long. By the time the woman who first heard the howling returned with others bearing pails of water, the howling had stopped. The flames still licked at the stone steps leading up out of the cellar. But when they called to those inside, the calls were answered with silence. Still, the door was ajar.

And when the embers had cooled, they counted out the bones to make bodies and found just nine, meaning one got free. That part is also true.

2

CELLAR SPIRITS

How could we know we'd never leave the root cellar? We were on the verge of hope when our journey was halted, not by dogs or pattyrollers, but by fire. Our dreams hang stagnant for centuries, till Girl comes and stirs the dust. She smells our sorrow, hears our songs echoing inside her mind. For all her life, when she thinks of us, Girl's heart will beat in rhythm to one word:
 Almost.

Whittaker House

Boston and Monterey, Massachusetts, May 1983
"Girl, you best not be sulking about Marcus." Tisha sucked her teeth and gave Pam an affectionate swat across the aisle of the van. "We're going to have us some fun on this trip."

The vehicle's battery coughed and died before they could so much as leave the curb. Miss Bell and Miss Wanetta, chaperones from the Columbia Point housing project youth center, ushered the kids off and made them stand in the blazing sun while the driver got a jump start. It was unseasonably hot: nearly 90 degrees and barely 8:00 a.m. Pam was already sweating.

Tisha and Shay got loud, showing off for the boys with their rendition of "Last Night a DJ Saved My Life," but Pam stayed quiet, in her thoughts. Marcus was supposed to say goodbye in person. She could imagine him sixteen flights up in his mother's apartment, gazing down at her with his mouth twisted.

Until she found out Marcus wasn't coming, Pam had been excited about going to Whittaker House in the Berkshire Mountains. Tisha, Shay, and Walt all had family down south whom they visited, and Marcus had lived a year with his great-grandmother in New Jersey. But Pam had never been anywhere. This was her big chance to see something new. And Whittaker House was supposed to be a big deal. It wasn't a museum, but it had something to do with Black history, which was cool. Pam imagined it would be fancy like the places she admired in the issues of *House Beautiful* that they used to keep at the salon where Mama had worked before she got too sick. The magazine rooms were full of bold-colored sofas and mirror walls, or pink-and-purple-flowered Laura Ashley curtains and throw blankets. Marcus had always laughed at her tastes and aspirations, but Pam loved picturing the two of them walking hand in hand through some fine, high-ceilinged room with deluxe gold-trimmed wallpaper.

Then Marcus got caught with weed on him and was disinvited from the leadership trip. So there went that.

"Forget his tired ass." Shay laughed and pulled Pam by the arm, forcing her to join their dance.

The van broke down again on the way to Monterey. The boys hooted profanities at the driver while Miss Bell and Miss Wanetta shushed them. Pam didn't mind the stop. Through the window on her right, she saw trees climbing up a mountainside. To her left was water, shining silver through a proscenium of greenery. Far from Dorchester, not a crumbling brick to be seen. The van's *eau de piss* scent recalled the housing project's elevators, but looking at all that green, Pam could breathe.

They were expecting Whittaker House to be pearly and pristine, with pillars out front and maybe a swimming pool in back. A rose garden closed off by gates that only a groundskeeper had access to. A first-class joint, predicted Randy, who knew about rich people from his cousin who worked at a country club in Marblehead.

Whittaker House was nothing like that. Owned by a family named Burke, it was red with peeling paint, though not what you'd see on a storefront in Dorchester. This paint peeled like it meant to, in tasteful spots here and there. "Distressed," the magazines called it. There were no gates, no roses, but wildflowers growing every which way on either side of the gravel driveway.

Their hostess was a big, tall, proud-smiling white woman in a long black dress and a purple shawl with shimmery silver fibers woven throughout. She wore her black hair in a towering bun atop her head, which made her appear even taller. Beside her was a white man clutching a coffee mug, and three teenage boys.

"Welcome to Whittaker House." The matron spread her arms, palms facing the arrivals as if she were blessing a congregation. "I am Leigh-Ann Whittaker-Burke."

"That's a witch right there," whispered Shay, earning a sharp look from Miss Bell.

The hostess continued. "This is my husband, Calvin, and these are our boys."

Mr. Burke, shorter than Mrs. Whittaker-Burke, bald and pink-faced, wore a rigid smile, which gave Pam the impression that the invitation had come from his wife, not him.

The Columbia Point boys—Randy, Davis, and Walt—stared at the white boys and the white boys stared back. If they were in Dorchester, Pam thought, they'd fight because that's what you did. Here in the Berkshire Mountains, no one knew what was expected when Black and white met, so everyone nodded or said "Hi," without smiling. Then Big

Mrs. Whittaker-Burke announced that she was taking the Columbia Point kids and their chaperones on a tour of the grounds.

"This way." She gestured toward the side of the lawn that was open, free of trees, and wrapped around the house. In Mrs. Whittaker-Burke's arm—though white and modestly cloaked—Pam detected the shake and swing of copious flesh shared by the arms of mothers she had known all her life. Mama's arms had moved like that—as she combed and braided and twisted her clients' hair—before cancer had sucked the substance from her bones.

Mrs. Whittaker-Burke led them around back, to where a sunporch and patio looked out on an enormous yard. *Yard* was a misnomer. It was a meadow with flower beds, little hills, and a pond—like the Public Garden gone wild. Instead of a stone wall for a border, there were real woods on the far end.

Mrs. Whittaker-Burke beamed at them all—a stiff-jawed smile like you'd make for a camera. "Our family built this homestead in 1794, not long after the Commonwealth of Massachusetts was established. The Whittakers were well-known abolitionists. Does everyone know what that means?"

She said it like a teacher looking around for a show of hands, but no one wanted to be a know-it-all. Mrs. Whittaker-Burke took their silent stares for ignorance.

"Abolitionists were opposed to slavery and fought bravely to end the practice." Mrs. Whittaker-Burke's smile remained firm and bright. "On these very grounds, my family harbored numerous runaway slaves making their way to Canada." She elaborated, creating circles in the air with her generous arms, offering a narrative about how her ancestors had supported the kids' ancestors on the way to freedom. Miss Bell and Miss Wanetta stood by, lips stretched into beatific smiles as if they were in church, chins lifted, senses on high alert for disrespect among the kids. One snicker or suck of the teeth would be met by a fierce glare.

Mrs. Whittaker-Burke walked them over the hills and around the pond, then stopped to point out a wooden door in the side of a hillock, several yards from the woods.

"This leads to the root cellar, where runaway slaves hid until they were able to secure safe passage to Canada." The door was latched from the outside, Pam observed. Anyone hiding inside would need someone to let them out. It was both prison and sanctuary.

Pam said, "Can we see inside?"

Mrs. Whittaker-Burke turned to her abruptly, gaze at once intimate and appraising. "Would you like that?"

"I don't know," said Pam at the same time that Shay said, "Why not?"

"It may be unsettling." Mrs. Whittaker-Burke ignored Shay, continuing to study Pam. "Perhaps you will see the inside at a later point this weekend. Perhaps not."

"So, this is where y'all are going to hide *us*?" said Walt as Miss Bell hushed him.

"Not a chance!" Their hostess chuckled, taking the jest in stride. She moved her guests along, drawing their attention to a pretty cottage at the top of a hill. "That's where you will be staying for the weekend—when you're not swimming, sightseeing, or hiking, of course."

Pam was crushed. She'd envisioned telling Marcus all about her stay in the big, luxurious house, imagining an enormous canopy bed with Laura Ashley sheets. She walked behind Mrs. Whittaker-Burke then, wondering about the fugitives who'd been hidden in the root cellar, about the abolitionists who had taken charge of them, choosing when to fasten and when to unfasten the latch on the cellar door.

⁓

That first night, after a cookout dinner of burgers and hot dogs, Mr. Burke said they could have a bonfire in the meadow behind the house. Two of the Burke boys got it going while the other played funk and R & B out of a boom box. It was a good mix. The boys had put some effort into accommodating Black kids from the city.

"Bet they watched them some *Soul Train*," Shay guessed under her breath, making Pam giggle.

By the leaping orange flames, under the spell of Teddy Pendergrass, everyone began to relax, including the adults, who retreated to the indoors. When "Get Up, Get Down, Get Funky, Get Loose" came on, Shay jumped up to dance, shaking her skinny hips till Pam and Walt joined in. Pam was a good dancer. Unlike Shay, she was not skinny. Pam was short, but had curves in all the right places, which made her moves graceful and sultry.

Shay whispered to Pam that one of the white boys, the older one with brown hair hanging long around his chin, kept staring at her. "Marcus wouldn't like that."

"Wouldn't he?" Pam felt bold enough to smile the boy's way.

∽

When the moon was high, the embers of the bonfire dwindling, Mr. Burke escorted the Columbia Point party up the hill to the cottage—a renovated barn with three large guest bedrooms, two baths, and a kitchen. The girls were to sleep in one bedroom, the boys in another, while Miss Bell and Miss Wanetta would take the third. In the girls' room, there was a bunk bed that Pam shared with Tisha— Pam on top—plus a separate twin, which Shay claimed for herself. The sheets, Pam noted, were crisp and white and printed with tiny green leaves. They smelled fresh and mildly floral. Pam checked the label, which was faded but still clear enough: LAURA ASHLEY. In charismatic block letters embroidered inside an oval.

"For real?" Pam said aloud and laughed. Tisha kicked her mattress from beneath and told her to knock it off.

After Miss Wanetta shut off the light, Pam stayed awake, relishing the softness of her down pillow, the freshness of the night breeze that billowed pale lavender curtains through the open window. From where she lay, Pam could see the full grounds of Whittaker House, illuminated by a nearly full moon.

And here came Mrs. Whittaker-Burke—dressed in a long, dark robe, candle in one hand—striding from the patio through the gardens, across the meadow. By the door to the root cellar, Mrs. Whittaker-Burke reached into a pocket and took out a second candle, which she lit with the first, kneeling, burying the butt in the ground. Mrs. Whittaker-Burke repeated the exercise again and again, removing candles from her pockets, lighting and planting each one, until she had created a large circle in front of the root cellar door. Standing amid the ring of light, she raised her arms to the sky.

"Y'all, check it out!" Pam swung her upper body over the rail to reach Tisha's bunk, shaking her friend's limp arm. *"Tisha."* Who would not be roused. Nor would Shay, so Pam returned to the window, marveling alone at their hostess's performance.

Mrs. Whittaker-Burke was dancing. Really dancing: waving her arms, swinging her hips, twirling around so the ends of her robe and nightgown floated around her slippered feet. Her voice came faintly through the window, chanting against the wind. She threw back her head like a wolf howling at the moon.

"Y'all," Pam said again without taking her eyes off the scene. Still no response from Tisha or Shay. There was no way Pam would be able to describe this in a way that her friends would believe. "Damn."

Mrs. Whittaker-Burke continued her dance till the candles melted down to the height of the grass, then stopped and clapped her hands. She spun and faced Pam's window. Pam kept still, hoping the woman would not see her with the darkened room at her back. But Mrs. Whittaker-Burke lifted her face toward the girl, raised one finger, and placed it to her lips.

In the morning, when Pam shared her story of the late-night spectacle with Tisha and Shay, the former was skeptical, the latter vindicated.

"Told you she was a witch," said Shay.

"Right?" said Pam. "What kind of spell you think she was doing?"

Tisha laughed. "Both of y'all calm down. Rich white ladies don't dance around in the woods with candles. They just *don't*."

"I know what I saw."

Taller, heavier than the other two, Tisha was the maternal one, the voice of reason. She put an arm around Pam. "Trust me. You were dreaming."

When they joined the family for a pancake breakfast on the sunporch, Pam wondered whether she would be singled out with a meaningful glance from the hostess. But Mrs. Whittaker-Burke—looking decidedly un-witchy in a yellow oxford tucked into sky-blue pleated pants—had only wide, indiscriminate smiles and pleasantries for them all.

Pam allowed herself to be distracted by the day's endeavors: a woodsy hike in nearby Sheffield, a picnic and a visit to a chicken-and-llama farm in Otis, a swim at Lake Garfield right in town—all facilitated by three volunteers from the town. Pam and Tisha complained about the many bugs and sharp branches on the hike. Shay and the boys were displeased by the stench of the chickens and the advances of the llamas, who accosted them with curious velvet snouts. Everyone loved the lake, though town regulars cast suspicious glances at the inner-city visitors, heads shaking at the volume of their laughter, the roughness with which they pushed and shoved each other into the water.

Late afternoon saw the Columbia Point group back at the cottage, exhausted, falling into beds for a nap before supper. As Pam drifted into slumber, she saw the root cellar door in the moonlight once again. Mrs. Whittaker-Burke was nowhere in sight, but Pam herself stood amid the circle of candles on the patch of grass in front of the cellar. Their lights flickered and switched in the wind as before, but rather than dwindling, they grew until they were at least Pam's own height. To her horror, faces began taking shape in the wax, followed by human bodies. They surrounded her, eyes mournful and somber, lips uttering unintelligible words, arms reaching for her. As Pam searched for an escape, the door to the root cellar swung open, revealing the formidable specter of Mrs. Whittaker-Burke. The whites of the hostess's eyes gleamed like embers as she pressed the same finger to her lips.

"Hey!"

Pam awoke to discover that Tisha was bouncing her mattress from beneath. "They're calling us! Get up!"

As Pam dressed for dinner, the image of human candles with reaching arms stayed with her.

⌒☉

Pam kept her distance from Mrs. Whittaker-Burke throughout the dinner, which consisted of barbecued chicken, baked ham, and beans. The hostess, wearing a red apron over her denim dress, was in high spirits, chatting amiably with any guest who crossed her path, collecting Styrofoam plates and cups as they got used and abandoned, refilling the potato chip baskets and lemonade pitchers as needed. Was Shay right? Was she a witch after all, able to infiltrate dreams?

Mrs. Whittaker-Burke passed in and out of the sunporch door, occasionally assisted by her husband or one of her sons, but none of the Columbia Point guests crossed the threshold into the main part of the house.

When the chicken and ham were eaten, tunes beginning to pump from the Burke boys' boom box, Pam relaxed somewhat, sitting with

Tisha and Walt on the edge of a planter on the patio. She felt a warm hand on her shoulder and looked up into the expectant face of Mrs. Whittaker-Burke.

"I thought we might speak."

Ignoring the curious glances of her friends, Pam allowed Mrs. Whittaker-Burke to escort her across the patio and sunporch, through a screen door, and into a kitchen straight from the pages of *House Beautiful*. The walls were tiled in a cool blue, the surfaces a finished pine, from the enormous kitchen island with bowls full of fruit to the lowered rafters with hooks from which pots and pans were hanging. The whole kitchen, Pam gauged, was as big as the apartment she and Pop shared in Dorchester. On one wall, a banner embroidered with daisies read BLESS THIS HOUSE. And clearly someone had. How white people lived!

Mrs. Whittaker-Burke took note of her awe. "Do you like it?"

"It's like a magazine."

Mrs. Whittaker-Burke gave an appreciative nod and brought Pam to the sink, where they each washed their hands with lemon-scented soap that scratched pleasantly but foamed up soft like shampoo.

"You are a dreamer," stated Mrs. Whittaker-Burke, proffering a clean blue hand towel. Pam dried her hands in silence, unsure of whether the hostess was referring to her recent dreams or making a general inference about her character. Mrs. Whittaker-Burke clarified: "You believe in the ghosts of your ancestors."

"Ghosts?" said Pam.

"Yes, ghosts." Mrs. Whittaker-Burke took several bakery boxes from a cabinet, directing Pam to the kitchen island, where they arranged an assortment of miniature cakes on a pair of white oblong platters.

"As I recall," said Mrs. Whittaker-Burke as they worked, "you were the one who asked yesterday about seeing the inside of the root cellar."

"I didn't say anything about ghosts."

"But you think about your ancestors a good deal?" said Mrs. Whittaker-Burke. "Those who toiled in the plantations, who escaped and faced such peril on their way to Canada?"

"Not really," said Pam, guarded. The truth was she had not given much thought to her ancestors at all until learning the story of the house and the root cellar. Her own present life was enough to handle: keeping Marcus's attention, distracting herself from the ache left by her mother's passing, caring for Pop the best she could, saving her last bit of attention for schoolwork. There had been no room for ancestors or ghosts.

"What do you think those fugitive slaves would make of you and your friends if they could see you today? All the liberties you have, all the access, the opportunities?"

"Opportunities?" said Pam. "You mean like coming here?" For the trip had been touted to Pam and her friends as a great opportunity. It was the only one she could think of offhand.

Mrs. Whittaker-Burke stared at her in surprise. "Why yes. I suppose it is indeed an opportunity. To be here of your own free will. For the sake of pleasure." She gave a perfunctory laugh. "I hadn't recognized the irony in that. You make an excellent point."

Pam had not intended to make a point but smiled nevertheless as Mrs. Whittaker-Burke tilted her head.

"I've just given it a bit of thought," she said. "I have decided not to allow you inside the cellar after all."

"Why not?"

"It would be too distressing for you and your friends to come so close to such a painful piece of your history." Her voice dropped on the last syllable of the word, indicating that there was to be no dispute. Indeed, before Pam could question her decision, Mrs. Whittaker-Burke set down the last cake and brushed her hands free of powdered sugar.

"I'll be back in two shakes." She gave no explanation but disappeared into a room beyond the kitchen, leaving her young guest alone.

Pam could hear the music outside—"Hot Stuff" by Donna Summer—and longed to rejoin her friends. Though the day's heat had lingered through dinner outdoors, it was getting chilly in the kitchen.

Pam shivered, noticing a book of matches and a fat yellow candle on the counter by the stove. She stepped over and ran a finger along the smooth wax surface. If she lit it, would it grow and reach for her? Before Pam knew it, she had done the thing and was staring into the flame. The candle didn't sprout arms or a face, but there was magic in its shape-shifting light. It stretched tall like a woman in a cream-colored cloak, shrunk short and squat like one of Snow White's dwarfs. Now in the flame's halo, there was Mama, strong and whole like before the illness came, giving Pam *the look*—full of warning and reprimand, but love all at once. Pam missed *the look* more than Mama's smile. Strange, how a little shoot of fire could dance as if alive, making you see things that weren't there.

The chill persisted, a darkness falling around Pam's shoulders, seeping into her bones as if the moon had invaded her chest. She heard someone's breath catch just behind her, turned, and saw a girl. Close to her age, her own height. Light skinned, with a cloud of wild, softly curling hair. The girl was at once there and not there, a projection of the candlelight, an image in the space between Pam's mind and eyes. The girl smiled a laughing smile, and then vanished.

A door slammed. Mr. Burke had just come in from the sunporch, face blanched and stern.

"I can't have you doing that in here." He pointed at the candle, and for a moment, Pam thought he was addressing the girl with the cloud hair. But there was no girl, none besides Pam. Mr. Burke added, "This old house is a tinderbox."

"I'm sorry." Pam blew out the candle, awash in shame. What craziness in this place had made her strike that match, see that girl?

"You shouldn't even be in here." Mr. Burke folded his arms, pitching back his neck in the authoritative manner of white men—storekeepers, doctors, cops—whom Pam had known all her life.

"*I* asked her to help me." Mrs. Whittaker-Burke swept back in from wherever she'd been. Exchanging a look with her husband, the hostess took the candle from Pam and dropped it into the pocket of her apron. Pam heard it clack against something already there—another candle? Several more? "Let's bring these sweets outside before they're forgotten."

Shamed and confused, Pam lifted her platter and followed Mrs. Whittaker-Burke out to the patio. She had no desire for dessert, only to escape from her hosts, their creepy house with its living candles and ghost-girls. All she wanted was to get down with her friends and lose herself in the music. But dancing made Pam more visible. Tonight, it was not just the oldest Burke boy watching her, but his parents too. And there were others. From the branches of trees, from the banks of the pond, from the stars that once led her ancestors north, Pam could feel invisible eyes following her every move.

∽

The Columbia Point contingent went to bed on the early side; the van back to Boston was scheduled to pick them up right after breakfast. But Pam was up late, watching the grounds for Mrs. Whittaker-Burke. Instead, it was the oldest Burke boy who came to the window and called to her, coaxing her to join him outside under the soft moonlight. Pam knew she'd been noticed, took responsibility for the encouraging smile she'd offered the night before. Still, it was strange to be alone with a white boy.

"Look up," he said, sensing that she was a stranger to clear country-night skies. Never in her life had Pam seen so many stars. The boy identified the constellations: Orion, Sirius, the Big and Little Dippers. He led her to a grassy spot where heavy willow branches formed a canopy. They crouched low and crawled underneath.

The boy had a joint, which he lit and shared with her while they talked. By the time the joint was gone, slippery gray clouds had swallowed up the moon. The boy continued flicking his lighter so they could see each other's faces. They were both smiling giddy eye-crinkling smiles that would not shut off. It was the weed, combined with the stars. That's all it was at first: the prospect of fun, of something new and daring and secret from Marcus, even from Tisha and Shay. Pam spoke boldly.

"What's with your mother?" Pam had once heard that white boys didn't defend their mothers like Black boys did. "Is she a witch or something?"

"Nah." The boy laughed. "But she'd take it as a compliment if you called her one. She goes in for tarot and Ouija boards and all that occult crap."

"Does she light candles a lot?"

"Drives my dad nuts." The boy rolled his eyes. "He says Mom's going to burn down the house one day."

"I saw her dancing last night. In a ring of candles in front of that root cellar."

"That sounds like Mom. She swears the cellar's full of ghosts. The house too. She was probably trying to summon them."

"She asked me if I believed in them," said Pam, then sat up straight. "Let's go. I want to see inside."

"The root cellar? Now?" The boy's eyes widened as he interpreted her meaning. "*Hell* yes."

He brought Pam down a path to the back grounds of the big house, stopping at the door in the hillock. The boy lifted the latch, pushed it open, and lit their way down a flight of stone steps.

"Tell me if you get scared," he said.

"I'm not," said Pam. But then the lighter faltered, shooting out little sparks before dying completely.

"I'm right here," said the boy.

"I know."

The pitch darkness made them speak in whispers. His hand found her shoulder, but it was Pam who pulled the boy close. The notion of encountering real ghosts did frighten her, but Pam's curiosity—about the cellar and its past, about the boy himself—outweighed that fear. Besides, if there were such things as ghosts, didn't that mean she might one day meet Mama's?

The boy took Pam's clinging for desire, which was not far off. What was the difference, really, between wanting someone to protect you and simply wanting them? The boy touched her, gently at first, a tentative hand slipping underneath her T-shirt.

"Is this okay?" he said. "Are you okay if I—?"

And Pam said, "Yes." Marcus never asked, just sensed what Pam wanted before she knew she wanted it, then took what she was happy to give. Now, though she liked the adventure of being here with a boy who did not exist in her world—the freedom, the lack of consequence—the closeness served the same purpose as with Marcus. Pam felt less alone, more whole—like before Mama died.

Though blinded in the dark, Pam darted her eyes all over the cellar, imagining things. Twisted roots hanging down like witch fingers, human skeletons rising from the ground. Whose would they be? Pam's curiosity about the slaves who hid here began to surpass her attention to the boy, who continued to touch her, then to ask if the touch was okay. The ground was hard, so they remained standing, Pam's back against the wall as he fumbled with his belt, her shorts. And when she said yes again, he found his way inside her.

Only then did a thin column of light—like the candle flame in the kitchen—leak through a crack in the wall, illuminating a host of brown and black faces. There they were: the life-size candles from her dream, eyes wide and imploring, hands reaching for Pam. Their touch was ice cold, yet soft—as if they feared harming her. Their mouths spoke words that Pam strained to make out. Then she understood.

"I was ready . . . I kissed the old woman . . . I ran . . ." Voices, layering over one another. *"I hid . . . I heard the horse hooves . . . I saw the men . . . We remembered . . ."*

$$\sim$$

Girl being close brings us to awakening. The first thing we see is them together: just another white man taking a Black girl for his own. An old song with too many verses, each ending the same way. Girl knows who we are. She's entranced by us, forgetting the boy and the timeless rhythm of his hips. We make a wall of souls—each clamoring. There are too many of us, too many, just like before. But those who catch hold find our voices.

"I was ready to die for my freedom."

"I kissed the old woman who loved me goodbye."

"I ran."

"I hid behind the hanging vines, made my breath silent as my heart."

"I heard the horse hooves thundering, the dogs closing in."

"I saw the men stop, squint, and spit."

"I ran."

"I hid in the swamp with its thick stench till darkness drank up the woods."

"We ran."

"We followed the stars, repeated the songs."

"We remembered the names of the places. Dawn, Dresden, Shrewsbury, Puce."

"We all remembered, still remember."

We plant pictures and stories into her body. Girl feels our hunger and, as the boy finishes, we hear her pray for us. By the time she and the boy ascend the stairs, Girl can hear us singing. The bygone songs her people made, creating hope from dust.

Condition

Boston and Manhattan, August 1983–February 1984

Three months later, Pam couldn't deny what was happening to her body. She hid her changing form under large, roomy tops that had belonged to her mother. Marcus noticed the change in Pam's shape but assumed he was responsible. He surprised her with a cheap ring, promising that they would raise the baby together. Marcus kept referring to the pregnancy as *him*. Our son. Pam thought of saying yes. There was a chance her melanin would translate for this poor child, that Marcus would never guess about the white boy with hair that fell around his chin. Then again, Marcus was darker than Pam herself. What if the baby turned out really light skinned like some mixed people she knew? Marcus wouldn't want the baby, or Pam for that matter. She put off answering him, gave only a smile as a placeholder.

As for Pop, if he were still his old self—sober, thoughtful, yet quick with a belly laugh—Pam would have told him about her situation in a heartbeat. But losing Mama had torn Pop apart. It was as if cancer had taken him away too, leaving in his place a childlike stranger who could barely see beyond the bottle in his hand. No use burdening the man with her troubles.

"You doing good?" is all Pop would say when they passed each other coming in and out of the bathroom, squeezed around one another in the kitchenette, or during commercial breaks when they watched reruns together on opposite ends of the worn beige sofa. Pam could not tell whether it was a question or a statement.

Her response was always, "I'm all right." Neither true nor completely false.

On the last night of August, Pam sat up in bed, hopeless, the sound of her crying muted by the neighbors' pounding music. Beneath that beat came another, unexpected rhythm: Pop's footfalls. Pam hadn't heard him come home. The nights he worked as a janitor at the community college, Pop didn't usually get in till morning. Pam hastened to dry her eyes.

"Thought I heard something." He walked in and sat at the far end of her bed, as far away from her as he could get. Pam knew shame made him keep his distance. Pop never wanted her to smell his breath if he'd been drinking. Still, he placed a gentle hand on the lump in her bed where her foot was. "I'm sorry."

She wanted to ask him, *For what?* But Pam feared if she spoke right then, he'd hear her voice catch. She couldn't bear for him to be any sorrier than he already was.

"A girl loses her mama," Pop said, "her father should be there for her. I haven't been."

Pam shook her head, comforted by the pressure of Pop's hand on her foot. It didn't make it okay, but it showed he was aware that a girl her age needed something. And he uttered her mother's name.

"Kaye was a good woman. She would have wanted me to be better for you." Sorrow thick in his throat. "What would she think?"

Pam sobbed aloud then. Though Mama's absence dwelt in each dust particle, though Mama's clothes remained hanging in the closet, her slippers unbudged from their spot by the door, neither Pam nor Pop ever talked about her. Between them, there were no stories or songs, or even candles lit, to remember her. As if mentioning the loss would break what was left of them. So when Pop moved closer, then held open his arms, Pam leaned into them. She soaked his shirt, which smelled musty, in need of laundering, but like the old Pop. In his embrace, Pam could not hold her belly in, knew there was a chance he would feel it, the life growing inside, and would question her, but she would not mind. She might tell him. He would help her figure it out.

"I gotcha," Pop said, and rocked her as he had when she was small. "I gotcha." But regarding the new thickness of her middle, he did not ask.

And by mid-September, Pop—Pam's sweet, sad Pop, who had never so much as been in a bar fight, though he'd witnessed plenty—wound up incarcerated. He had been in Brookline at the time of the assault, which had gone down in Washington Park, but Pop was identified by the victim in a lineup. He could afford neither an attorney nor bail, which had been set high due to the nature of the crime.

Marcus was over when Pam got the call. As she stood frozen, unable to think or breathe, he took the receiver from her hand and called his mother, who said Pam must not be alone.

So Pam packed one bag and rode the elevator with Marcus to the sixteenth floor, where his mother welcomed her into their noisy home. There were already three adults, an infant girl, and two little boys as well as Marcus living there. Pam stayed two sleepless nights, during which she lay awake, envisioning a bright moon and stars forming pictures in the sky. Whittaker House, on whose wide, green grounds her child had been conceived, was summoning her. Hadn't Mrs. Whittaker-Burke singled Pam out and introduced her to the ghosts of her people? Didn't that connect them? Wouldn't she be welcomed by the only grandmother her baby would ever have?

On the third day, Pam borrowed money from Shay and got on a Greyhound bus to Great Barrington. From there, she hitched her way to Monterey. It was after ten at night when she arrived at the farmhouse. The whole place was dark and still. When Pam rang the doorbell, a second-floor light went on, soon followed by another downstairs.

Mrs. Whittaker-Burke opened the door, towering and stately in her navy-blue satin bathrobe. Her hair was in the same extravagant bun she'd worn back in May.

"Can I help you?" Her tone was low and cold, as if they had never prepared dessert together in the pretty blue-and-pine kitchen.

Pam stammered, aware too late that coming here was a bad choice. "I visited here this spring, with the Columbia Point Youth Leadership group? My name is—"

"I know who you are." Mrs. Whittaker-Burke hesitated a moment before stepping back and letting her in. In the light, Pam felt self-conscious as Mrs. Whittaker-Burke's gaze probed her body. If you knew what you were looking for, Pam's short stature left little surface area to hide a pregnancy at this point. Only the top three snaps on her denim jacket were fastened.

"I know what happened between you and my oldest son that night," said Mrs. Whittaker-Burke. "I saw you together. Afterward I confronted him and he confessed." Her face remained tight as she informed Pam that the boys were away on a camping trip and that Mr. Burke was traveling on business. "It's just the two of us tonight. Have you eaten?"

Pam hadn't. In the kitchen, which felt darker and less welcoming than it had in the spring, Mrs. Whittaker-Burke emptied the contents of a Tupperware container into a saucepan. Minutes later she presented Pam with a bowl of thick beef stew and sat across the table from her while she ate. Halfway through the meal, Pam mustered her courage, finding the question she'd buried.

"Why did you invite me inside that night? Why me and no one else?"

Mrs. Whittaker-Burke lifted an eyebrow. "I had a notion about you, I suppose. I thought—I don't know what I thought." She rose, washed the saucepan, then turned back to Pam. "I have only myself to blame for the situation we find ourselves in. It was my miscalculation."

"What did you miscalculate?" said Pam, recalling the ring of candles. Had the hostess uttered the wrong spell? Sent the wrong son to Pam's window?

"Nothing worth dwelling on," said Mrs. Whittaker-Burke. Pam was afraid to press.

"Thank you for the stew."

"You can stay here tonight," Mrs. Whittaker-Burke said. "In the morning I will drive you to New York. One of my sorority sisters owns a group home for girls in your condition, as well as an adoption agency. The baby will be well placed." This wasn't up for debate.

When Pam was shown to her room—a beautiful powder-blue bedroom with lace curtains and a basket of unnaturally fragrant fake flowers on the dresser—she considered bolting, hitching her way back home and being free from Mrs. Whittaker-Burke and her complications. Instead she flopped on the lush bed in the center of the room and fell asleep.

Twice during the night, Pam stirred to half consciousness, aware of a chill in the air around her. She heard, she could have sworn, someone's deep breathing right beside her in the bed, along with whispers that might have been a dream. *I was . . . I ran . . . I hid . . .* Then, in her drowsy state, she saw the light-skinned girl with the cloud hair resting in a chair at her bedside. Pam felt comforted. She was not completely alone.

On the way to New York, Mrs. Whittaker-Burke was nearly silent—cool but not hostile. Pam was not a person so much as a cumbersome task to be dealt with and crossed off. At last Mrs. Whittaker-Burke pulled up in front of a narrow but elegant building on East Ninety-Fourth Street—smooth, cream-colored concrete with tall, thin windows.

"This is where we part ways," said Mrs. Whittaker-Burke, keeping her gaze on the windshield.

"One day," said Pam, "you might meet your grandbaby. Too bad you'll never know." She stepped out of the car, slammed the door, and turned toward the residence.

༄

There were five girls already living there. Two looked Spanish while the others were Black, each at a different stage of pregnancy. Miss Shirley was the group home's guardian. She was not the owner but a retired nurse employed by Mrs. Whittaker-Burke's sorority sister to live in the home with the girls, acting as a parent.

The girls did not attend high school but were offered modest encouragement to study for their GEDs. They were well cared for, fed, clothed—mostly to benefit the babies they carried, each of whom was destined for better than what the residents of the home could provide. By the time each girl was in her eighth month, she would have spent enough time perusing an album full of photographs of waiting couples to select one for her child.

"What if you want to keep your baby?" Pam asked another girl one day.

"Then you can't stay here," she was told. "The couples pay for us to live here. They pay for everything so they can get our babies. That's the deal."

Pam hadn't understood that she had no choice in the matter. The deal did not sit well with her, but she could not come up with a better option. New York was a strange place where she knew no one outside the group home. When she imagined running away, perhaps finding a church with ladies like those in Dorchester, who might help her and offer guidance, Pam remembered that those women had always considered her an especially good girl. She'd never skipped school, had always been discreet with Marcus, refusing to do anything with him in public but hold his hand. Pam could not bear to disappoint even unknown church ladies, to be seen as tarnished, though now she was.

Besides, the group home had a parlor with smooth white-and-yellow wallpaper, a crystal chandelier hanging over a pair of cream-colored love seats. In one corner, there was a white cast-iron spiral staircase whose banister formed an intricate leaf pattern, all of which pleased Pam's aesthetic sensibilities.

The linens at the home were always fresh and clean, as were the lush bath towels. Clothes arrived in a donation bin from which the girls could select what they liked as their waistlines expanded. And the food, though bland, was plentiful and nutritious. The girls themselves were reserved with one another, but nice enough, Pam found, with minimal gossip and little drama between them. They knew there was no point in forming true friendships, as each was but a smudge on the landscape of one another's lives. After her baby was delivered, each young mother would become a closed chapter for the remaining housemates.

Still, Pam liked that there was always someone to talk to. Always another girl available to grease and braid her hair. She stayed.

Months passed. The child grew inside Pam in a healthy, normal pregnancy, according to the obstetrician to whom Miss Shirley brought all the girls for prenatal care. During her eighth month, Pam sat with Miss Shirley, looked through the family photo album, and woodenly selected a couple. They were white, like all the couples in the book. The woman had kind eyes.

A Plan

Manhattan, March 1984

The baby girl made her way into the world on the first of March. Miss Shirley was transformed into a kindly grandmother for the delivery, accompanying Pam to the hospital, holding her hand, wiping her forehead.

"Push!" said Miss Shirley. "*Push*, my dear!"

"I'm dying!" Pam cried out over and over as Miss Shirley assured her that she wasn't. And then it was done. Pam heard her child cry and sobbed herself as Miss Shirley patted her hand and told her she'd done well.

In the recovery room, the nurses washed the baby, swaddled her, and placed her in Pam's arms. The baby was pink as a strawberry, but the flesh around her tiny fingernails—Pam knew this was how you could predict her future shade—was the color of peanut brittle.

There was brief disagreement among the adults over whether Pam should nurse the baby. Miss Shirley said absolutely not; it would make the separation too difficult. The older nurse agreed. The younger nurse countered that Pam *must* breastfeed, claiming that the initial milk contained something called colostrum, a magic formula that would protect the baby from a wide range of ills later in life. This angered the older nurse, who accused the young nurse of confusing Pam and causing trouble.

"You people need to keep your politics out of our ward."

This Pam did not understand. *You people?* Both nurses were white, as was Miss Shirley. It was then revealed that the young nurse was not a nurse at all but a lactation specialist—an interloper, who identified herself as a member of La Leche League. The white women's discord freed Pam to decide for herself.

"I would like to breastfeed."

Miss Shirley and the older nurse wore matching scowls as the lactation specialist positioned the baby girl across Pam's body.

After a few false starts, the baby latched on and began to suck.

"She's an expert," said the specialist with a laugh. "And so are you."

Pam smiled, her insides surging with energy and affection. As they wheeled her into a proper hospital room, with a window and a painting of sailboats, she heard Miss Shirley click her tongue and the older nurse humph with disapproval.

Pam could not take her eyes off her daughter. Even when the new mother became drowsy, she insisted that the infant be placed in a plastic bassinet at her bedside rather than removed to the nursery. Pam had no idea how much time elapsed before Miss Shirley cleared her throat and shook her into a state of alertness.

"Mr. and Mrs. Taylor have arrived to meet their daughter."

Pam had not understood that she would be expected to meet them, especially not here, in the hospital room, where she was raw, exhausted, half-naked, and more vulnerable than she'd ever been in her life. Yet here they were. Younger looking than their photographs, Mr. Taylor—in khaki pants and a navy blazer—held the elbow of Mrs. Taylor, in a pink high-necked dress, blonde hair feathering at the sides. The Taylors approached the baby's bassinet and hovered.

"Oh, look at her!" Mrs. Taylor placed both hands up to her mouth in a manner most precious. "Our little Alice. Honey, she *looks* like an Alice!"

"She's beautiful," said Mr. Taylor, and wiped his eyes. A moment later he remembered his manners, turned to Pam, and asked how she was feeling.

"Fine." It was the only word she could manage without releasing the tears swelling their ducts.

When Mrs. Taylor told her how grateful they were, it was more than Pam could bear. *How can these white people claim my child?*

Sensing Pam's emotional distress, Miss Shirley coaxed the couple out of the room to wait for the surrender document.

"There's nothing to worry about anymore," Miss Shirley told Pam. "Just sign right here." She pointed to the line on the paper, at which point Pam began to wail, clutching the baby to her breast.

"You are making a scene," Miss Shirley informed her in a soft, firm tone. "This behavior will not do."

"She's *my* baby," Pam blurted out between sobs.

"We've been through this." Miss Shirley kept her voice calm, but the tension in her brow was unmistakable.

"Please." Pam could feel the baby's heart, her breath, her being. She had Mama's wide forehead and curving lips. Everything about her was familiar.

"The Taylors will give her what you cannot," said Miss Shirley. "You can't change your mind now. It's unfair."

The older nurse came in, suggesting a sedative. One was administered before Pam could respond.

When she came to, there was yet another white woman in the room, standing beside frumpy Miss Shirley. This one was tall and slim, in a neat pantsuit with a stylish paisley scarf and a flip of silver hair caressing each ear. She introduced herself as Miss Edith, owner of the group home and agency, sorority sister of Mrs. Whittaker-Burke.

"How are you feeling?" said Miss Edith, pulling a chair close to Pam's bedside. "Better?"

Pam nodded, because it felt like the right response. The baby was no longer in the room.

"She's in the nursery," said Miss Edith, as if reading her mind. "They're bathing her and giving her a vaccination." Miss Edith leaned forward. "Mr. and Mrs. Taylor have gone home for now. They would like to give you time to think about whether you want to go through with the placement or not."

"You mean I can still decide?"

"Of course. She is your baby."

Pam must have misheard or misunderstood. "But I thought I had to sign. Because you let me live in the home."

Miss Edith's smile did not waver. She reached for Pam's hand. "Oh, my dear. No one would make you give up your baby. It has *always* been up to you."

Pam exchanged a glance with Miss Shirley, whose face betrayed nothing of the harsh message she'd delivered earlier, and for months prior. Miss Shirley spread her jowly cheeks wide in imitation of Miss Edith's elegant beam.

Pam's distress eased. Surely Miss Edith was sent by someone from above, either God or Mama.

But then Miss Edith tilted her head to one side. "We can speak now about your plan."

"Plan?"

"For supporting the baby."

The older woman's tone remained warm, calm, and patient as she rattled off questions. Had Pam any extended family to help her with childcare? Did she have a livable income? If not, had she applied for public assistance?

Pam's answer to each query was no.

Each time the girl spoke, Miss Edith gave a slight nod. At last she said, "Well. It seems you haven't a plan for raising this baby at all, have you?"

Pam shook her head, blinking as the tears swam once again. Miss Edith rose, gesturing for Miss Shirley to do the same.

"You've had a deeply overwhelming day," said Miss Edith. "We'll give you some time to rest and think things through."

With this they were gone. Pam was alone until an orderly wheeled in the baby's bassinet.

"She needs to nurse."

Pam reprised the position she'd learned from the lactation specialist. As her tiny daughter got to work, a name came to mind:

"Ayesha. Not Alice. Ayesha Kaye." *Ayesha* was the prettiest name Pam knew, and *Kaye* had been Mama's name. Pam murmured it aloud several times over. She said to her child, "That's who you are."

⤳

Sometime during the wee hours, Pam awoke and noticed that the curtain around the second bed was drawn. Someone must have given birth and joined Pam while she was sleeping. Amid the nighttime hospital sounds—the beeping of monitors, the opening and closing of doors, the droning voices over the intercom—Pam heard the woman singing softly, a lullaby for her newborn in a minor key, at once sweet and mournful. The words she could make out were familiar: *Dawn, Dresden, Shrewsbury, Puce.* The curtain rustled in rhythm: her neighbor must have been rocking her child. *Dawn, Dresden, Shrewsbury, Puce.* A chill came—both from within her and from outside. Pam rose to make sure her sleeping Ayesha was well covered.

Now her neighbor's curtain moved as in a great breeze. The voice ceased its singing and urged her, "Go!"

Pam stared, one hand on her baby's chest. "What did you say?"

"I said go! Go before they take her from you!"

"Who's there?" Pam approached the curtain.

"Something wrong with your ears, Girl?" Again, the voice sang, "*Dawn, Dresden, Shrewsbury, Puce.* Find the star, follow it. Take her and run before they come back."

Befuddled, Pam stepped closer. When she pulled back the curtain, there was a rush of bitter air and an acrid smell. No one was in the bed.

"*Go!*"

Dawn

Manhattan, March 1984

Outside in the darkness, exhausted, scared, open to the elements, cloth between her legs rubbing against the place where she's torn. Baby tied to her, hidden under her cloak. She prays there's body heat for them both.

Girl looks up. The moon and the moving lights—white, red, blue—are too bright to see the stars. How will she find the one pointing north? We feed her the songs till her lips move in time. Follow the Drinking Gourd; Dawn, Dresden, Shrewsbury, Puce . . . The chill inside her persisting, muscles straining with fatigue. She knows the feel of fever, wills it away. Steal Away to Jesus. Swing Low, Sweet Chariot.

Babe at her breast fussing. No question of turning back, no good to abandon course. Keep moving, Girl. Keep singing. One star will always glow bright enough to light your way. Girl sees it now. That's the one. Hope stirs her heart.

⁓

It wasn't like the sky in Monterey, which was full of stars that the long-haired Burke boy had named for her. At first, only the moon and the flashing lights of airplanes broke through the smog. But once her eyes adjusted to the city sky, Pam was able to make out a single bright star. She alternated her gaze between it and the street signs—East Seventy-Seventh, Park Avenue, East Seventy-Eighth, East Seventy-Ninth.

The buildings here were enormous and stately, with uniformed men guarding the entries, their gazes hardened, aiming past her when she glanced their way. A wild-haired man staggered along the sidewalk, the lips of a bottle emerging from a bag in his hand. As he passed, Pam recoiled from his scent, nearly losing her balance.

She clutched a street sign just as a taxicab paused to release a fur-clad woman into the care of one of the doormen. Pam looked down to avoid notice. A woman, even one in a fur coat, would be curious about her bundle, would sense the baby and want to take her away. Pam crossed Park Avenue, a double street with garden islands in the center, and continued walking on Seventy-Ninth Street. Soon she stood on Fifth Avenue, Central Park on the horizon. Pam knew about Central Park, what it was and how big—big as Boston proper, someone once told her. At night it was lawless, dangerous. No young girl should be in there alone. Pam crossed Fifth, holding tight to her baby, reasoning that she was *not* a young girl alone. She was a mother traveling with a child who was hers to protect.

On a bench by an entrance to the park was a trio of old Black women. By the light of a streetlamp, Pam could see that they were sleeping, leaning on one another. They stirred as she drew close but did not open their eyes.

They could have been grandmothers from Dorchester: tired, hardworking, practiced at running threadbare homes with no money. Bartering, sharing, pooling what little there was, relying on ingenuity for the survival of those in their care. They would not offer help but would provide it if asked. What could Pam ask of them? How could she begin to explain her mission?

"Go on, Girl." These words came from one of the women as Pam stared, though the speaker had not lifted her head. Pam could feel their cold. She could smell a whisper of the root cellar. The cellar spirits, the candle people, would follow her anywhere, Pam understood. They would stay with her while they needed her. At once guardian angels and parasites who clung to their host. No matter. Their interests dovetailed. If Pam was safe, they were.

Pam shifted Ayesha inside her jacket, tightened the sheet, and proceeded into the park. It was wild like a forest, raccoons and rats and men lurking, scavenging, hunting. Pam kept low, dodging from tree to tree, trying to keep one eye on the star.

∽

Look to Girl now. She comes to a clearing and sends her gaze high over the tops of the trees. The chill in her bones spreads out, tingles, turning warm, then hot. The star fills her feverish vision. She spreads her arms and rides the rays of light to the places in the song. Dawn, Dresden, Shrewsbury, Puce. She's a vessel, the chariot, the riverboat. Sail away, Girl, sail away to that sweet, sweet shore.

She follows the will of the star to a door made of glass. Rings the bell, waits, and finally collapses on the step with the babe across her lap. Too cold to fall into a proper sleep, the fever takes her to a place just beyond.

∽

In the morning—still chilled and shaky, with searing pain between her legs—Pam was inside the place where the star had brought her. She was lying on a rank and lumpy mattress, under a scratchy blanket in the corner of a room with cracked gray paint. As pieces of the night patched in, Pam observed that her arms were empty. Horrified, she forced herself to stand, searching the bed for Ayesha Kaye.

"My baby!" Pam's eyes met the blank faces of several women and children, also in beds lining the wall, at varying levels of dress and wakefulness. "Where is my baby?"

One of the women snorted and turned away. But Pam heard the unmistakable squall of a newborn infant nearby. She spun around, too weak to run, yet managed to propel herself in the direction of the sound, down a hall with mildewed carpeting and dirty glass doors demarking run-down offices. The last door was ajar. Inside was a woman—Black, neatly dressed, unlike the disheveled crowd in the open room Pam had run from. The woman was pacing before a desk, cooing, and bouncing Ayesha Kaye.

Pam lunged at her. "My baby!" Stumbling, floundering to the floor.

"Yes," said the woman. "She *is* your baby." She shifted the still-squalling Ayesha to one shoulder, assisted Pam to her feet, and helped her to a chair. The woman removed a bottle from an improvised warmer—a mug of steaming water—and offered it to the baby.

"She doesn't take a bottle," said Pam.

But the woman was patient. Ayesha felt the nipple at her lips, fussed, then opened her mouth and began to suck.

"She's hungry," the woman said. "Babies adapt."

Pam's breasts ached. Her heart sank. "You'll mess her up. She needs me. She needs my—" Pam had forgotten the word the lactation specialist had used.

The woman sat across the desk from Pam, cradling Ayesha in her lap. She held the baby so naturally that Pam relaxed a bit, as if the confident, comforting arms were caressing her own body. The woman was brown skinned, with her hair styled in short finger waves of which Mama would have approved.

"Do you own this place?" Pam said.

"Own? Lord, no," said the woman. "I'm a case manager."

Pam had been a case before. She felt some solace in the notion of being managed.

Then the woman said, "I'm Dawn."

Dawn! Dresden, Shrewsbury, Puce! Oh! It was all we spirits could do to keep from rejoicing, filling the room with our hope. We believed in those places again.

Almost.

"Dawn Leeds," the woman added. Then her face grew stern. "And you, a little girl with a newborn infant. How could you bring her here of all places? You've exposed her to all kinds of germs."

"I ran away from the hospital," Pam said, eyes downcast. It was horrible, horrible what she had done, she now saw. She'd put her own child in danger. "They were going to take her from me." How foolish, how selfish it seemed in the light of day. She could not tell Dawn Leeds about the whispers, the voices of the spirits.

Dawn asked for her name and wrote it down along with notes, the way case managers do.

Pam made sure to add, "The baby's name is Ayesha. Ayesha Kaye."

"Ayesha *Kaye?*" Dawn smiled unexpectedly, looking up from her notepad. "*Kaye* was my mother's name."

"Mine too," said Pam, surprised at this connection between them. But Dawn was frowning again, back to case managing.

"She has to see a doctor," said Dawn. "And so do you. Did you tear badly?"

"Yes."

"Got stitches?"

"Yes."

"Pain when you walk?"

"Yes." Pam wanted to describe the weakness, the vertigo. How she was hot and cold at the same time. But she struggled to find her voice over the whispers of the cellar spirits.

Dawn shifted Ayesha Kaye again. "Have you got any family?"

Pam shook her head, and the tears she'd been holding back since she left the hospital began to flow. The case manager reached out and touched her arm.

"Goodness, you're feverish! We have to get you to a doctor now."

"Please," Pam said. "Don't let them get her."

Dawn looked quizzical, bouncing Ayesha. "Don't let who get her?"

"The people. I don't remember their name." Words choking their way out of her. "They wanted me to . . . I couldn't . . . They tried . . ." Pam fought the fog of fever, desperate to tell about Miss Shirley, Miss Edith, and the white couple, about the lactation specialist who said she was an expert at caring for her daughter. Pam could feel the room rotating, her tale an incoherent gumbo. She could not make Dawn Leeds understand. Nor could she stop her from calling an ambulance.

⁓

Pam awoke in a hospital bed to take in the smiling faces of Miss Edith and Miss Shirley. The pair stood at her bedside, hands clasped, heads tilted in a twin show of benevolence.

Pam tried to sit up but found she was restrained by straps attached to her bed. The smells were different from the place where she'd given birth: less earthy, more astringent. There were no pictures of sailboats, no windows. It was less a room than a cell. The whispers, Pam observed, had gone silent.

"Where is she? Where is my baby?"

"She is perfectly safe," said Miss Edith. Miss Shirley nodded.

"Did they take her? That couple? But I didn't sign! You said I didn't have to—"

"You *did* sign," said Miss Shirley. "Don't you remember?"

"They took her?"

Miss Edith responded. "The Taylors decided they were not comfortable adopting her, given the confusion."

"So where is she?"

"Perfectly safe," Miss Edith reiterated. "Thanks to Mrs. Leeds from the Hope Center. She called the hospitals in the area to find out where you'd delivered. The ward contacted us as quickly as they could. Thankfully. You made a terrible error. Compromising your health and endangering the welfare of a child."

"Where is Ayesha Kaye? She needs me!"

"On the contrary," said Miss Shirley, expression turning sour. "You've shown that the baby is not safe in your care. You are unstable and unwell."

Miss Edith elaborated. "You are here recovering until you can go home. Meanwhile, the baby is making a lovely adjustment to her wonderful new parents."

"No! She's mine! She's *mine!*" With her limited strength, Pam wrestled her restraints in vain.

Miss Edith reached out and pressed the nurses' call button. "Perhaps," she said, "it will give you comfort to know that they are Black. This way, she will never know."

Pam continued to scream and writhe as a large nurse, one she'd not seen before, arrived with gloved hands. Without a word, the nurse leaned over Pam's bed and emptied the contents of a syringe into the girl's upper arm. Pam's vision blurred. The world blackened.

∽◉

Pam awoke in the company of a man standing over her with tears in his eyes.

"Pop?" He was so changed, his face thinner, drawn from his months locked up. "How'd you get here?"

Pam's restraints were gone, allowing her to sit up and throw her arms around him. Overcome with relief, confusion, joy, dread—Pam could barely order the questions she had for her father. Pop had been exonerated, he said, after the true perpetrator was caught committing a second assault and confessed to the first. Not only had Pop dried out while incarcerated; he'd made a lucky connection that led to a steady job and membership in the maintenance contractors' union.

"We're going to be okay," he said. "I'm going to take care of you." Pop reached out to smooth the frizz coming off Pam's hair, which hadn't been properly braided since she'd left the group home. He added, "I kept thinking you'd visit when I was locked up. I kept writing. When I heard you were gone, I didn't know what to do. I thought I'd lost you along with your mother. Don't know what I'd have done if that social worker hadn't finally tracked me down."

"Social worker? Mrs. Leeds?"

"You know how I am about names." Pop shrugged. "No matter. I'm taking you home as soon as they say you can go."

"Where is she?" said Pam. "Where is the baby?"

Though Pop was now clear-eyed and present, it was evident from his expression that he knew nothing about Ayesha Kaye, or even the source of Pam's affliction.

When he asked her, "What baby?" Pam found she did not have the words to speak the truth.

ᔆ

Instead, she returned to Boston with her father, fabricated a story for Marcus, and resumed what she could of her life there. She wrote letters to Ayesha Kaye that she would save, but not send, hoping in vain that the act would heal her heart. She took comfort in the cellar spirits' silence, mistaking it for a long-awaited, hard-earned peace.

~ෙ

And Baby Girl? She grows up without knowing where she came from, in a good home, with a good name, Kaye Ayesha Leeds. Mrs. Dawn Leeds and her husband, Elgin, raise her as their own. Wonderings plague Kaye, but she can't form the questions. She's got a longing, deep and strange, a third eye, searching without meaning to, without knowing what it seeks.

Sometimes it's quiet and leaves her be. Other times, Kaye's yearning is a crack in the world, a window filled with pictures—of strangers, of loved ones, of the ancestors who took hold one spring night in the dark underground.

3

THE OBELISK

Coffee Shop

Brooklyn, February 2018

Kaye tears her attention away from the young breastfeeding mother seated diagonally across the café to gaze at her own children. Though Kaye weaned each of them years ago, she remembers the weight in her arms, the oneness of her body and theirs. When Miles was born, Kaye left the financial consulting firm where she and Andy were both employed. Andy rose in the ranks as Kaye devoted herself to motherhood. She did not begin her entrepreneurial venture—a networking platform for high-end Black hair-care specialists and consumers—until Miles and Billie were both in school. Kaye still arranges her hours around their needs, attributing her children's poise and self-assurance—at least in part—to her constancy. It is a luxury her middle-class parents lacked, a bittersweet luxury, to be taken for granted by your kids.

Miles's eyes are glued to his iPad while Billie leans into him, chin on his shoulder. Whatever game he's playing reflects red and blue swirls on both their faces as half-eaten elephantine croissants languish before them. Her children thus absorbed, Kaye catches the eye of the other mother and sends her a smile—the warmest, most sisterly I've-been-there-honey smile she can muster. The woman's face remains stonelike. The babe at her breast is a snowy shade of mixed—just how Miles was as an infant. Mom is brown, as brown as Kaye if not more so, and Kaye *feels* her. Needs the woman to know it. What wouldn't Kaye have given, back when Miles was new, to have someone smile at her and let her know she wasn't alone among the bright-white mother-mass of their little Brooklyn enclave? Oh, the Slope is woke politically. Everyone who lives here is liberal. It's diverse too, Kaye will admit, but on an aesthetic rather than cultural level.

Kaye remembers herself in the woman's shoes, sitting alone and nursing, but not at ease, not relaxed like the white breastfeeding mothers of Brooklyn. Kaye's clothes had been neatly pressed, the baby blanket soft and fresh, Miles's onesie clean, bright colored, and adorable. His five strands of hair were impeccably combed, as was Kaye's own perm. The white mothers pushed their Bugaboo strollers, confident in dingy, unlaundered new-mom clothes, their hair carelessly bound in sloppy new-mom ponytails. With impunity they could dress their infants—whether white like they were, or adopted: Black, brown, or Asian—in ill-fitting, spit-up-stained clothes. The only other Black women Kaye saw were the white women's Caribbean babysitters. The other mothers smiled uncertainly, did not befriend her on the park bench as they did one another. The babysitters also looked at her askance. Kaye looked as if she should be Miles's babysitter, but there she was nursing him. The pair of them made no sense to anyone.

Finally, after a Music Together class for infants, Kaye was in the lounge area with three other mothers who had lingered to chat, change diapers, and nurse. Almost simultaneously, the four of them—Kaye included—turned their babies horizontally to face them and pulled their shirts sideways as the infants latched on. All four shared smiles of recognition, sharing in this sweet *pas de deux* of early motherhood.

There was relief in their camaraderie, or so Kaye thought, until one of them spoke to her.

"Please don't be offended." The mother—short, thin, and pale, with mousy brown hair and incongruously enormous breasts—had the kind of soft, unassuming voice that downplays the boldest of statements. "*How* can you breastfeed that baby? There's no *way* he's yours."

Kaye was momentarily shocked into silence. Another mother, a chunky brunette with acne-pocked cheeks, said under her breath, "*Lexi.*" It was the fact of Lexi's friend's mortification that gave Kaye the courage to find her sense of humor. Kaye leaned forward slightly, squashing Miles enough to pop off her breast, face pink with exertion.

"Well, of course not," Kaye said, beaming unblinkingly at Lexi. "I'm the wet nurse!"

Lexi's mouth dropped open, but the other two mothers erupted in approving guffaws. Soon even Lexi applauded her bluntness. And just like that, Kaye was in. She had a group of mom friends.

When Kaye was honest with herself, she would acknowledge that she belonged with this set only as long as she adhered to a scripted role: the bold, no-nonsense Black Mama. The fearless one who defended and supported, who told it like it was in a loving way. Kaye had become what she swore she'd never be: the only Black friend of a slew of white women. Each of them could point to her—to Gabriella, a Puerto Rican mother who joined them, to Tessa, another mom who declared herself one-quarter Vietnamese—and consider their group diverse.

But there have been no Black women friends to come her way. Kaye's sorority sisters moved out of the city to places like New Rochelle or Maplewood, New Jersey. They're close enough to visit occasionally but too far away to be fixtures in her children's lives. And, while Kaye's sister Michelle moved in four years ago with no inclination to move out, Michelle isn't like having a *girlfriend*. Michelle has no children and is currently between girlfriends herself, since the last one broke her heart. There is no one around to go *Girrrl!* and settle in for a real talk. Another reason Kaye feels so warmly toward the stone-faced woman nursing across the café.

Billie glances at Kaye, then follows her mother's gaze. Billie is eight and a fan of babies. She nudges Miles, who's ten and oblivious to things that are not electronic.

"You can see that lady's booby!" Billie whispers.

"Shut up!" Miles, fearful of losing his game, barks at his sister. And the nursing woman's eyes focus momentarily before going blank again.

"Booby," says Billie once more, cracking herself up.

"Billie." Kaye gives her daughter a look, which makes the girl stop mid-giggle. "That's not a word we use."

"Sorry, Mama." Billie takes a slurp from her smoothie. "Mama?"

"Yes?"

"That's a cute baby, right?"

"As far as I can see. The baby's face is pretty busy right now."

Billie grins. "Did you feed me like that?"

"You know I did. Till you were a year old."

"And Miles."

"Miles too." Kaye feels a momentary echo of the despair she'd felt on the first birthday of each child, the mourning of infancy, where she was the sole source of comfort and nutrition. Both children were ready to move on before she was. As the mother across the coffee shop sighs, Kaye exhales along with her, vicariously living what she recalls as pure exhilaration.

If he were paying attention, Miles would voice his dismay over all talk of bodily functions, the transfer of fluids. The kind of talk Billie cannot get enough of. Their quirks, their differences, never cease to surprise and amuse Andy and Kaye. Will that nursing mother get this same kind of pleasure as her child grows? Of course she will. She just doesn't know it yet. Life is still all spit-up and diapers and sleepless nights and no sex. The woman barely nods as a cheerful ponytailed server bearing a menu and glass of water attempts to chat her up. When the server moves on, Kaye decides to try. She rises, tells the kids to sit tight for a few minutes, and crosses the café.

"Hi," she says, boldly sliding in across the booth from the mother, whose eyes widen, broadcasting alarm and fear. *Why fear?* Kaye wonders. Then evaluates her decision to join the woman as ill advised. Who knows what kind of sister she is? Lean and long necked, with full fashion-model lips and straightened hair terminating in a polished flip. The massive ring on her finger along with the pale tint of her baby suggest she married a white guy, as Kaye did. But why would Kaye assume this lady is yearning for friendship with another Black woman? What if she's stuck in a place of self-loathing? What if she knows too well that a Black woman alone in these parts is acceptable diversity but that two Black women together—perhaps laughing, chatting with audible familiarity—are viewed as a threat? Kaye knows this too, but has learned not to care.

Don't worry, she wants to tell the woman. *I won't blow your cover.* But she doesn't. Nor does the woman return her greeting. She simply stares.

Flustered, Kaye introduces herself. She adds, with a nod toward her brood, "Those two over there are mine." Which should be more than enough to explain her reason for connecting.

The woman's eyes shift from Kaye to Miles and Billie. Billie is still looking over her shoulder at them. She flashes a sweet Billie-smile and waves. The woman looks back at Kaye. No wave back at Billie, no smile for a friendly little girl in pigtails. Kaye's blood heats up instantly. Be cold to me all you want. What kind of monster can't return the greeting of an innocent little girl?

Kaye keeps her eyes on the woman's. As she's thinking of what to say to extricate herself, tears flood the woman's eyes. She blinks, and rivulets pour down her smooth cheeks. By now the baby—a girl, judging from the rosy tint of her sweater—is done nursing and has fallen asleep. The woman weeps noiselessly, letting her child drop from the still-exposed breast into the cushion on her lap.

"Careful, she's going to—"

Kaye swings her body to the other side of the booth, just in time to save the infant from rolling off her mother's lap onto the hardwood floor. The woman doesn't move. The child, still in a post-nursing stupor, merely stirs as Kaye lifts the tiny figure onto her shoulder. There's a well-worn space there, carved out by Miles and then Billie, that the infant relaxes into. Out of habit, Kaye rubs her back in small circles. An audible breath escapes the lips of the mother as Kaye covers her breast with a section of the baby's blanket.

"Are you all right?" Kaye says.

The woman shakes her head as if awakening from a trance. "Yes, I'm fine. Thank you." She opens her hands to take the baby back. Kaye hesitates only for a second, places the child in her mother's arms, and returns to the other side of the booth.

"I'm sorry," says the woman, righting the blanket, bouncing the baby on her shoulder like any ordinary new mother would. "I'm a little out of it. Sleep deprivation, you know?" Expression flat but almost normal.

"Please," Kaye says, smiling with relief at the reference to common ground. "My two never slept at this age. What is she, six weeks?"

"Seven. No—eight." The mother's smile is weaker than Kaye would like, her laugh a bit too forced to inspire confidence. But she's speaking at least. The woman adds, "I can't keep track of anything these days."

"Oh, I know how that is," Kaye says with exaggerated warmth to make up for the woman's oddness. "It gets easier. Then you forget and have another!" She laughs at her own joke.

"That's what my sister says," the woman tells Kaye. "She's got two as well and makes it look easy."

Again, her words are appropriate, but the tone, the "as well"—it's all too strained to trust. But what can Kaye do? Call Child Protective Services? For what, exactly? It crosses Kaye's mind that perhaps she's created some narrative about this woman out of her own need for companionship.

She tries, "Hey. I know it can be isolating at your stage. You want to join us over there for a bit? Miles is lost in his game, but Billie is a sucker for babies and always good for a laugh."

"Oh." The sad woman's eyebrows knit, mouth twists briefly. "It's just . . . I think maybe—"

"No need," says Kaye, brightly brushing off the rejection. She shouldn't have asked, should have left it alone. "I understand."

But as their eyes lock, Kaye's sight splits as it used to when she was young—a pillar-shaped window opening before her. She sees a blast of images: a Black woman—this very same young, sad mother—lying still on her back, on a dark wood floor, eyes frozen white as death, a white man with his throat cut, a knife beside them, a pool of blood, and of all things, a spinning wheel on its side. Now the window zips shut, leaving Kaye in a state of panic over the content as well as the very fact of her reverie. She had thought these visions were behind her, the affliction a thing of the past. Kaye swallows her horror as a question flickers in the eyes of the Sad Woman. Without another word, and with too much haste, Kaye returns to her children.

Billie, ever observant, says, "Mama, what was wrong with that lady?"

"Nothing, sweet. Just tired like everyone else with a new baby." Her voice shakes and Billie notices.

"Mama, are you okay?"

"I am fine, baby." Kaye's voice comes out hard, her *no further questions* tone. Billie stays watchful but leaves it alone.

Kaye and her children file out of the café fifteen minutes later. The woman is nursing the baby again, staring straight ahead.

Obelisk

Manhattan, 1988–1998

Kaye is five, maybe younger, the first time it happens, sitting in the bathtub when the wall splits between the tiles. She sees an image of a big red farmhouse, an older girl in a jean jacket, hair in cornrows, waiting outside the front door. When the vision disappears, the tiles fused back together, Kaye opts not to tell Ma or Daddy.

The next time, Kaye is seven, lying in the bunk bed she shares with her sister Michelle, when she sees her paternal grandfather—seven hundred miles away in South Carolina—collapse, clutching his arm. Remaining calm, guided by her own old soul, Kaye phones her grandmother and wakes her.

"Call 911, Nana," she says.

Nana, a woman of utmost faith, questions nothing and calls, saving Pop-pop's life. Nana declares afterward that Jesus had intervened.

As the years pass, the visions keep coming. Kaye gives her secret a name, "the Obelisk," because the opening always starts out shaped a bit like Cleopatra's Needle in Central Park. An exclamation point, a lighthouse flashing.

Most of the time, the Obelisk shows Kaye images that she can do nothing to remedy, like Ma grieving over Gordy's small body years before his actual death, a scene that breaks Kaye's heart but that she can share with no one. Kaye has no language to describe her visions, at least no believable terms.

There are other times when the Obelisk reveals Ma and Daddy, looking younger and thinner than Kaye remembers, gazing over a pink bassinet. Ma has tears on her cheeks, and Daddy has a hand on the small of Ma's back. Somehow Kaye is sure it's *her* in the bassinet, not Michelle or Gordy.

Ma whispers to Daddy, "If only." It's the first time the Obelisk offers up words. "If only."

With that Kaye knows, despite being the firstborn—the one who gets good grades, who's popular, who's pretty—that her parents have a wish about her just like they do for Gordy (to be healthy and normal) and Michelle (to be less awkward and odd). *If only . . .* there's a regret about each of them.

Kaye senses too what her defect is, even if no one ever says it aloud. The family story is that Gordy and Michelle look like Daddy while Kaye favors Ma. But looking at herself in the mirror alongside her mother, looking at family photographs, *really* looking beyond her complexion— at facial features, the curve of her jaw, her hairline, her body type—Kaye knows it's a lie. Her *if only* is that she favors no one. But every time Kaye considers asking her parents about her origins, she recalls the vision from way back, remembers the sorrow in her mother's shoulders, gazing at the baby girl who was Kaye.

She will not ask them, cannot ask them: *Whose was I before I was yours?*

Peppermint Bikini

Manhattan, 1999
Ma keeps banging on the wall, yelling that the music is disturbing Gordy. Kaye restarts the Destiny's Child CD but turns the volume way down.

"You can stay there," she tells Michelle, who is sitting on her bed, "but only if you promise not to annoy me."

Michelle cannot promise. She never knows what will annoy her sister. But Kaye is too distracted by her own image in the mirror to pay the younger girl much mind. She is packing, imagining herself in each outfit, ranging from cute to downright sexy. She's sixteen now, with a job for the summer, a *position*—as a live-in mother's helper. She'll accompany the Gifford family to their summer house on Martha's Vineyard, keeping an eye on six-year-old Evie and eight-year-old Stevie, but also hanging out with her friend Ruthie Everson, whose parents have a place on the Vineyard too. Both residences are walking distance from "Inkwell Beach," lovingly named for the multitude of well-off Black families—like the Giffords and the Eversons—who frequent the place. Ruthie has promised summer nights jamming to sweet R & B in the company of some fine lifeguards—boys their age whose families have been summering in Oak Bluffs along with Ruthie's since before they were born. This, Kaye and Ruthie have agreed, will be their summer of boys. And it's going to be *fun*, Kaye thinks, swaying her hips in time to the music like Beyoncé Knowles.

The Vineyard will be a much-needed break from the grimness and gloom of home. No one speaks of anything these days but Gordy's health, and even that comes in whispers and hushed fragments.

Daddy will say to Ma, "Is he—?" or "Has he—?" and Ma will give him a look, cautioning him not to let the girls hear. Ma will say, "No" or "Yes." Meaning anything, but certainly nothing good.

Gordy is eight and will not survive till his next birthday. He has never walked or spoken, but his large, heavy-fringed eyes see inside your soul and speak to your heart. He can nod and shrug. His tiny fingers reach for your face and transmit love. His smile is wide and full and gracious. No one but Kaye expected him to be here, no one expected to know him the way they do. When he was born, the nurse offered Ma a chance to hold him, to kiss him, to name him before she said goodbye.

Daddy went next. When it was Kaye's turn, she looked down at the baby's weak, blue form. Then the window in her mind showed him to Kaye as he is today. A sweet-faced boy in red pajamas, head tilted at the unnatural angle that's natural to Gordy. Just for a moment. Then Kaye handed the baby back to her mother and he coughed and began breathing on his own. The blue tint left his skin and he was theirs for a time.

But now, packing for the Vineyard, with Destiny's Child pumping from her player, Kaye blocks out the Gordy worries, replacing them with visions of lifeguards. She clutches her prize, the much fought-over peppermint-striped bikini that her mother finally let her buy at Macy's. Holding it against her body, Kaye can imagine sand between her toes, the eyes of a cute boy drinking her in.

"I wish we were going away together," says Michelle, annoying her older sister. Kaye twirls, humming a few bars of "No, No, No," still holding the bathing suit, trying to keep her exuberance pure, untainted by guilt. She's as glad to have a break from Michelle as she is from the rest of them. The mopey, awkward twelve-year-old sister who's now as tall as Kaye but has no grace, no art to the way she carries herself. No sense of *pretty*—she doesn't even try. Kaye was already chasing and being chased by boys at that age.

"Come on," says Kaye, finally placing the swimsuit in her bag. "You'll have a great time. You're going to the mountains!"

By this she means the Berkshire farm of their father's old college roommate, Dan Iler, a white artist with a beard, knobbly shoulder bones, and a long mouse-brown ponytail. Mr. Iler, along with his wife, left the city to raise their children among trees and lakes rather than subway trains and skyscrapers. Daddy used to take the girls there about once a year, while Ma stayed home with Gordy.

"Going to the mountains" was Daddy's phrase, romanticizing the place for a pair of New York City girls growing up in Mitchell-Lama housing, a stone's throw from the projects. And it did thrill Kaye and Michelle when they were younger. By the Ilers' farm, you could run barefoot through a meadow and dig up Queen Anne's lace "carrots" by the side of a winding mountain road, breathing in sweet-green smells unknown on Amsterdam Avenue.

Then, three years ago, when the girls were visiting on their own, Kaye discovered Mr. Iler himself peering through the bathroom window as she showered. She refused to go after that. Kaye was, and remains, too shame-filled to explain her new aversion to the place. Her parents chalk it up to adolescent stubbornness and don't press. Nor have they contemplated sending either girl back there till this summer. Kaye doesn't worry about Mr. Iler, or anyone else, peering at Michelle. Michelle's not someone you peer at. She's too young, too big, too un-pretty, Kaye thinks. All these things will keep her baby sister safe.

This summer, Kaye knows Ma and Daddy need her and Michelle gone. Their parents want to devote 100 percent of their parenting to Gordy and don't want the sisters to have to witness his decline. They don't know that Kaye has seen Gordy's upcoming exit already. She's seen the numbness that will descend upon her parents, felt the impending freeze on affection in her home. She has bawled alone—selfish, adolescent tears—anticipating her own losses, of Gordy but also of what little she's had of Ma and Daddy.

"You hate the mountains," says Michelle, raising an accusatory eyebrow. "You didn't used to but now you do."

"I've outgrown them," says Kaye. "That's all."

∽

When Mr. and Mrs. Gifford, along with Evie and Stevie, come to pick Kaye up, she hugs sweet Gordy, kisses his fingers, hugs Ma and Daddy. Then she turns to Michelle, who is trying not to cry.

Feeling charitable, Kaye wipes a tear from her sister's cheek.

"It's going to be a great summer for us both," she says. When she embraces her sister, Michelle clings to her so tightly, Kaye has to pry herself free. "Michi. *Michi.*" She turns and joins the Giffords, wheeling her bag toward the elevator. Michelle sniffles, but Kaye doesn't look back.

⚬

Kaye has Sundays free. Mrs. Gifford drops her off at the Eversons' at ten, where Ruthie is waiting. After primping, tying back their beaded braids to protect them from the salt, the girls gather their towels, magazines, beach chairs, and umbrella, then set off down Seaview Avenue to the beach.

They choose a prime spot in full view of anyone who might matter, spread out their things, and lie out to get hot before they go splashing on into the calm waves. The boys they've set their sights on soon arrive, bearing a badminton set and a pair of big black inner tubes for floating on. In no time, Kaye—in her peppermint-striped bikini—is sitting in the center of one of the inner tubes, legs dangling over the sides, head thrown back as she shrieks in glee. The boy she likes best is spinning her around in the tube. She splashes him with each revolution, commanding, "Faster!"

Then comes a game of chicken, Ruthie and Kaye on the boys' shoulders, trying to pull each other into the surf. Next the girls challenge the boys to badminton, moving the hilarity onshore, with nary a pause in the strutting, flirting, and preening.

When the sun is at its highest point, the four race back into the chilly foam. Kaye propels herself into an oncoming wave, meeting nature's energy with her own.

But now a crack opens amid the sandy floor, and she sees her sister Michelle running, clothes torn—then sobbing into her elbow as large, knotted white hands explore her body, prying, probing, forcing.

The water paralyzes Kaye. She can do nothing to help, but her mind screams at the image of her sister, *Run, Michelle! Kick him! Grab anything you see to fend him off! Please!* She cannot see Mr. Iler's face, but she knows it's him. Kaye remembers his hungry eyes on her, remembers the shame, the fear as fresh as it was that day in the shower. How could she have been so stupid? How could she have let her sister go there alone?

"Michelle!" she screams aloud as she's lifted from the water. The boy she likes is carrying her onto the beach. Kaye thrashes, still calling out to her sister, as Ruthie and the boys wrap her in towels, sit her under the umbrella, fetch her water to drink. Finally she's quiet.

"Are you okay?" says Ruthie.

"My sister's not." Kaye finds the strength in her legs to stand and grab Ruthie's arm. "We have to go."

Back at Ruthie's, Kaye calls her parents, who aren't home. From the information operator, she gets the number for New York-Presbyterian Hospital, then waits on hold for the proper ward.

"I'm sure she's fine," Ruthie keeps saying. "Why would you think something's wrong all of a sudden?"

"Because there is."

Kaye won't explain more, just paces back and forth in the Eversons' kitchen, winding the telephone cord around her arm, then unwinding it again. Finally, *finally*, a nurse locates her father and puts him on.

"Kaye? I promised I'd let you know what's going on with your brother if anything happens. Why are you calling me here?"

"You need to go get Michelle."

"What's wrong with Michelle?"

"Just go get her, please! It's Mr. Iler. He's hurting her. He's going to if he hasn't already. Daddy, *please*!"

"That's absurd."

She tries persuading him, voice growing shrill, hysterical, hard to take in, let alone believe.

"Baby girl, she'd call us if anything was wrong."

"But you're not home!"

Daddy responds with phrases aimed to calm, encouraging her to relax, to enjoy herself. He promises to call Michelle at the Ilers' as soon as he can.

"Hey," Daddy says. "We're all on edge this summer. I know being scared for Gordy probably has you thinking something's wrong with Michelle too."

His voice is so patient and comforting. And his words make sense. Of course Kaye is concerned about Gordy. But it wasn't him she saw through the Obelisk this time; it was Michelle.

"It's natural," Daddy goes on. "You love your brother and sister. And I love you." Which he uses as a segue to get off the phone.

Next Kaye tries calling information in Egremont, Massachusetts, only to learn that the Ilers have an unlisted number.

But that night, Daddy calls her at the Giffords'. "I spoke to your sister and she's fine." Kaye sighs with relief, then Daddy adds, "I spoke to Dan Iler as well, and he says Michelle's having a great time. Helping out on the farm, cooking and planting, even working in the art studio."

Daddy sounds so sure, it eases Kaye's fears just a bit. Michelle would have told Daddy if something was wrong, wouldn't she?

"Daddy, can you give her my number here in case she needs help and can't reach you?"

"Sure I will." Then he shifts gears. "I need to talk to you about Gordy now."

Kaye lets the topic of Michelle go. Perhaps this time she misunderstood what she was seeing in the Obelisk. Maybe it could be like a dream sometimes: just pictures based on worries, but not real, not true.

∞

But it does turn out to be true.

One week later, Daddy calls Kaye at the Giffords', summoning her home to be with Michelle, who's already returned from the mountains. Kaye wants to know why, but Daddy talks over her, detailing Gordy's continued need for both parents' presence at the hospital.

"It's not fair to leave your sister home alone," he says, as if he expects Kaye to complain.

She packs while Mr. Gifford arranges for her to be on the next available ferry. There's no chance to say goodbye to her favorite lifeguard, but Kaye rides across the Vineyard Sound replaying the heady kisses they shared one night over sticks of drooping roasted marshmallows. She cannot resent Michelle. Kaye's brief time away was sweet.

The moment they're alone after Kaye arrives home, Michelle tells her about the horrible thing that happened to her. Kaye holds her sister, cries with her—tears of her own that are many more parts guilt than sympathy.

"Daddy went and got you after it happened?" Kaye says. Even if their father heeded her warning too late, perhaps it staved off further damage.

"No. Mrs. Iler drove me home." Michelle's head is buried in her sister's shoulder, voice muffled. "I asked Daddy to come before. He couldn't."

"I know. I asked him too."

"You did?" Michelle looks up at her. "Why?"

"I mean I didn't—I don't know. I just had a feeling."

"About me?"

"I always think about you," Kaye fudges, remorse pounding in her chest.

"I didn't tell Daddy or Ma," says Michelle. "Because of Gordy. They can't handle anything else."

"No, they can't," Kaye agrees. But wishes she could confront Daddy, take him to task for dismissing her fears. "Maybe it's better for you that way anyhow. It's good you told me so you won't keep it inside, but now you should try and erase the whole thing from your mind." It's the only advice she can think of. "Tell yourself it didn't happen. And then it *won't* have happened."

She hugs Michelle extra tight to wring the horror, the shame from them both. "Anytime that horrible thing comes into your mind, come find me. Squeeze my hand as hard as you can so the thoughts will go out of you and into me. I'm stronger and I'll destroy them."

Kaye believes the words she is uttering and can hear the gratitude in Michelle's breath as the younger girl clings to her.

Regarding the Obelisk, her visions themselves, Kaye told no one in the family. She knew her parents would dismiss the notion of clairvoyance as dramatic teenage fantasy. She couldn't explain it to Michelle, nor could she speak about Mr. Iler spying on her in the shower. Therefore, Kaye could neither ask for nor receive her sister's forgiveness.

The only person Kaye ever told about the Obelisk was Calliope, the therapist who was hired two years later to help with Michelle's darkening moods and slipping grades. Ma suspected Michelle's issues were somehow linked to the loss of Gordy and signed Kaye up for sessions as well. At her very first meeting with Calliope, Kaye—who had not realized that she needed to—blurted out everything about the Obelisk, from the first vision in the bathtub right up to—but not including—the ghastly images of Michelle being pursued and assaulted by Mr. Iler.

Kaye wanted Calliope to teach her to eradicate the visions. Calliope—who was more spiritual healer than clinical therapist— refused, encouraging Kaye to embrace her gift, to harness her power for good. Instead, Kaye asked Ma to stop making her see Calliope, pointing out that Michelle needed the sessions more.

As the Leeds sisters passed from adolescence into adulthood, Michelle squeezed Kaye's hand with diminished frequency. Kaye spent the next decade teaching herself to shut down the Obelisk. Ultimately, she found that it faded with an aspirin or a drink.

And now that Kaye is in her midthirties, with two kids, a husband, and a start-up business, she believes she's managed to obliterate the Obelisk. The alliteration amuses Kaye, making her just a bit too smug.

Ninth Street

Brooklyn, March 2018

But after the day in the coffee shop, the visions return. The Sad Woman and her child have torn off the Obelisk's seal. Anytime there's a lull in Kaye's chores, her work, or her dealings with the kids, the window opens. The visions are intense, full of shifting images. Like the complex adventure dream you have when you doze off reading the news, then wake up to find that only five minutes have lapsed. There's no telling whether she'll have revelations from the past, present, or future. Kaye's been on ships, in kitchens, in a meadow with moonlight streaming over a barrier of trees. She's danced, laughing, holding hands with other Black women she doesn't recognize. She's seen a boy the same age Gordy lived to be, but healthy, able, unbent, playing with a spotted dog. Often the visions end with the same house—big, red, flanked by wildflowers and birch trees.

The pictures are frenetic, unsettling, disorienting, with no apparent connection to one another. Sometimes Kaye is an outsider, watching scenes unfold. Other times she's in the thick of the activity. Some visions seem innocuous—a bridge over a shining river, a garden full of colorful blooms. Others are frightening, like when Kaye finds herself in darkness, chains binding her wrists and ankles, vanquished by the stench of human sweat and feces, of death itself—or running from dogs through deep, wet woods—images to whose meaning no Black person on earth is ignorant. On those occasions, Kaye returns to consciousness in a state of terror that takes several minutes, maybe a cup of tea, or something stronger, to shake. The fear never fully leaves her, but it fades to a dull dread. Kaye won't let herself dwell on why these apparitions have chosen her.

The kids have tae kwon do at Champions Martial Arts after school on Thursdays. Most of the mothers stay in the waiting area to watch, to be on hand for meltdowns or snack breaks during the one-hour classes. Kaye's kids have no need for that, so she usually dashes across the street to Russo's to pick up something for dinner—fresh pasta, cheese, and Andy's favorite black olives. As she's opening the door to the Italian delicacy shop, the giant front tire of a baby jogger emerges and Kaye ceremoniously steps back, holding the door for whoever's pushing it.

It's automatic, the way you hold the door open, feeling your own sense of hard-earned liberty, to have been parenting long enough to have kids independent enough to participate in martial arts classes while you shop unencumbered. Kaye smiles at the baby, not the mother. Because she knows with white moms, some smile back—*most* smile back—but those who don't affect Kaye in a deep kind of way. It's a reminder that she is still *the other*, no matter how cute her clothes, no matter how big her brownstone. Kaye spares herself the pain and saves her smiles for the babies.

But at the last moment, noticing that the hands pushing the stroller are brown, Kaye looks up into the face of the Sad Woman she saw a month ago in the café, whose terrifying image Kaye saw in the Obelisk.

Flustered, she rummages for words to warn the Sad Woman. Such as . . . what? *Beware the spinning wheel?* Like some psychotic fairy tale prophet? "How are you, girl?" is all Kaye comes up with.

The Sad Woman doesn't respond, not even to thank Kaye for getting the door. She continues pushing the baby jogger outside and turns right, heading up Seventh Avenue.

"Wait!" Propelled by the old remorse over dismissing the Obelisk back in the summer of '99, of failing Michelle, Kaye goes hurtling after the woman. She dodges through traffic, past oncoming vehicles, around scowling pedestrians, to get to her. It dawns on Kaye, as she continues the chase through the intersection of Seventh Avenue and Tenth Street, narrowly missed by a Poland Spring delivery truck, that the woman is not running from her but simply running for exercise—possibly to combat the depression. In any case, the Sad Woman, whose endless legs carry her like a gazelle, is a real runner. Kaye, who is not, chugs after her, panting, aware that she still needs to shop and make it back before the children finish class.

At the next corner, the Sad Woman glances from right to left, then sprints across the street on a diagonal, vanishing up Ninth. As Kaye lunges onward, the Obelisk opens wider than ever before, engulfing Brooklyn in a thick green mist. Kaye continues running as unruly branches swipe and scratch her face. She hears the rush of a stream, the barking of hounds, the concussive thud of horses. Kaye's heart races, matching the beasts' footfalls. In a flash, someone's black arms push through a curtain of willow vines and pull her to safety, folding her into a strong, soft embrace. She sees a dark, smiling face, feels the other's warm breath on her cheeks. Now a car horn honks and the image evaporates, replaced by pavement and flashing lights.

In a too-sudden effort to avoid a man on a scooter, angling herself between him and a pair of mailboxes, Kaye skids on the curb cut, twists her ankle, yelps, and goes down. A yellow cab swerves as she drags herself out of the street, attempting in vain to stand. Kaye's ankle throbs, weak from the trauma. She hasn't the wherewithal to assess the damage as yet. She remains seated on the cold late-winter sidewalk, eyes beginning to tear. Proximity to the gutter is transformative; Kaye internalizes it as people step blindly by. Her favorite wool coat—a Marc Jacobs splurge—is smeared with soot and waste from the street, creating instant shabbiness, she imagines, a vagrant appearance. Kaye is no longer an affluent mother, co-owner of a brownstone. She's a Black woman in a ruined old coat, sitting alone on a street corner. Friendless. Pathetic.

"Kaye?" A familiar voice, alarmed, vaguely tinged with judgment. "Oh my God! Yo, *girlfriend*, what's *up?*"

It's Lexi of all people. Lexi—who's lately been trying out Black slang in Kaye's presence—pulling her up. Regardless that this is her least favorite mom-friend, Kaye's heart swells with gratitude at being recognized. Tears of relief rush freely as she embraces the tiny white woman.

"Are you okay?" Lexi says.

Kaye sobs, unable to speak.

"Here." Lexi offers an arm—spindly, even in her thick puffer coat—to help her up. There's no nearby bench, but there's a protective red awning in front of Smiling Pizza and, next to that, the fence demarking the subway entrance. Kaye hops, weight partly crushing Lexi's shoulder, till she's propped against the fence, where she can lean and try to wiggle her foot.

"Thanks," Kaye says, catching her breath. "I'm okay." She notes her reflection in the pizza store window, attempting to fix her hair, which is askew in a way that can't be remedied without a sink and some Aunt Jackie's Frizz Patrol.

"What were you running for, girl?" says Lexi, laughing, doing a cringeworthy neck slide. "You were going all Usain Bolt on me! Did someone swipe your phone or something?"

"No. Nothing like that. I just thought I saw an old friend. It wasn't her."

"Oh, bummer." Lexi's nose wrinkles in sympathy. She looks more closely at Kaye's face and drops the cool-girl act. "Hey—I do stuff like that all the time." She brushes some muck off Kaye's coat, and Kaye realizes she's never been with Lexi when there weren't other mothers around to perform for. "You've just got mom-brain, that's all."

The understanding in her tone lets Kaye reset and feel normal again. She succumbs to a smile.

"Wow." Kaye places a hand on Lexi's shoulder. She looks around. "That was crazy, right? To chase a total stranger through the streets of Brooklyn."

Lexi laughs with, not at her. "Kind of crazy, yeah. But like I said—"

"I know: mom-brain." It's a relief to brand it, accurately or not.

"Hey," Lexi says, "your kids are over at Champions with Ethan now, right?" Referencing her son, who's in Miles's tae kwon do class. "If you want, I can bring them home if you just need to, you know . . ."

Kaye is about to decline, say she's fine—which she mostly is, thanks to Lexi. But now they're joined at the corner by a small group—an older woman whom Kaye recognizes as Meg, the Realtor who helped her and Andy find their brownstone, two men forming a hand-in-hand couple, and one infant, too large for the carrier she's been stuffed into, worn by one of the men. Kaye, still shaken by her fall, shamed by the smears on her coat, is nonetheless about to greet Meg, perhaps with an explanation about her appearance, when Meg snorts.

"Good *lord*." Shaking her head, Meg steers the hopeful homeowners away. Adding at a reasonable volume, "That's an anomaly. In this neighborhood, you hardly ever see that sort of thing."

That sort of thing. The words, vague yet pointed, dissolve what's left of Kaye's dignity. She chokes up again just as Lexi squares her shoulders.

"Excuse me?" Lexi speaks as if from Kaye's own mind, the words she'd use if not muzzled by shame. *"Excuse me?"*

Meg turns, startled, as the young men with the baby cower beside her.

"Yeah, *you!*" Lexi stands firm in her size 5 Doc Martens. "*What* sort of thing do you hardly see around here?"

And Ninth Street slips into the Obelisk, replaced by a dusty road with scraggly overgrowth on either side. Kaye sees a green-eyed white man on a horse, holding the end of a rope that leads to the right of the horse's flank. There stands the Sad Woman, bound by her wrists and neck. The man kicks at the horse, who in turn kicks the Sad Woman. She collapses, crying out in pain as howls of glee erupt from her captor. The road fades and Ninth Street reappears.

"Holy *shit*!" Lexi is laughing, clutching Kaye's hand. Meg the Realtor and the young fathers are nowhere in sight. "Did I not *school* that old bitch? Did you see her *face*? *Did* you? I thought she was going to die right there!"

Kaye makes herself laugh along, though she did not see, did not hear Lexi's schooling of Meg. Lexi continues to gush and gloat over her rescue of Kaye. Over Lexi's head, Kaye spots a slim Black woman with erect posture and a gleaming inch of straightened hair poking demurely from under a white knit beanie.

"Hey!" Kaye calls out. Lexi turns. The woman stops to stare at them, and Kaye recognizes with dismay: it isn't her.

⁓

Kaye can't give up, though. The duty to warn impels her to search for the Sad Woman, walking the streets of the Slope, into Russo's and the neighboring businesses, peering into coffee shop windows, nosing around the vestibule at the Music Together place on First Street, every baby clothes and infant supply store. Turning to the internet, to Facebook and LinkedIn, Kaye realizes she knows nothing about this woman aside from a guess that her husband is white. But scouring interracial couples pages and multiracial families groups on social media proves futile.

At night Kaye dreams of the scene with the spinning wheel, dreams of the Sad Woman's tearful face staring at her over the form of her sleeping infant. By day, Andy, Michelle, Billie—even Miles—notice Kaye's distraction, but it's nothing she can reasonably explain. Kaye smiles brightly, enacting a facsimile of good humor to avoid worrying her family.

In desperation she takes to staring at walls or into blank spaces, vain attempts to conjure fresh visions—anything that might help her save a life. But the Obelisk refuses to be manipulated.

The Damn Mountains

Brooklyn, June 2018

The Damn Mountains Again, reads the subject line of Michelle's email. Anticipating some new revelation about the Horrible Thing, which the sisters rarely discuss anymore, Kaye puts off opening it. Just for a bit. She reminds herself that Michelle is stronger now, thanks to many years of work with Calliope. There was even some exposure thing where Michelle had to go back to the Berkshires, to those same "Damn Mountains" and live, reclaiming the narrative, as it were. It seemed to work too. Michelle "reclaimed" the place, her power, herself—even fell in love along the way. When the relationship fell through, Kaye and Andy opened their home to Michelle indefinitely.

The idea had come from Andy, who didn't know that he—at least what he represented—was the cause of the latest rift between the Leeds sisters.

Michelle had come out right around the time that Kaye brought home her first white boyfriend, each sister recognizing the start of a breach. Michelle, then fourteen, experienced Kaye's choice as an outright betrayal.

"Our history," Michelle told her older sister, in tears after the boy had gone home following an awkward family dinner, "is full of rape at the hands of guys like him." Kaye understood her full meaning, that *our* history meant Michelle's history especially. But it was not Kaye's. She could not assign past crimes to her beau.

Ten years later, Michelle responded with disdain to the news of Kaye and Andy's engagement, referring to the nuptials as the "colonization of my sister." Andy—whom Kaye considers to be aware and savvy, cognizant of his privileges, whose Jewish ancestors arrived long after slavery—would have been devastated by the remark. Kaye never told him.

Eight years after the wedding, Andy suggested Michelle move in.

"She's got nowhere to go," Andy said. "She's your sister, and we've got plenty of room. If you're okay with it, I am." The summer of '99 compelled the "yes" from Kaye's lips.

Michelle accepted the invitation to share their home, along with Kaye and Andy's offer of an interest-free loan for a master's program in social work. Four years later, Michelle still lives in the spare room. Now that she's working, she pays rent and shares the grocery bill. She's doing okay. Still, any mention of "the Mountains" sets Kaye's heart racing.

∽

"You didn't read the link I sent?" says Michelle later on, dissecting a head of broccoli in preparation for dinner. "About the murder in the Berkshires?"

"What link?" Kaye, rinsing greens, turns her head away, distracted for a moment by the voices of the children in the next room, fighting about something. Without intervention, perhaps sensing their mother's alertness, Billie and Miles settle down. "Oh. Right," says Kaye. "'The Damn Mountains Again.' Wait—did you say *murder*?"

"You did *not* read it." Michelle sets down the knife. "Well, you better sit down for this."

Kaye leaves the greens in their colander, pulls a stool out from the kitchen island, and sits.

"It's an article from the *Berkshire Eagle*," says Michelle. "D sent it to me," referring to her ex, who still lives in Massachusetts, raising the little boy she had with the guy she cheated on Michelle with.

"Are you and Dominique talking again?" Kaye sees her sister's chest contract at her articulation of the woman's full name. When Michelle was dating her, Dominique's friends were part of a cultish group called the Seekers, obsessed with contacting their ancestors via séance. They were all sleeping together, as Michelle learned too late. It sounded so messy to Kaye.

"Not really," says Michelle. "She sends me stuff sometimes. Articles about house hauntings. Pictures of her kid." She shrugs like she's not still hurting. "So, this couple goes on vacation Memorial Day weekend. She's Black; he's white. Sound familiar?"

"Shockingly." Kaye rolls her eyes.

"And they have a little baby girl. Anyway, they go up to stay at an Airbnb in the Berkshires—a big, old farmhouse with a pond out back. Two days later, the couple is found slashed to death and the baby is gone."

"Oh my *God*!"

"The murder weapon is on the floor beside the couple, but there are no fingerprints on it aside from both of theirs."

"That's just gruesome, Michi."

"Yeah. First the cops thought it was domestic violence. That he was attacking her and she stabbed him and then herself, or the other way around. But the problem with that is, where's the baby?"

"Abducted by the real killer?"

"But then it turns out that the lady who owned the Airbnb is gone without a trace too."

"So obviously she killed them."

"They say she abducted the kid, but they don't think she killed the parents."

"Why not?"

"No prints linking her to the crime. Plus, she didn't fit the profile."

"The profile of what? A slasher, or a baby swiper?"

"The first one."

Michelle gets the link open on her phone and hands it over to Kaye, who scrolls past the text, past the image of the Airbnb owner—a plain-looking older white woman—stopping at the photograph of the young couple smiling on their wedding day. *Dr. Robert Campbell and Dr. Galen Lord.* Dr. Campbell is a big dude, bearded with red hair, looking awkward in a tuxedo, more like an alpinist than a physician.

Dr. Lord—thin and regal, elegant in her strapless gown, with a face that's snap-your-fingers familiar, like a neighbor you take a second to recognize because they have a new haircut or—

Kaye's breath cuts short: It's *her*. The Sad Woman from the coffee shop, from the Ninth Street chase, is Dr. Galen Lord.

On this side of the Obelisk, Kaye collapses into Michelle's arms. But on the other side she is in pitch darkness as a woman prays, "Rest eternal grant them, O Lord. Let light perpetual shine upon them. May they rest in peace, amen . . ." over and over. Now a door opens, light streams in, and Kaye sails along a hallway, hears quiet footfalls taking her consciousness into a room with a chair, a cradle, a fireplace, and an overturned spinning wheel. All over the floor, blood pools from the bodies of a white man and a Black woman in a heap, knife inches away from the woman's open hand.

The footfalls cease, but the prayer continues in the same hushed, even tone.

"Rest eternal grant them, O Lord . . ."

Kaye floats downward as a pair of thin arms lower her into the cradle, where she fits comfortably.

"Let light perpetual shine . . ."

A frail-looking white woman in a blue gingham dress steps around the cradle and over a splash of blood to sit in the chair. Kaye sees her lips moving lightly around the words of her chant.

". . . shine upon them. May they rest in peace, amen."

The woman's leg extends to rock the cradle. She gazes down at Kaye with soft gray eyes.

"Hush now, Birdie," she says. "Sweet Birdie. Hush."

Kaye won't remember that part. For next come rapid flashes of light and color interspersed with shadow. Kaye is floating again, over grassy terrain, over rainy sidewalks, where people's heels click and thud, splashing through puddles. She is swaddled tightly with someone's heart beating close by. Kaye senses that this body is everything she needs: love, life, nourishment, though she cannot see the other's face. Now they are huddled together beside a concrete stoop on a city side street. A glass door opens, and there is a brown skinned woman with a furrowed brow, a look of worry Kaye would know anywhere. *Ma.* Which means that the other—the one holding her—is not Ma.

The vision ends as Ma's face ages up to the present day and Kaye and Andy's bedroom materializes around them. Ma is sitting on the bed, with Michelle in a chair pulled up close, Andy standing at the footboard.

Kaye covers her face with her hands. "How long have I been here?"

"Three hours?" says Michelle. "Three and a half? I called Ma and Andy as soon as you passed out."

"The kids are fine," Andy says, knowing it's Kaye's next question. "They ate. Now they're playing that computer game with the butterflies."

Michelle says, "You were shouting about the *Berkshire Eagle* article in your sleep."

Michelle's mention of the article reminds Kaye of her failure to avert yet another Horrible Thing. "Can I talk to Andy alone?"

Her mother and sister slip out.

"Michelle showed me the article." Andy usurps Ma's spot on the bed, taking Kaye's hands, rubbing her palm with his thumb. "It was pretty upsetting, especially with the baby missing. I understand."

"No, you don't. Michelle doesn't either. Andy, I met her. I held that baby."

"How is that possible?"

She tells him about the coffee shop encounter, about the recent visions. He listens, patient, nodding, continuing to massage her hands.

"How could it have been the same woman, though?"

"I don't know, but it was. I should have done something. I should have warned her."

"Kaye—"

"I swear it was her." Kaye feels herself getting agitated, which won't help her credibility. "I know it's crazy, but it's true."

"Okay."

"You're humoring me."

"What else can I do?"

Gently he suggests she get in touch with a therapist to see if a professional has any thoughts about the situation. Kaye bristles, turning away, though she knows he's right. Not that Calliope is what Andy has in mind when he says the word "therapist." Still, Calliope, if she's still around, is the only one Kaye could share this with.

⁓

"I didn't know if you would remember me." Kaye sits on the seafoam velour sofa between two oversize throw cushions printed with a black-and-white geometric pattern. The sofa is unfamiliar, but Kaye remembers the collection of Senegalese masks and Shona sculptures. On the coffee table is a red clay sculpture depicting four tiny women with their arms around each other's shoulders. Each woman's headdress has a hole into which Calliope has inserted a stick of incense. Calliope herself is in her seventies by now, shorter, thicker, the locks that reach her hips a pale gray. She wears square gold-rimmed glasses, enhancing her wise-woman air.

"How could I forget?" Calliope lowers herself into an upholstered rattan chair. "You came just a few times, but your sister talked to me about you for years."

"I suppose she must have."

"I saw your mother too."

"I didn't know."

"You never told either of them about your visions, about what you called the Obelisk."

"I guess you didn't either."

"I never break a confidence." The old woman's smile reveals a gold front tooth. Kaye can't recall whether that's new or not. "What brings you here today?"

Kaye explains about her meeting with, her visions of, the Sad Woman, Dr. Galen Lord, the recent tragedy in the "Damn Mountains," and the disappearance of the baby, whom she held in her own arms. The tears come as Kaye concludes, "I know. If I'd listened to you all those years ago when you told me to harness my power, I could have stopped this from happening. That little girl would still have her parents; she'd be safe."

Calliope slides the box of tissues closer, contemplating her response. "Maybe you couldn't have harnessed anything back then. Maybe because there was a piece of you missing that you weren't ready to look for."

"What kind of piece?"

"I think you know what I mean." Calliope eyes Kaye over her glasses. "I'm talking about where you come from. Maybe now you're ready to put it together and find out why you have this gift in the first place."

Kaye's anxiety rises. This is definitely not what Andy had in mind vis-à-vis therapy. "Gift," she snorts. "It's a curse."

"Either way, it's a responsibility and an honor." Calliope rubs her hands together, then reaches forward to light the incense. "Acacia and sandalwood. What if you tell me what you saw in the Obelisk after your sister showed you the article."

Kaye closes her eyes, inhaling the rich incense smell, trying to recapture the vision. She describes the closeness, the warmth of the anonymous loving being, the concrete stoop and her mother opening the glass door.

"That was where it ended," says Kaye. "My mother was there on the bed with me in real life."

"Your mother was?"

"Yes."

"What did she look like in the vision?"

"Herself. Younger." Kaye takes another deep breath in an effort to stop her heart from racing. "Why?"

"And who do you think was holding you when your mother opened the door?"

"I don't know." Kaye holds one of the throw pillows, a barrier between herself and whatever truth Calliope is trying to pry out of her.

"But whoever it was 'felt like love,' you said."

"Yes."

"Well then, she's your missing piece. You find out who she is and you'll know how to use your gift."

∾

When Andy asks that evening, as they're washing dishes and Michelle is reading to the kids, Kaye shrugs and says that therapy was fine.

Then: "We talked about the baby from the article. The one who went missing. The one I held."

"Oh, Kaye honey."

She meets his eyes, tears visible in her own. "I just can't get her out of my mind."

"I know. There's nothing more heartbreaking than a lost baby." Andy puts his arms around her. "The question is: What does she have to do with you?"

∾

Months pass. Kaye follows the story, which by now consists mostly of interviews: with detectives who seem largely stumped, with a librarian at the Monterey Historical Center who knew the Airbnb owner, with the parents of Dr. Robert Campbell, the murdered husband, and lastly, with Delia, the sister of Dr. Galen Lord, the murdered wife—an on-screen favorite, pretty as her unfortunate sister Galen with high cheekbones, long burgundy box braids, and an uncanny ability to speak coherently through tears. A mother herself, Delia is devastated, desperate for information regarding the disappearance of her infant niece, whose name is Olivia. Delia talks right into the camera, wide-eyed and imploring: if anyone has any information at all—please, *please*. The baby belongs with her grieving auntie. The station offers a contact number.

Kaye writes it down on a Post-it, then squirrels it away in her sock drawer. She knows nothing for certain. If she were to call, she'd only upset Delia further. Kaye has no proof, only a few visions she can't begin to make sense of. None of that is a lead. Still, her heart aches for Baby Olivia.

Soon, Delia's tearful face becomes a staple image in Kaye's brain, along with the sight of the yellow Post-it in her sock drawer, crumpled, pushed aside, but still there every time she puts away her laundry. Why would she call the number? What exactly would she tell the police?

As for the Obelisk, it's unpredictable at best. Kaye can't summon it at whim, but it continues to show her glimpses of the baby. Kaye assumes it's Baby Olivia, though the pictures aren't always clear. Sometimes the little girl lies in an old-fashioned cradle tucked under flannel bedding. Other times, Kaye sees her in the same sling that sat beside her mother in the booth that day. Wearing the sling is an older white woman—not her mother. Kaye only catches a glimpse, never enough for a police sketch.

Every so often, Kaye sees the baby on a concrete city doorstep, with someone's body wrapped protectively around her. The other is a teenage girl in a worn denim jacket. Kaye comes out of those visions with the same old question on her lips, the one Baby Olivia will share one day: *Whose was I first?*

The Truth

Brooklyn, September 2019

The kids are at school when the results of Kaye's DNA test arrive via email. Kaye knew it was a shady idea: to spit into a little vial and send it off to a company that would forever have access to her genetic material. But thanks in part to her recent visions, curiosity defeats prudence. Kaye clicks on the link and reads all the information. She registers the percentages of her "DNA Story" with shock and disbelief—that her European roots outpace her African ones. She does not call Ma. She does not tell Michelle or even Andy. There is a box to check if you would like to be contacted by your matches—people who are cousins, or closer. Kaye hesitates, then checks it.

Less than a month after that, a woman messages Kaye through her Ancestry.com profile. Could it be you? reads the heading. The woman's name is Pam. She shares a story about her infant daughter, who was taken by social workers in New York and given to an anonymous family. Pam was a teenager at the time. She'd run away from her home in Boston.

Concluding her narrative, Pam writes: I've been waiting years. Our DNA matched as mother and daughter, so I know it's you. Your last name is the same as my case manager's. I believe she's the one who took you. But you were my Ayesha Kaye.

It takes Kaye more than a week to write back, I must be.

Pam writes, Would it be okay if I sent you something?

Kaye responds, Yes.

Five days later, a package arrives, full of envelopes addressed in the same hand. Out slides a single loose photograph of a young girl in a denim jacket with one elbow rested on the shoulder of a man who is clearly her father. Kaye recognizes the girl, the jacket too, from her visions. On the back of the photograph, in the same penmanship, it says *Pop and me, Dorchester, 1984.* They are both somewhat darker than Kaye, but their faces, their *faces!* They are the spitting image of hers. She rummages a bit and finds more loose photos: Pam, as a younger girl with Pop and a woman who must be her mother, *my grandmother.* Pam, in a wedding dress with Pop giving her away, looking giddy but dignified in a tuxedo. Pop, older, grinning on a dock holding up a fish he's caught, the other arm around a small boy with a matching grin. *My brother?* Feeling short of breath, Kaye crams the photos, along with the envelopes, back into the package and presses her eyes shut. *Pop and me.* She can see them still, side by side, smiling her own smile.

Kaye stashes the package under her dresser but retrieves it the next day while the children are at school and spreads its contents out on the bed she shares with Andy. Tissue box at her side, she opens the envelopes one by one, anticipating every word of the story that has hovered all her life—*If only*—waiting for her to know it.

> Your name was Ayesha Kaye. You were conceived in the root cellar of a big red farmhouse in the mountains of Massachusetts . . .
>
> Your mama was me, a poor Black girl from a troubled housing project in Boston. Wherever you grew up was nicer by far, so no regrets about that. Your daddy was a rich white boy who I haven't laid eyes on since the night we made you. He didn't force himself on me, in case you wondered, but we were both young and dumb and didn't think any of it through. And

your daddy's mama was a great big, rich white lady who probably wishes neither of us was ever born. If you're tall, it's because of her, not me. That red farmhouse in Massachusetts belonged to her family, so it kind of belongs to you too . . .

Something happened I never told anyone before. That night I got pregnant with you, I saw the spirits of our ancestors. Your daddy's mother believed the house and the root cellar were haunted, and that night, I found out it was true. I saw them. I thought they were coming for me, but they weren't. They were runaways, still trying to get to Freedom. They thought I could help. Nothing more I can say about that, but I wanted you to know . . .

Kaye sets down the final letter, clutches a pillow, inhales, exhales, keeping the sadness and anger at bay.

∽

She lets another week go by, trying to behave and feel like the person she's always known herself to be. Finally she calls Ma, who answers the phone with her full name, like she does at the Hope Social Service Center, where she's worked for nearly forty years.

"Dawn Leeds."

"I know, Ma," Kaye begins. "I know about Pam."

Ma's silence lasts for the entire speech Kaye has rehearsed. Then she coughs.

"What do you want to know?" Ma's voice is husky, and Kaye knows she's fighting tears, knows that Ma will win, that Ma will not cry, because she never does. "That girl came to the agency when you were barely a day old. She was sick. She had exposed you to all manner of germs." Ma's story meshes with Pam's, but it chills Kaye to the bone.

"Ma." Kaye can find no other words.

"What I did was wrong, but it was for the best. I held you and loved you at once. I couldn't let you grow up in squalor and poverty." Ma's voice shakes, then steadies again. "And I kept the second name she gave you, did you know that? The girl said her mother's name was Kaye. Same as your grandma's. That's how I knew you were destined to be ours."

"Ma." Kaye's tears fall for them both.

"I am sorry," Ma says and hangs up.

Kaye sits on her bed, staring at the window, thinking about her first mother, how Pam must have wondered and searched. Calliope's words about her "missing piece" come back to her. Now that Kaye has unlocked her secret, can she control her gift? Should she try? Kaye settles her body and wills the Obelisk to transport her back to the time and place where she was taken. She needs to see herself, to pull down the blanket and take just one glimpse of the infant she was before Dawn and Elgin Leeds claimed her. When Kaye opens her eyes, there's nothing at first but the bedroom curtains, pale yellow—the same color as the Post-it crumpled up in her sock drawer with the precinct's contact number.

Now the curtains ripple; the Obelisk relents at last. Kaye finds herself on a neatly paved walk on a sunny day. Her view tracks slowly past benches and tended shrubs, lush blooms, the occasional squirrel. She's bouncing in rhythm to the irregularities of the ground as sunlight glints through tree silhouettes. People glance down in her direction, smiling. *I must be in a wheelchair,* Kaye thinks, based on the angle of their gazes. *Or a stroller.* And here, off to her right, a giant bridge materializes—the Golden Gate, the most recognizable bridge in all the world. And alongside its magnificent shadow, Kaye sees her own. She's just a tiny girl whom fate has taken from her mother. The stroller stops and a middle-aged white woman appears before her, crouching to fix the canopy. The woman touches her cheek and smiles.

When the Obelisk closes, Kaye's heart is pounding. She grabs her phone and brings up the link from the *Berkshire Eagle*, verifying that the face of the woman in her vision matches that of the Airbnb owner.

Kaye retrieves the Post-it from her dresser drawer. "Baby Olivia," she says to the air. "Let's get you home."

4

A Gift from the Earthbound

Walkway

San Francisco, September 2019

The sun beams down on the walkway in the imposing shadow of the Golden Gate Bridge. Maxine kneels before Olivia's stroller to fix the canopy. The little girl smiles.

"Hi, Mama." Which melts Maxine's heart each time she hears it. Attachment, she has read, is an amazing thing, the way it is transferred from one loving caregiver to another. Maxine touches her daughter's cheek and straightens up to resume their daily walk.

How funny: on the day they met, Maxine was disappointed that Olivia was not browner. Now she knows that the child's fair skin is what has kept them anonymous. The perfect cover.

Anticipating Guests

Whittaker House, Memorial Day Weekend 2018

Charcoal gripped between her index knuckle and sturdy, round thumb, Maxine studies the boy's face projected on the wall from her computer screen. After the Rhodes family left—without saying goodbye—*fled*, frankly—Maxine copied their photo, then edited out everyone but Timothy so she could one day capture his likeness. That was three years ago: 2015—it must have been. Obama was still in office.

Timothy must be ten now. Is that fourth grade? Fifth? Kids are meaner by that time. They notice when your speech seems lifted from an encyclopedia, when your conversation is limited to details about prehistoric marine reptiles. Second graders might let such a thing go, but ten-year-olds find ways to target and humiliate.

Upon the family's arrival, Timothy, their youngest, was impervious to Maxine's cheerful greeting, her offer of cranberry scones. The child stared blankly when Maxine gave his family a tour of the house. He came to life, however, laying eyes on a watercolor of a leaping dolphin, the largest painting in Maxine's *Cape Cod* series, the only one that had not sold.

"An ichthyosaur!" the boy exclaimed and began rattling off facts. "Warm-blooded, air-breathing marine reptiles who existed from the late Triassic through the early-late Cretaceous. By the mid-Jurassic period, ichthyosaurs had attained lengths exceeding eighty feet. They were deep swimmers who ambushed their prey in . . ."

Maxine didn't have the heart to disabuse him of his discovery. "It is *indeed* an ichthyosaur!" she said when he paused his monologue. Because, in that instant, her bottlenose subject had become one. Maxine shared a smile with his mother and experienced a devastating, if not unexpected, stab of envy.

"Timothy." His father's voice was gentle but firm and full of we've-talked-about-this intent. "Timothy, that's enough now."

But Maxine was captivated. She had been from the moment she'd seen the family's Airbnb profile photo months earlier. It was a Christmas card picture: a mother, father, and three boys. The parents and two of the boys were white. As in Anglo-Saxon white, a very different kind of white than what Maxine considered herself to be. The granddaughter of Russian Jews who had escaped the pogroms at the start of the twentieth century, arriving in the United States when Jews were deemed not *entirely* white, Maxine had grown up learning how hard her grandparents had worked to fit in and assimilate, minimizing their culture, failing to teach their children Yiddish. Whereas Timothy's family—with the exception of Timothy himself—was gleaming white, alabaster white, *Nordic* white: tall, blond, blue-eyed. To be fair, Maxine's frizzy bob had at times been blonde. But it was an apologetic blonde, a self-conscious, never-quite-the right-shade of bottle blonde.

There was nothing self-conscious about Timothy's parents, who looked eerily like brother and sister—corporate types with neat hair, sharp jaws and cheekbones, exquisite, no-nonsense grooming. The older boys—Grayson, Maxine recalls, and Barrett—were spitting images of both parents. Timothy's wide-spaced, thickly fringed eyes looked out from his brown face, hungry—Maxine was sure of it—for a kindred spirit. In this photograph, Timothy stood in the center of the family as the others leaned toward him, creating a gold-headed halo around him, a shield between this small Black boy and the harsh world. They failed to recognize that Timothy appeared in the spot that a pet might have occupied. Their mascot. As soon as the thought struck her, Maxine shook it off. But another materialized in its place: *he would be better off with me.* Afterward, she would fantasize about an impossible life—where Claude had survived and agreed to adopt a child, where that child was a sweet, strange, and brilliant Black boy. How Claude would have taken to a child like Timothy. How he would have relished teaching him things!

There's another notion that remains to this day: had Maxine gone ahead with an impulse she'd had one night, about a year after Claude's death, this little boy might indeed have been hers. Adoption, Maxine reasons, is arbitrary like that. Who is to say where a given-away child winds up? What sort of life he'll have? Suburban or rural. Artistic or sports-driven. Offbeat or conventional. Timothy would have thrived in the farmhouse, surrounded by this history, among these hills and the souls buried beneath them.

Maxine was hurt when the family vanished so quickly. But she understood. She understood very well. And now, three years later, Maxine is drawing Timothy, marking, rubbing, furiously shading, focusing only on the eyes to start with. Next she allows a broader field, creating the whole of his face. By the time she's finished pulling Timothy's essence from the page, the late spring's afternoon rays have lengthened through the skylight. Maxine steps back from her easel, heart quickening with the rush of generativity. Timothy's eyes, anxious and full of intent.

A few minutes later, setting up the French press, Maxine glances out of the window at the burgeoning magenta rhododendrons and pink azaleas marking the path from her cottage to the farmhouse. The landscapers have outdone themselves this year. When she's finished her coffee, she'll head down to prep for the new guests: an interracial couple from Brooklyn and their baby girl.

A Marriage

Maxine Ross Whittaker's late husband was the author Dr. Claude L. Whittaker, twenty-two years her senior. Maxine had attended one of his talks back in '98—or was it '99?—and, smitten, introduced herself when it was over, boldly dropping her phone number on the lectern. For years afterward, Claude would embellish the story at dinner parties, describing Maxine as "the lissome artist who threw herself at me after a lecture on Proust." It was his *voice*, Maxine explained to her sister later, the way Claude measured his words, by turns impassioned and reserved as he argued on behalf of the Kilmartin translation.

When Claude brought her to the house for the first time, Maxine was bowled over by its size and the acreage upon which it sat. It was springtime, and the grounds, crawling with members of a landscaping team, gave off a smell of renewal and hope.

"You live here by yourself?" Maxine was then renting a tiny studio apartment on Manhattan's Upper West Side. Claude had nodded and given a rare shrug—eyebrows lifted in acknowledgment of the absurdity.

Claude came from money and did not fret terribly about earning it. The house was one of several that had belonged to his family for over a century. His older sister, Leigh-Ann Whittaker-Burke, had raised her family here. When her three boys had left for college, she and her husband, Calvin, had moved to the city while Claude had taken residence along with his first wife and daughter. By the time he and Maxine met, the daughter was grown. She and the ex-wife had moved out west. Each behaved as if Claude didn't exist, except as the provider of funds.

Claude made it clear to Maxine from their first date: he would father no more children.

And, though Maxine was just thirty-two at the time, that was that. They'd wed a few years later, in the summer of '02, and Whittaker House—the name had always felt too stately, too stuffy for a sprawling red farmhouse—had become Maxine's home. Though it had enough bedrooms to accommodate a bustling family, Claude and Maxine dwelt there alone. He wrote. She painted and drew. They enjoyed trips to Great Barrington or Stockbridge for dinner, then strolled hand in hand, savoring the crisp mountain air, discussing politics and music. They attended open-air concerts at Tanglewood, summer dance performances at Jacob's Pillow in Becket. Claude was kind and affectionate. Maxine loved him deeply, loved their intimacy and the interests they shared. What need had they for children?

Until Maxine's fortieth birthday, when she awoke feeling terrified, as if a train she'd been watching from the platform all her life was suddenly leaving the station. *She wanted a baby.* Desperately. She wanted to share the beauty of the world, the things she loved, to see it all through the magical gaze of an innocent child who was hers!

But how would she persuade Claude, who was already sixty-two? Maxine spent several days plotting the best way to confront him. She would not be coy but strong and insistent. She would not ask but would tell him: she wanted to be—she must be—she *would* be a mother. "So it's settled," she'd planned to say. "You will let me have my way on this."

One afternoon, angular frame wrapped in a short black kimono-style robe, bearing a bottle of Beaujolais and two glasses, Maxine found Claude in his office. It was raining in sheets outside, drenching the property. Chopin was playing on Claude's refurbished antique Victrola. All was perfect for the ambush she had intended.

But without warning, something contracted within her, as if a pair of powerful hands were squeezing her abdomen—compressing from the outside, pulling from within. Along with the sharp pain, Maxine felt a wet, sticky warmth between her legs, looked down to see the blood. Maxine cried out and collapsed as Claude whirled around in his chair, jumping to action.

How heroic he was that afternoon! Sweeping her into his arms, running with her down the stairs, dressing her in his warmest raincoat, then racing out into the downpour to bring the car right up to the doorway. He recited her favorite passage from *On Golden Pond* to ease the bumps as they sped along the mountain roads to Fairview Hospital.

Uncanny the timing. Maxine's ectopic pregnancy and subsequent hysterectomy settled everything once and for all. She took it as a sign and therefore did not consider exploring other avenues—adoption, for example—though nearly everyone she knew was traveling to Romania or Cambodia to adopt orphaned children. No, the Whittakers' marriage would continue as planned. Claude's way. Which was always best.

Claude suffered a massive heart attack five years later and—at the age of sixty-seven, after ten years of marriage—was no more. Maxine, at forty-five, was a childless widow in a 220-year-old Berkshire County farmhouse, owned by her late husband's family.

Once Claude was in the ground, Maxine's tears dry, and the thank-you notes sent, she rationalized that she was indeed better off childless. To have a child on her hands right now—it would be too much. Maxine saw how her younger sister Deborah, a hard-working CPA, slaved over diapers and playdates and pots of cooked carrots with dinosaur-shaped chicken nuggets on the side. While Maxine was like the mother they'd lost as teens—a whimsical, mercurial artist—Deborah was pragmatic, the good soldier, who followed their father's conventional path to financial success. Still, Deborah complained that there was no room in parenthood for breathing, let alone a creative soul like Maxine's. Maxine agreed with her, convinced herself she was content with her choice.

Then, the house began to cry.

The Wailing

It started in the summer of 2012, after Claude had been dead just one week. Maxine had been turning in earlier than was natural for her, taking refuge from her solitude and despair. Several hours into a deep slumber, she was jolted awake by a human sound: one long wail followed by a series of short, staccato yelps, the unmistakable cries of a newborn. Maxine sat up in bed, tuning in to her body first to determine whether or not this was a dream. She could feel the crease of the sheets under her thighs, the heft of the comforter, the mountain chill from the windows Claude always insisted on leaving open.

This was no dream. Maxine grabbed her robe and equivocated briefly: Should she carry something—a broom? Claude's cane? But the sound of a baby spurred the impulse to rescue, not confront. She raced for the stairs.

The cries were gaining volume and urgency by the time Maxine reached the bottom. Heart racing, she dashed from room to room, flicking on lights. Wherever Maxine went, the sounds were coming from someplace else. She called to it.

"Where are you? Please! Let me help you!"

Around and around the farmhouse Maxine chased the newborn voice, on the verge of panicked tears herself. Somewhere in her own home—on its own plane, in its own dimension—was a child who needed her.

At last, Maxine found herself standing in the birthing room, in the portion of the house that had not been altered or updated since it had been built in the late eighteenth century. The cries went silent. The house was still. And then the antique cradle in the center of the room, the cradle that held nothing but old, folded flannel blankets, began to rock—ever so slowly, gently, as if to deter another round of howling.

"You're safe now," Maxine said, because it was nearly four o'clock in the morning and she didn't know what else to say. She gathered her robe around her and crept back up to bed.

In the morning, however, Maxine was frightened—not of ghosts or spirits haunting the farmhouse, but for her own sanity. She made an appointment with a grief counselor and another with a psychoanalyst. Then she phoned Claude's sister, Leigh-Ann, widowed by then, and a docent at the Salem Witch Museum. Maxine recalled Leigh-Ann intimating once that she was skilled in the art of "cleansing" homes that retained what she called "earthbound spirits."

Leigh-Ann questioned her about rooms where she thought she'd heard the crying. Maxine described the path she'd taken, how the cries had ceased so abruptly in the birthing room.

"*Hmph,*" said Leigh-Ann when she was done. "Frankly, I'm not surprised. Why wouldn't they make a stir—now that Claude is gone?"

"They—*who*?" Maxine said, lowering herself into an armchair.

"The mother and child," said Leigh-Ann as if it were obvious. "I learned about them from my grandfather's sister, my great-aunt Helen.

I always hoped to encounter them when our father would bring us here as children, though I never did. On the other hand, when Cal and I were raising the boys at the house, I'd hear their ghosts—the house ghosts along with the ones from the root cellar—all the time. No one else did—just me."

"You did? You heard what—"

"Why do you think I went and learned the art of cleansing?" Leigh-Ann said. Maxine could hear the soft clink of ice cubes in a glass. There was a pause and then a swallow. "Perhaps it's an exaggeration to say I heard them *all* the time. I never did when Calvin was around. But when Cal was traveling and the boys were small, those spirits made a ruckus." Leigh-Ann sighed. "Of course, we moved out when the last of the boys left for college, and I never got a chance to test out my skills. Claude moved in, and there didn't seem to be a point. They've got an aversion to men. Which is why, I imagine, you're hearing them for the first time now."

Maxine sighed, unsure of how to terminate the call. It had been a mistake to contact her sister-in-law, who would spew paranormal gobbledygook ad nauseam if given the chance. Maxine would be seeing the psychoanalyst in two days—a true professional who might succeed in cleansing *her*.

As soon as Leigh-Ann gave her an opening, Maxine made something up about a contractor arriving to repair a leak and said goodbye.

But the house continued to wail. For hours, every night. It began with the baby; then its squalls would be joined by a woman's voice, moaning in anguish. Occasionally, as Maxine fought to make her way back to sleep, she would see them, or imagine she did. A slight Black woman in a dress, a child—who sometimes appeared as a tiny infant in the mother's arms, other times as a toddler, or a little girl of six or seven. Desperation drove Maxine to call Leigh-Ann again.

"Please come."

A Visit

"So Claude never told you the legend of Whittaker House," said Leigh-Ann, sweeping in, draped in black velvet and chiffon, gliding through the house to the living room, where she planted herself on the sofa.

At seventy-five, Leigh-Ann was still a woman of grand stature, five feet eleven inches, weighing an even three hundred pounds—silver hair wound into a magnificent top knot with a well-crafted ringlet hanging beside each ear. She requested tea.

"Lemon verbena." Which Maxine's cupboard possessed. How Leigh-Ann had been certain of this, while Maxine herself had not, spoke to the difference between them. Leigh-Ann did not have an equivocal bone in her body.

"The legend," Maxine repeated, joining her sister-in-law in the living room when the tea was ready. "I didn't know there was one."

"Claude wasn't as taken with our great-aunt Helen's ghost stories as I. He found them entertaining, but I devoured every word." Leigh-Ann shut her eyes, inhaled deeply, then exhaled. "The scent is powerful."

"I don't smell anything besides the tea," said Maxine. "And the usual house smell. Old wood."

"I have trained olfactory glands," said Leigh-Ann. "The usual house smell you detect is death, my dear. Very strong in this room." She shifted her body to face Maxine's chair. "Claude did tell you the house was part of the Underground Railroad?"

"Yes."

"The runaway slaves mostly hid in the root cellar, but at least two of them died inside the house."

"I see."

"*I* smell." Leigh-Ann gave a chuckle at her own rejoinder.

"How can you smell someone who died more than two centuries ago?"

"I'm not referring to the decomposed body," said Leigh-Ann. "I mean the spirit. Spirits. Mother and child. When we first spoke, you said you'd heard them both."

"Yes."

"According to my great-aunt Helen, there were two slave women fleeing north. One was pregnant and near her date. They were hidden out in the root cellar—like all the fugitives who passed through—but came into the house, into the birthing room when the baby was coming. My great-great-grandmother—Great-Aunt Helen's grandmother, Jane Whittaker—performed the midwifery."

"She met them before they were ghosts!" Maxine could hardly contain herself.

"Great-Great-Grandmother Jane wrote all about them in her diaries. Great-Aunt Helen read them."

"Diaries? Do you have them still?"

"Sadly, no. They were on loan, along with records from other families, to Williams College, as part of a course on the abolitionist movement. Somehow, Jane's diaries vanished, if you can believe it. They suspected some student had managed to steal or—more likely—lose them, though no one was permitted to remove any of the documents from the library. My grandfather wanted to sue Williams, but no one else wanted to make a fuss. So all we have is the legend, the oral history, as it were."

"Please, tell the rest. Your great-great-grandmother was delivering the baby."

"Slave catchers arrived just as the baby emerged. The other fugitive woman ran off, but the new mother grabbed a dagger from the belt of one of the catchers, fatally stabbed him and then herself—to avoid being returned to the plantation she'd fled. Great-Great-Grandmother Jane survived the raid by hiding herself in what's now the broom closet inside the pantry."

Maxine absorbed the tale, artist-sense prickling with gruesome, dramatic images. "And the baby?" It was the only question, of the dozens percolating, that gelled enough for her to ask.

"Birdie," said Leigh-Ann.

"Birdie?"

"That was the baby's name. I always imagined she was called Birdie so her spirit could fly up to heaven."

"How marvelous," breathed Maxine.

"According to Great-Aunt Helen," Leigh-Ann went on, "her grandmother's stories were full of ambiguities. Jane Whittaker had suffered an illness in her teens which left her mildly confused for the rest of her life. In some passages, she wrote that the infant was stillborn. In others, the mother killed Birdie along with the slave catcher and herself.

"In still another entry, Jane wrote that Birdie survived but, with no mother present, would have starved to death had Jane not prayed for her own breasts to fill with milk, enabling her to provide the child sustenance. But then little Birdie died anyway."

"Birdie," Maxine murmured, feeling a rush of maternal affection. To know the name—that was something.

Leigh-Ann finished her tea, handing the cup to Maxine. "I once read a theory about the spirits of stillborn children. That they can appear to the living in different forms, at different ages."

"I didn't know." Maxine considered sharing her visions—of the woman, the infant who shape-shifted, trying out stages of a childhood never claimed.

But then Leigh-Ann added, "Great-Aunt Helen told me that when she was a girl, Birdie appeared to her all the time, growing along with her. They were always the same age, companions."

Which brought on jealousy in Maxine. She rose and carried Leigh-Ann's teacup to the kitchen. When she returned, Leigh-Ann was still speaking.

"When Calvin and I were still living here, I had a notion of placating the house ghosts by inviting a cohort of Black teenagers from Boston."

"Placating them?" Maxine sat on the sofa beside her sister-in-law, but perched on the edge, alert.

"Well, I knew nothing about spirits back then, but I thought it would be nice to introduce the ghosts to some of their own kind." Leigh-Ann said it as if she were connecting two girlfriends with a shared passion for needlepoint. "I thought, if the ghosts could see that—I don't know—their descendants were doing fine, then maybe they'd feel some peace."

"Did it work?"

"Calvin wasn't comfortable with all those inner-city kids in the house. They were awfully rowdy, you know. They slept in the barn up the hill. So we never found out." Leigh-Ann placed her hands on her thighs, leaning forward in preparation to stand. "I've got my kit in the trunk of my car. If you'd like, I'll fetch it and get started."

"Started?"

"With the cleansing. Isn't that why you invited me here?"

"If you cleansed the house, would they—Birdie and her mother—would they go?"

"That is the goal. Earthbound spirits are earthbound for specific reasons. Something is incomplete for them in this world. Or they fear what awaits in the next. Cleansing mobilizes them and assists their passage into the great beyond. Sometimes it's successful. Other times, if I am unable to make contact or if the pull to stay is too complex, it's not."

"What if we leave things as they are?"

"Then things remain as they are."

"I have to think about it," said Maxine.

"Of course," said Leigh-Ann, eyes softening. A gentle smile emerged. "You miss him, don't you?"

"Yes." Maxine looked away, checking herself, willing back the tears.

"You miss him a great deal." Leigh-Ann extended one well-upholstered palm to pat Maxine's knee. "If we don't cleanse, the spirits will keep you awake at night. They'll absorb and sap your energy. Then again, you may not be ready for yet another goodbye so soon."

Maxine nodded. She had not mastered her tears, and here they were in abundance. Tears for Claude and the cavernous absence she lived with in this enormous house. Leigh-Ann held her as she wept, allowing a light gasp and sniffle of her own. Claude had been her baby brother after all.

"It's so damn hard," Maxine said. And Leigh-Ann began to rock her as if she were a child. Maxine allowed it, relished it. Leigh-Ann, who had lost her own Cal more than a decade prior, said simply, "I know." And these were the right words.

The women ended their visit not long afterward. Leigh-Ann kissed her sister-in-law on the doorstep and drove off without removing her kit from the trunk. Maxine closed the front door, returned to the living room, and collapsed onto the sofa, which was still warm and compressed from the fading presence of Leigh-Ann. Maxine sobbed, loudly and wetly. How she missed her Claude!

At last, exhausted by the physical labor of bawling, Maxine let her breath slow and surrendered to sleep. The last thing she noticed was a chill against her arm, then someone's icy breath—a comfort to her grief-hot cheek.

Companions

In the days—nights and wee hours—following Leigh-Ann's visit, Maxine learned to coexist with the spirits. She had no more visions, though part of her wished badly to see them again, Birdie and the mother whose name was lost in history. Maxine wondered if they were concealing themselves on purpose to punish her curiosity. She continued to hear them, however, and would lie in bed, pondering: "Do I hear a baby crying? *How* could I hear a baby crying? Well, I *do* hear a baby. Do I hear a woman? Why, yes, I believe I hear her too."

Sometimes the cries were faint enough and brief enough for Maxine to simply roll over and return to sleep. Other times, the cries were sharp and so disturbing that there was nothing to do but go downstairs.

Loathe to jar the eyes of someone who'd lived long before the advent of electricity, Maxine never turned on the bright overhead lights.

Instead she would carry a battery-operated lantern and pad around the downstairs, speaking softly, first to the young mother.

"It's all right. You're all right. The baby is all right. We're all safe." Then she would try to soothe the child. "Birdie? Birdie, love, you're okay. I'm here."

The first week or so, Maxine's voice would quake, her heart pounding as she repeated the phrases to comfort herself as much as, if not more than, the spirits. But as no harm ever came to her, as no doors slammed, no lights went on and off, no utensils flew madly across the kitchen, Maxine relaxed, recognizing that hers was the position of comfort. She was alive, corporeal, existing in the world where she belonged. The poor spirits were stuck in transit. At least this was so according to Leigh-Ann and the websites she recommended, which Maxine perused during the day.

The worst part was that the internment of the spirits mirrored the very bondage that their bodies had escaped. Maxine had, of course, learned about slavery in school, read books about Harriet Tubman and Frederick Douglass and Nat Turner, but had she ever truly considered the horror of it? The beatings, the murders, the rapes, the ripping apart of families, the negation of one's humanity? There were parallels to the atrocities her own forbears had fled in Europe, Maxine knew, which heightened her kinship with the spirits. But their plight had occurred right here, in this "free" New World!

How strong they had been—all of them!—ancestors of today's African Americans. How many of them had untold stories, legacies erased into oblivion? It broke Maxine's heart to think of the young mother and her child Birdie, the female companion who had fled. They deserved to be known, Maxine felt passionately that this was so. Oh! If only Claude were here to share these new ideas with. Claude, who expounded at least once daily on the importance of some male European thinker—be it Voltaire, Nietzsche, or Churchill—would have found it fascinating to ponder and debate the value, the personhood of those claiming African descent. What fun it would have been to be the patient mentor for once, rather than the eager student. Moreover, Maxine would have urged Claude to mine the memories of each night he'd spent here as a boy. What, if anything, had he witnessed of the spirits?

Maxine made a trip to the Monterey Historical Center, where she located a large volume about the town's position during the abolitionist movement. But, aside from inclusion on a list of safehouses, there were no special details about Whittaker House, no registry of slaves who had passed through or perished there.

Maxine began reading slave narratives and diaries. She read *There Was Once a Slave* by Shirley Graham and *Twelve Years a Slave* by Solomon Northup. She read someone's dissertation called "Modern Dialogue and the American Age of Enslavement."

She learned that it was wrong to think of them as "slaves" and began to think of her spirits as "enslaved African Americans" instead, as "freedom seekers" rather than "runaways." Maxine felt virtuous and respectful as a result of these semantic adjustments.

When she went into town and passed the rare Black person or couple, she made gentle eye contact, where she might have avoided it in the past, feeling guilty when she saw someone Black, then feeling guilty for feeling guilty in the first place—not knowing why. Of late, however, she would offer any person of African descent what she believed to be a welcoming nod, sure that they recognized the newfound affinity she had for them.

Mostly, Maxine had become obsessed by the lives of her spirit companions, particularly the woman, who had actually lived life enslaved, as opposed to the infant, who had been born and had subsequently died free. Maxine was obsessed by their deathly existences as well, doing everything in her power to provide them with peace and comfort.

Maxine leaned into her role as host, protector, and nurturer. When the baby squalled but the woman—whom Maxine thought of as "E.S." for "Earthbound Spirit"—remained silent, Maxine would pace the birthing room, cooing, "*Shh*, Birdie. *Shh*. I'm here." She would sing gentle lullabies, which she shocked herself by recalling from childhood.

"Go to sleep my baby, someday there may be, a land that's free for you and me . . ."

Drawing Black People

Caring for Birdie and E.S. initially filled the void Claude had left, but soon the nightly disembodied wailing had become a horrible, painful tease. There were times when it was unbearable, being a mother yet never laying eyes on your children. At night, in the darkness of her bedroom, Maxine strained to recapture the images she'd seen in the early days of hearing them, before she'd learned the story from Leigh-Ann. She tried meditation, tapping into her own spiritual self, with the hope of luring the ghosts out of hiding. She tried lighting candles in the library, the birthing room, even out in the root cellar, calling to them: "Show yourselves!"

What did you look like? Maxine would demand of the ether, of the space E.S.'s and Birdie's essences inhabited. Leigh-Ann had offered no physical descriptions from her great-great-grandmother's diaries. So Maxine devoured the stunning charcoal illustrations and etchings that decorated the covers of the volumes she read on slavery, then attempted sketches that always fell short of her imagination.

Back when Maxine was getting her MFA, she'd studied figure drawing and painting, but the models were always white. So when she attempted to create a person of African descent (she'd practiced saying "person of African descent" rather than "Black person" with such rigor that it had become as natural as breathing), the features were all wrong, though Maxine couldn't pinpoint why.

One afternoon, she drove all the way out to Pittsfield, to a section of the city that had a large Black community. Maxine walked among them, eyes downcast mostly, *feeling* them, listening to their footfalls, the rhythms of their speech, glancing up at the faces here and there, absorbing the shapes of lips and noses, of brows and chins. And hair! *Goodness,* thought Maxine, *such glorious hair!* Such diversity of styles, each a work of ingenious creativity. Such an unsung medium of human expression!

At home, Maxine Google-searched local and semilocal drawing classes that had Black models—which, of course, no studio would openly advertise. What did she think? That it was 1820, when they advertised African-descended people? She shook herself. She was becoming desperate. But in Lee, not eleven miles away, there was a listing Maxine found promising. A life drawing class on whose website one could find headshots of the instructor as well as the models—three young women, one of whom was of African descent. The names of the models were listed separately from the photos, so Maxine had to play detective. There was a Michelle Leeds, a Trish Polaner, and a Dierdre Johnson.

Maxine ruled out Trish right away. She could not fathom that there might be a Black "Trish." "Pat," maybe. "Patricia," yes. But "Trish" felt trite, lacking dignity. "Michelle"—for some reason—sounded Black to Maxine, while "Dierdre" did not. Then again, "Johnson" sounded Blacker than "Leeds." So Maxine went to the class on a Sunday and found herself sketching the rosy-faced, snowy-thighed, sandy-haired Dierdre Johnson. Michelle Leeds, who was indeed Black—as Maxine gleaned from the conversation of two regular students—only appeared on Saturdays.

Six days later, Maxine sat in class, breathless, eager, as Michelle Leeds strode in, removed her robe, and positioned herself on the covered stool in the center of the room. Whereas Dierdre, who was younger and plumper than Michelle, had seemed self-conscious, averting her gaze from the artists, Michelle seemed comfortable, sharing a joke or two with the instructor and one of the experienced participants.

Michelle's hair was natural and full, bound at the crown with a colorful head wrap Maxine proudly recognized as kente cloth. The only jewelry she wore was a trio of tiny gold hoops on each ear—two on the lobe and one high at the top. *She's magnificent,* Maxine thrilled.

In the middle of class one week, a memory struck Maxine. As a young child, she had longed for a Black doll. Her politically progressive parents thought it an odd and inappropriate request—that a white child would want to *own* a Black doll, to manipulate as she saw fit. So Maxine had asked her babysitter, who was Black herself. Maxine's parents were mortified and expected the babysitter to be offended. But the babysitter was touched and offered to buy the doll herself. Maxine's mother would not allow this. The babysitter was let go shortly thereafter.

Maxine attended the drawing class in Lee every Saturday, gaining new skills each week that she would apply to the studies she had begun of E.S. and Birdie. She worked hard in the class, harder at home. She would not show or sell the new pieces. They were her own private collection, for her eyes only. Though her skills were growing.

About three months after that first night of disembodied wailing, Maxine completed an enormous charcoal drawing that made her breath catch. She stood back and gazed at them, E.S. in a drab gray version of the robe Michelle Leeds shed at the start of each drawing class, the baby Birdie naked in her mother's arms. But there they were. Her offspring. There they were!

A Scheme

One Sunday, Leigh-Ann returned unannounced, cleansing kit—a sturdy carpet bag—in hand.

"I'm checking up on you," she told Maxine, who hastily invited her into the kitchen for a cup of lemon verbena tea.

"I'm fine," Maxine told her sister-in-law. "I've decided the cleansing won't be necessary."

"Suit yourself," said Leigh-Ann. "But you're not fine. They're depleting you. I can see it. You've fallen in love with them."

Maxine was not one to blush but did so. She could deny nothing.

"It's not uncommon," said Leigh-Ann. "Especially when one is grieving." She smiled. "Well, I won't take them from you. But you must take a break. Go on a vacation. Visit New York, Paris. Someplace where you'll be surrounded by the living."

Maxine's first thought, which she had the sense not to articulate, was, *How can I possibly take a vacation when the baby needs me here?* And this thought—the very notion that she was capable of such a thought—jolted some clarity into her. She did need a break. Some distance from E.S. and Birdie, if only there were a way to keep them from feeling abandoned.

The gears in Maxine's brain clicked into place. There was indeed a way.

Before Claude had died, he and Maxine had talked about turning the big house into a bed-and-breakfast, moving into the guest cottage up the hill, where Maxine now had her studio. With a constant stream of visitors, E.S. and Birdie would have no shortage of society. Leigh-Ann received the plan with enthusiasm and secured the approval of her three adult sons—attorneys practicing in Los Angeles—who were the official owners of Whittaker House.

It was five months after Claude's death that Maxine hired a contractor and commenced the yearlong designing and construction journey of carrying out their dream. She struggled to attract a regular flow of guests until listing the place on Airbnb, at which point things took off. Now, there are skiers who flock to Whittaker House in the winter, antique hounds in the spring, lake hoppers in the summer, and deer hunters in the fall.

While Maxine has been discreet regarding the secret of the house, the spirits have not been. A young lesbian couple includes in their online review the description of a strange encounter in the living room: the rocking chair moving on its own. A pair of elderly sisters reports something similar. Someone posts a link to Leigh-Ann's recently created web page, "The House Cleanser," on which "Lady Leanna" offers a much-embellished version of the Whittaker House legend she shared with Maxine.

Rather than a deterrent, the legend is a draw. Maxine answers questions about "the ghost" when she gives vacationers the tour. She plays along, enjoying their curiosity, knowing that E.S. and Birdie will likely keep to themselves if there are men present. People continue to give the house—and Maxine herself—rave reviews on the Airbnb site.

Maxine's only regret is that people of African descent rarely contact her. Are Black people less interested in homes with "ghosts"? Maxine recalls Eddie Murphy's old routine about *Poltergeist* and *The Amityville Horror*. The comedian had made much of the notion that—unlike white people, who stay to investigate—Black people would have had the sense to flee at the onset of paranormal happenings. On the other hand, perhaps it's simply that fewer Black people are interested in New England vacations.

Maxine tweaks the house's profile, highlighting the fact that it was an Underground Railroad safehouse. She's clear about her language too, scrupulous about writing "enslaved African Americans," and "freedom seekers." Maxine gets the home listed on sites dedicated to African American heritage and the history of the abolitionist movement. She excises every review that mentions spirits and "paranormal incidents," every link to "Lady Leanna's" site. She waits.

And waits in vain. The only Black people who contact her are historians and activists, interested in tours of the house, not in being guests. The only exceptions are Black people who are part of mixed-race groups of friends or of interracial families. Maxine hunts for those groups, gives preference to them, eager to provide her "children" with the society of brown faces, but something always falls through. In Maxine's four and a half years of guesthouse proprietorship, Timothy is the only person of African descent who has spent the night.

And that was three years ago.

The Brooklyn Family

The husband is white, redheaded, bearded. The wife is Black but thinks she's cleverly concealed this fact online. Their Airbnb profile photo is a solitary portrait of the man—a technique, Maxine knows, that Black vacationers employ to fool racially biased hosts. Maxine was onto the family right away, followed her suspicions to a Google search of the man, which turned up a wedding photograph, revealing the wife's rich brown skin. Feeling triumphant, Maxine canceled on a white family to make room for the Brooklyn folks.

Finally it's the Friday before Memorial Day. Maxine has been giddy, waiting out the months between the booking and their arrival, curiosity brimming over the appearance of the baby. No one can argue, Maxine thinks—*no one*—that mixed-race babies are the most breathtakingly beautiful creatures in the world!

In the farmhouse kitchen, Maxine sets out a basket of navel oranges and a plate of blueberry muffins. A bottle of sauvignon blanc chills in the refrigerator along with a six-pack of beer.

The click of the front doorknob startles her, though she's left it unlocked.

"Hello?" A young man's voice.

"In the kitchen!" Maxine calls, reminding herself of comedies from the 1950s, where the mother was always in the kitchen. And now a Viking-size, red-bearded man with bright green eyes is standing before her. He has on an orange T-shirt with lots of writing on it—too much for anyone to actually read.

"I'm Rob." He extends a hand, which Maxine clasps in welcome. "My wife is in the car with the baby. I know we're early. Olivia has us up by five, so we figured we'd beat the traffic."

"Of course. No worries." She offers him a muffin, which Rob accepts, then the grand tour. "Or should we wait for your wife?"

"Galen will be a while. The baby is napping and then she'll probably need to nurse."

Maxine is momentarily still, aching to meet his wife, admiring the fondness in his tone when he pronounces her name. *Galen.* A cross between a gale and a violin. Musical, powerful, free.

"This way," Maxine says, gesturing. And commences the tour, interior first, followed by the grounds—root cellar included. They use their phones to illuminate the grim, dank cavern.

"Galen will love this," Rob tells Maxine as they descend the stone steps into the cellar. "She did a DNA thing and found out some of her ancestors escaped through safehouses in New England."

"It's mind-boggling," says Maxine. "How much they all risked."

Returning to the sunlight, they circle the house and cross the front walk just as Galen is getting the baby out of the car. Rob's wife is tall, fine-boned, and lean, wearing a decorative "athleisure" ensemble. Galen turns to face them as the breeze blows off Baby Olivia's hat, revealing—to Maxine's surprise and profound disappointment—what appears to be an ordinary white infant. Maxine has read that it happens sometimes—mixed children turning out all-the-way Black or all-the-way white—but it's jarring somehow. That this stunning Black woman's child should be so pale. Maxine recovers from her shock and introduces herself, making a point of gushing over the baby.

Then Rob holds out his arms for Olivia, insisting that Galen take the tour. Though eager for some time alone with Galen, Maxine finds it rude, extremely rude, that Rob doesn't ask whether she minds showing the house again. It would be common courtesy to ask, but Rob simply ducks into the house cradling the tiny cloud-white child. Maxine wonders, watching after him, whether he is similarly thoughtless in his marriage.

Maxine takes Galen first to the modern upstairs, followed by the high-tech kitchen, gradually working their way to the old wing of the house. Galen's demeanor is cool, aloof. In the sewing room and library, the younger woman asks few questions, but Maxine can see her observing every detail, running her fingers against the dark wood bones of the walls, the smooth curve of a ceramic yellowware urn. Maxine is discreet, monitoring the house and its rhythms in response to Galen's presence. She can feel E.S. waking, stretching, detecting a shift in the air. Birdie will sense it too. Maxine considers for the first time how Birdie will take to the notion of another baby visiting Whittaker House. Will she be jealous? Is she capable of harming the child? Maxine's mind goes briefly to the memory of the Rhodes family's flight, the blood on the stair to the root cellar. But it wasn't Birdie, Maxine reassures herself. It couldn't have been.

Galen slows their pace as they enter the birthing room with its cradle, spinning wheel, rocker, and tiny fireplace—quaint wrought-iron tools hanging from the mantelpiece. A poker, a wire brush for sweeping ashes, bellows, and a knife on a leather strap. (For whittling, Claude had once explained to Maxine. His grandfather was a whittler of small figurines: birds, mermaids, miniature drums—that sort of thing. There's a box full of them in the attic.) Galen reaches one slim, elegant hand out to touch the strap of the knife, then slides a finger down the length of the blade. Maxine is mesmerized by the odd grace of the action—not alarmed. The blade is too dull to be a danger in any case.

"I'm interested in the history of this place," says Galen, continuing to stroke the knife. "I've read that it was part of the Underground Railroad."

"Yes," says Maxine. "But the runaways weren't hidden here in the house. It was too close to the road." Immediately she winces. *Runaways*—how could she? Maxine is about to check herself, emphasizing *freedom seekers*, but thinks better of it. She wants her young guest to recognize her empathy for the African-descended. But it would be inexcusable to be seen as trying too hard.

"The freedom seekers," Galen corrects her, and shame washes over Maxine. As the blade catches a bit of flesh on Galen's finger, the young mother appears oblivious. "I read that one died inside the house. Is that right?"

A drop of blood, rich and round, swells from Galen's finger to land on the stone base of the hearth.

Maxine gasps. "Are you all right?"

"Why?"

"You've cut yourself. You're bleeding."

"I didn't realize. It's fine." Galen places her finger in her mouth.

"I have Band-Aids in the kitchen."

"I'm fine."

Maxine stares, unsure of what to do. Artists are never fazed by a little blood, but Galen's interface with the knife, her stoicism—these unnerve Maxine. It would be patronizing to insist on first aid when it's already been declined.

Galen moves them forward. "You were going to tell me about the freedom seeker who died?"

"She died right here in the birthing room." Maxine forces herself to recover. "That's all I know about her. But I can show you the root cellar, where the rest hid, if you like." Galen's stiffness is contagious. Maxine wishes she could cure both the knife wound and the awkwardness with a joke—or an offer of muffins at least—but the only words that come are the stuffiest ones, the words of cold hospitality. "Or, if you'd rather unpack now, I can point it out and you can take a peek at your leisure." *A peek at your leisure.* Like a proper white woman from a Jane Austen novel!

Galen nods. "I would like to get settled."

There's something mournful in the way Galen rocks the aged cradle, as if she's lost in a memory far more painful than the cut on her finger. Possibly she is feeling the house and its history closing in. Perhaps it's too much. Maxine wonders whether the young woman is lonely, being the only member of her family with brown skin. Timothy felt lonely that way, as he blurted to Maxine on the only day of their acquaintance. But that was different. Timothy was a child whose loneliness would be addressed and presumably solved by his loving, competent parents. Galen is a mother, and a mother's loneliness is no one's problem but her own.

A sudden chill whispers through the room. Maxine inhales sharply, imagining Galen through E.S.'s eyes. What can the spirit think of this new presence? This fellow mother? Does E.S. recognize a comrade—kin perhaps? Maxine considers Rob's mention of the DNA test, which she knows better than to bring up with Galen. Rob clearly thought nothing about sharing that intimate detail, but Maxine understands. Until

Galen chooses to confide in her—and why should she trust a strange fifty-five-year-old white woman?—Maxine will respect her reserve. Though it breaks her heart.

The Gift

Maxine returns to her cottage upon the hill, giving the couple just enough space. She keeps an eye out from her window, registering the fact when the couple loads the car with towels and beach chairs. Galen leans inside the car, likely strapping Olivia into her infant seat. They pull out of the driveway, bound for the nearby lake. Maxine takes advantage of their absence, descending the hill, slipping back inside the farmhouse, hoping to sniff out signs of interaction between her guests and the spirits.

There's no such evidence yet; it's scarcely been an hour since their arrival. But in the birthing room, Maxine can smell the house smell, the death smell, which Leigh-Ann taught her to discern, more intensely than elsewhere. The tools hanging from the fireplace swing from side to side, clacking against one another like tone-deaf wind chimes. Poker, brush, bellows, knife. Clack-a-clack, clack-a-clack. There is a window open, but no breeze to create this motion. The curtains are quite still.

After a moment, the tools adjust their rhythm to swing in unison, with no clacking, which Maxine takes as a sign of contentment. The delivery of an African-descended woman clearly provides E.S. some equilibrium.

"Hello, my loves," Maxine says, in her mothering tone. "What do you think of these new people?"

She worries briefly about Rob, remembering what Leigh-Ann said about the presence of men driving the spirits into hiding. But Timothy's father didn't deter their emergence. The presence of African ancestry must embolden E.S., overriding her reticence. The tools swing just a bit higher.

"I thought you might like the woman." Emotion quickens Maxine's breath. This is the closest they have come to a two-way exchange in all their years together. "I thought . . ." She breaks off as the chill of E.S.'s breath envelops her. Maxine interprets it as a thank-you. "I thought she might bring you resolution."

Maxine hopes for it with her whole heart. She wants them set free, as hard as it will be to say goodbye.

Maxine returns to her cottage. She cleans up the French press, puts away her charcoals, showers, changes clothes, and heads into Stockbridge to meet an old friend for an early supper. Maxine drives home as dusk is settling. From her window, she can see the young couple on the patio, having a romantic drink as the shadows grow long. There is a pang in her heart, a memory of being in love with Claude, sharing the quiet notions they shared, the sexy laughs that only they would understand. They weren't young like this couple. Maxine had never known Claude young. But the feeling of love, of oneness with another, has no age. Maxine shuts the curtain and goes up to bed, leaving the Brooklyn family in the capable hands of E.S.—leaving E.S. and her baby Birdie to find their own way.

In the morning, Maxine takes the path down the hill to the farmhouse, arms laden with fresh towels, though they aren't needed. There are plenty of bath towels, beach towels, and dish towels in the house. But Maxine cannot keep herself away. Their car is still in the driveway.

She knocks as a courtesy, waits what she considers to be a reasonable amount of time before letting herself in, walking gingerly through the house till she hears the creak of the antique cradle. Now she ventures into the birthing room, where little Olivia is fast asleep, breathing evenly in time to the cradle's slow, easy rock. Just beyond her is the tipped-over spinning wheel and the bodies of the baby's parents.

Maxine sucks in her breath. Oh, she *could* scream. The scene is gruesome: blood everywhere, Rob's body atop Galen's, the whittling knife beside them on the floor. But mindful of disturbing the baby, of rankling the earthbound spirits of Whittaker House, determined to protect the peace they surely require to complete their transition, Maxine does not scream. There is no time, in any case, no place for emotion. She's been given a gift she dares not squander.

Maxine conquers her panic, her racehorse heart, and walks up the stairs to the nursery. She packs up the baby's things—diapers, rompers, stretchies, binkies, sleepers, and socks. Down in the kitchen, there's a case of organic baby food but no bottles. Rob said something about nursing, Maxine remembers. They'll stop somewhere for formula.

∽

Back in her studio, Maxine gathers her laptop along with the drawings of little Timothy Rhodes, Michelle Leeds, E.S., and the baby—all the pieces in her *People of African Descent* series. She packs them in a large portfolio, then fills a suitcase for herself. She's thinking of a fresh start. A new life. Perhaps California. San Francisco, which she's always fantasized about, but where she knows no one.

Olivia is still sleeping when Maxine returns to the house. The baby stirs only slightly when transferred to her infant seat, already fastened to the back seat of Maxine's Subaru. Olivia opens her eyes at the sound of the car door shutting, immediately beginning to squall. But soon the rhythmic, hilly drive lulls the child back to sleep. Olivia will wake again soon enough, at which point Maxine will have to improvise. But mothers always improvise, don't they? She'll find a way.

5

GIRL WITH THE CLOUD HAIR

Catherine

Monterey, Massachusetts, June 2015

They turned Whittaker House into a fucking Airbnb. It's hard for Catherine to wrap her mind around that, even being here in person with Pete and the boys.

For their last family trip before his Senate campaign swung into high gear, Pete wanted to go to his parents' place in Sagaponack, which would have put Catherine over the edge. Another vacation at the Rhodeses' Hamptons estate with their pristine, private beach and too-elegant-for-kids brunches surrounded by people who looked just like Pete's parents—white, tan, tastefully clad, and gorgeously preserved. Catherine would have been under constant pressure to explain Timothy—his neurodivergence, his Blackness—to tolerate everyone's attitudes, to hate herself for doing so. Then Pete would tell her that she was imagining things, "teaching Timothy to see racism and ableism where there isn't any," that she was making it worse.

Catherine suggested the Berkshires instead, selling it hard: the green, the hiking and swimming for the boys, the quaint little shops and farm stands. Wyndhurst Manor's much-celebrated, historic golf course in Lenox, which got Pete on board. He gave Catherine the go-ahead to check out some Airbnbs. And there on the site was Whittaker House.

Maxine, the owner or proprietress or whatever she is, leads the family through the kitchen—which has undergone a total renovation since Catherine was here last. And the library, where—*oh my God*—she ravished Lawrence Reeves sixteen years ago.

That was the fall of 1999. Catherine had signed up for the seminar on abolitionists to impress Lawrence, the only Black guy on the Williams College lacrosse team. Catherine was dating one of his teammates, but Lawrence was so hot, so cool, so different from everyone she'd ever dated, he was all she could think about. Catherine grabbed Lawrence's ass as they were passing through the Whittaker House dining room, making her intentions clear. Lawrence grinned but whispered that they *shouldn't*—it was disrespectful of the house's history—which made Catherine more insistent. She dragged him by the collar of his jersey into the darkened corner under the library staircase. While their class continued the tour, Catherine and Lawrence did it up against the wall, with their clothes on—more or less.

Catherine was fearless then and so alive. Now she's just tired—of their friends at the club, of the PTA—of everything except Timothy, her youngest, her light. Catherine has faded to the point where no one could remember which Catherine Rhodes she was—there are three in their town—until Peter announced his candidacy. She glances back toward the staircase, longing to recapture a shade of her radiant nineteen-year-old self.

"You'll note that the house creaks much more in this section," Maxine is saying as they pass through a small vestibule. "These are the original floorboards from 1794."

Grayson, their oldest, duly impressed, bounces in place to test out the wood. Barrett, their middle son, is oblivious, messing with his phone, while Timothy's eyes dart from right to left, up and down, as he registers everything around him. Catherine places a hand on his bony shoulder, transmitting calm.

She whispers, "We're okay."

Timothy whispers back, "It smells weird."

Maxine hears him. "That's the old house smell. The wood in these original rooms has been here for nearly two and a half centuries." She smiles as she points out more details, leading the way into the birthing room, which Catherine remembers from her first tour back in college.

The birthing room also featured prominently in Jane Whittaker's diaries, supplemental sources for the seminar. Those handwritten relics detailed the author's bizarre bond with the spirit of a baby fugitive slave.

Later, Catherine had stolen the diaries as mementos of her romance with Lawrence, but also because of her fondness for the abolitionist. Jane was just the sort of white person Catherine herself would have been had she lived in those days. Catherine would have chosen a man like Lawrence, would have fled with him north to Canada, where they would have lived in safety, raising their stunning mixed kids. The diaries spent nearly sixteen years at Catherine's parents' summer home in Maine. Now they're in her suitcase, here to be returned.

As they exit the birthing room behind Pete and Maxine, Timothy ducks out from under Catherine's hand and rushes ahead down the hall, where there's a painting of a leaping dolphin.

"An ichthyosaur!" Timothy cries out, identifying one of his favorite prehistoric marine reptiles. His error enchants Maxine, who tries to engage him in conversation. Pete takes the diversion as an opening to dash out to the car—where there's reception for some reason—to fire off another email to his team. What's draining Catherine most of all is Peter and his fucking campaign, which is turning the family into one big, smiling prop.

Birdie

Who are you, Boy? You call that white lady "Mama"?

My mama was a girl who worked in the big house. My daddy was a monster. Do you know what bad men, monsters like my daddy, do to girls like Mama? I do. I know what they do to boys like you too. Why don't *you* know? Where do you come from that you don't know?

You tell lies, Boy.

What I know, I know from my time inside my mama's belly. No one could see me, but I could see, smell, and hear all there was. The whole time I was growing inside her, I was learning. I know about stones, trees, dirt, and the pail on a rope that goes down in the well for water. I know about fire and the big pot where the house women boil lace linens clean. I know about cotton fields and sweat. I know about whupping. I know about branding and the smell of flesh and hair when they burn. I know about screams. I can even tell between the different kinds of screams. Some's for whups, some's for brands, some's for when they cut off people's parts to punish them. Some screams—the silent ones—are for what he did to Mama.

I'll tell you what they do to boys like you. They let you grow a little bit; then they take you away and get the best price they can. Then, you grow up some other place just like where you started out, only no Mama. No Daddy. No brothers. Just you in a place full of strangers. You might get whupped; you might not. But you'll be alone.

Mama ran before it could happen to me. She wanted me to be born free. And I might have been. Never had to obey any white lady. No white man ever touched me. Never breathed plantation air.

Tell me about you, Boy. Are you their only Negro? The only one they brought here? You do all the work taking care of four people when you're so small?

Why do you stare at me like that, Boy?

Timothy

Her hand is cold. I don't like to hold hands, but I don't mind holding hers because it is cold so that there's no sweaty, sticky feeling like when Barrett touches me after eating cheese, and when he stops touching me, there's still Barrett on my skin from the cheese. Barrett always eats cheese and then touches me, especially when I tell him about giant mosasaurs and plesiosaurs which he doesn't like. Barrett knows that I don't like him touching me with cheese on his hands, but he does it anyway to make me stop talking about Mesozoic marine reptiles.

Mom did not let anyone eat in the car while we were on the way here. We stopped at a restaurant for lunch and got burgers so there wouldn't be fighting between me and Barrett or tears from me because I don't like the way it smells when people eat in the car. Barrett's burger had cheese even though I cried because I knew he was going to touch the cheese and then try to touch me. Dad said it had to be okay for Barrett to eat cheese sometimes and that it wasn't fair for my issues to dominate what people ate.

I don't like when Dad talks to Mom about me as if I am not there, because whatever he says sticks in my mind. Like if Dad says to Mom, *If you keep indulging him, he's never going to learn to act like a regular kid,* then I will think and think and think about how a regular kid acts and then I don't know how to do it and that makes me so mad and sad. Then Mom says, *He's seven years old, not an infant. He can understand you!* And that makes me wish that I were an infant and not seven because then I wouldn't know what it was like to be me. It upsets me to hear them fight about me, and then I hit myself because it makes me hate me to cause them fighting. And when I hit myself it makes Mom and Dad stop fighting so they can grab my hands and stop me from hurting myself. I keep trying to hit myself until Dad gets my arms tight behind my back and holds me so tight which I like because then I know everything will stop.

Mom took me outside after Barrett's cheeseburger came because I screamed and hit myself and people at the restaurant were staring at us. Mom said Dad would make sure Barrett washed his hands before he got back in the car, which would leave Grayson alone at the booth where we were sitting but that's okay because Grayson is thirteen and knows what to say to waitresses and bus drivers and the men who come to fix things at the house when Mom and Dad are busy.

When Dad, Grayson, and Barrett got back in the car after lunch, Dad said he didn't want to hear a peep out of anyone for the rest of the ride. Grayson got in the way, way back of the minivan so he could keep an eye on Barrett and me. Barrett secretly waved his hand to pretend he was going to get cheese on me, but I ignored him like Grayson always says to do. It was easy to ignore Barrett because I could smell that he had no cheese on his hands and I didn't care.

The house was big and red like the *Big Red Barn* book I had when I was little. There were windows on the slanting part of the roof and flowers outside and a lot of birch trees with white bark and some balsam fir trees with green needles. There was a teacher in a long blue sweater waiting for us at the front door. I said that she looked like a nice teacher because she looked like Mrs. Rosen who is our reading specialist and has a not-too-loud voice.

Barrett said, "She's not a teacher, stupid. She's the owner of the house."

And Mom and Dad both told him that was enough. I wasn't upset, because the lady had a nice smile and I know that Barrett is the one who is stupid and not me.

The lady, Maxine, really is like a teacher. She tried to make friends at first by giving us juice and cranberry scones, but I hid behind Mom because I don't like cranberries and I was afraid Dad was going to say try one to be polite, but he didn't.

The house was cold and old and smelled weird, so at first I didn't like it. Maxine said the smell was old house wood, and then I didn't mind the smell anymore because I knew what it came from. But then I was afraid they were going to say I had to sleep in a room without Grayson or Mom, but then Grayson said I could sleep with him no matter what. It turned out that Barrett didn't want to sleep alone either and it seemed too risky for me and Barrett to share a room, so Dad wound up saying that all three of us would share a big room even though there are enough rooms for everyone to have their own.

Then things got even better because Maxine showed us a painting she made of a giant ichthyosaur. Barrett said it was a dolphin, but I knew it was an ichthyosaur and not a dolphin because of the elongated snout and the size of the eye. Ichthyosaurs had the largest eyes of any vertebrate species ever, measuring up to 244 millimeters in diameter, which allowed them to see through dimly lit seawater where prey and predator alike lurked. Ichthyosaur eyes were protected by sclerotic rings which enhanced motion and are well preserved in many fossils. Dolphin eyes are just regular. Barrett is so stupid that he cannot tell the difference.

The lady was happy that I knew her painting was of an ichthyosaur and then I was her favorite. Now Maxine is my friend and not Barrett's.

While we were still walking around the house, Mom went back into the library even though we had seen it already. She stayed in there for an extra-long look because she likes books as much as I like plesiosaurs and mosasaurs. Then Dad and my brothers went back to the kitchen to have scones, but I kept by Maxine and we kept walking together through the house. We talked and talked and I told her a secret about being me that no one in my family knows.

The secret is that it makes me lonely to be the only Black person in my family. It's mostly a secret from Mom because I know it would make her sad. Mom loves me the most and says that I am her handsomest boy even though I am the only one who didn't grow in her tummy. It felt very good to tell Maxine my secret because Maxine lives all alone and she says she knows what it feels like to be lonely. I said I am not lonely all the time, only sometimes when Barrett says stupid things. I did not tell Maxine that I hit myself when I am upset.

The smallest and oldest room in the whole house is called the birthing room, and it isn't really a room but more of a bend in the hallway with its own diagonal fireplace. It has an old wooden cradle and rocking chair and spinning wheel like in museums, and old tools hanging from the mantelpiece. I liked the birthing room best of everything in the house, except for the painting of the ichthyosaur, because the birthing room looked like a story of something old and secret and special. It also made me kind of sad, because it made me think of a thousand questions to ask but I couldn't think up the words for any of them and anyway, Dad says I pepper people with questions too much and I need to give it a rest sometimes.

The only question I peppered then was if I could sit in the rocking chair. Maxine said yes, so I sat there. When Maxine saw that I was happy rocking in the rocking chair, she said she was going to go find my parents to see if they had any questions. Maxine left me alone here in the rocking chair, which is how I still am when I meet the girl with cold hands.

She says hi and I say hi and I say I'm seven and she doesn't say how old she is, but she seems like she's seven too. She's Black but not as Black as me. She says her name is Birdie and I don't say that's a funny name, but I think to myself that it is. I don't ask what she's doing at the house either, because at first I think that Maxine is her mom. Maxine is white like my mom, and a lot of people think Mom's not my mom and ask rude questions like where is my mom when she's standing right next to me. But I remember that Maxine said she lived alone, so I don't know who Birdie is.

I say, "I'm Timothy," and then Birdie asks me to come with her and says she'll show me around the outdoors. She holds my hand with her cold hand and tells me things that don't make sense.

Birdie doesn't know the things that everyone knows. She asks, "What does that mean?" when I complain that there's no service here because of being up in the mountains. Birdie doesn't know what *online* means or *YouTube*. Birdie doesn't even know what the internet is! It's not that she's stupid like Barrett. Birdie is *ignorant*, which Barrett thinks means the same thing as *stupid* but it doesn't. Stupid means you don't know things because your mind can't hold them. Ignorant just means you don't know things because you haven't learned them yet.

Birdie is not like Barrett who says things to upset me on purpose. Birdie tells me things that upset me because she thinks the upsetting things are true. While we are walking around the hills, Birdie says that when I am bigger, I will get sold for a good price because my family is white and I am Black and that is the way it is.

I do not cry when she says that. I tell her that it is *not* the way it is. She says it *is* and then I do cry. I run inside the house and find Mom in the kitchen with Maxine and Dad and Grayson and Barrett. I am crying so hard it is hard to speak, so it is hard for Mom to understand me at first. When she figures out what I am saying, she yells at Barrett because she thinks he's the one who told me the upsetting thing and not Birdie with the cold hands.

Mom is very, very, very angry at Barrett, and I feel bad because he didn't do anything this one time, but I'm crying too hard to tell her and Birdie is gone. Now Barrett is very, very, very angry at me because I got him in trouble even though I didn't mean to because it wasn't him who said it. Later, when Mom is not with us, Barrett will hit me and won't get in trouble if he leaves marks because he will say I hit myself.

Barrett

I didn't do ANYTHING. Timothy was crying because Timothy always cries. ALL THE TIME. If something upsets him or looks like it might upset him, he freaks out and we all have to deal with it. It's not always someone's fault, but Mom has to blame someone and that's usually me.

Sometimes I mess with my brother on purpose because I'm going to get blamed anyway, and I might as well have some fun.

But this time I didn't do ANYTHING to him. I especially did not—*would not*—say that we were going to sell Timothy when he got bigger. I know about slavery and how bad it would be to say that to my brother because he's Black and we're white. And if I even thought of something like that, or wished for something like that, which I never ever really did (only sort of in my head), *I* would probably be the one they sent away.

Catherine

Catherine could use a drink. Once she's consoled Timothy, scolded Barrett, and fought with Pete—the same fight they've fought since Timothy joined the family—Catherine rages outside into the garden alone. She remembers the expanse of land from that visit in '99, how her red-tinted sunglasses exaggerated the already vibrant fall foliage. Today the early spring sunshine illuminates pink and yellow buds all over the property, new and unsullied and hopeful. She inhales, exhales, taking in the swirling aromas of flora and fauna, decay and renewal. Not as good as vodka but a placeholder.

Pete's final statement, the one that led her to storm out, echoes in her brain. Standing here by a pond full of frogs, half a meadow between herself and the house, Catherine can laugh out loud at the ambiguity of the sentence. "This was *your* idea." Pete's mantra, absolving him of culpability. It will be engraved on his tombstone one day. "It was Catherine's idea." She never asks for clarification. Never, *What* was my idea? The trip? Pete's campaign? Becoming a family? Getting married in the first place? The joke was that each one of these decisions had indeed begun with a comment, if not a push, from Catherine herself.

After the birth of Grayson—perfect, pink, fat, and full-term—Catherine's body was nonetheless wrecked inside. Her ob-gyn cautioned against a second pregnancy. But back then she was still her father's "tenacious girl," still believed Pete was the yang to her yin, the male version of herself—strapping, quick of mind, fair of hair and eyes, but with skin that tanned a smooth, even bronze in the summer—that together, the two of them were invincible. Catherine scoffed at the doctor's warning and, with Pete's support, timed the next pregnancy so that their second child (a daughter, they learned as soon as the evidence was in) would be born just after Grayson's second birthday.

Catherine was on bed rest by her twenty-fourth week and went into labor in her twenty-eighth. Six weeks before her due date, she delivered the little girl she'd dreamed of all her life, Ella. Lovely, peaceful, and cold. They had a funeral populated by family and friends, with a tiny pearl-white casket, just as if there had been a life, a brief childhood.

Against all medical and psychiatric advice, Catherine went off her birth control the moment her body felt ready to give it another try. Barrett arrived close to full term. There was an emergency C-section, several blood transfusions for Catherine, and three months in the NICU for the baby boy. He came home healthy at last, though fussy, colicky. A fitful, wakeful child, Barrett neither matched his handsome, amiable older brother nor healed Catherine's heart, which still ached for the daughter she'd lost. When children's clothing catalogs arrived in the mail, as they always did, she would scan the pages for the little girl, blonde and round faced with short bangs and freckles, that would have been her Ella. It was not Barrett's fault, but he was not enough to fill the void in Catherine's heart.

Catherine was not foolhardy enough to attempt a fourth pregnancy, but she raised the prospect of adoption when Barrett and Grayson were two and five, respectively. Pete said no. They already had behavioral challenges with Barrett. Wasn't Catherine wary of introducing someone else's unknown, possibly unstable genetic tendencies into the family? She wasn't. Among her four siblings, they all had quirks and complications—anxiety, dyslexia, kleptomania—yet all had the same parents. Still, to appease Pete, who was an only child, Catherine did some research, then assured him it was possible to learn all about the child's biological family members, their history, their mental health, their values.

So adoption was Catherine's idea too. As was her insistence that the child's race should not be a factor. The social worker at the agency suggested that they might have a shorter wait for a child if they were willing to consider one who was slightly older, one who had a disability, or one who was not white.

"Any race, any color at all is fine," Catherine blurted without so much as glancing at Pete for confirmation. "Just as long as she's healthy."

"She?" the social worker repeated.

"Our preference is for a girl," Pete said, placing a protective arm around Catherine's shoulders. He explained their loss, and Catherine felt grateful to him for understanding, for being the one to say it.

And that afternoon, Catherine opened her mailbox to find the Boden kids catalog, on the cover of which danced a little girl in a purple polka-dotted skirt. Her skin was light brown; her dark hair formed a magnificent halo of ringlets. Her face—freckled and full lipped—was that of an angel. Catherine traced the child's face with her little finger as the image of Ella evolved in her mind's eye.

She flashed back to Lawrence Reeves. Though Catherine had been over him since the turn of the millennium, during the heat of their romance, she'd contemplated what beautiful children they would have had together. Indeed, the girl in the Boden catalog—Ella 2.0—was just how Catherine's children with Lawrence might have looked. Catherine shut her eyes and imagined racing with her exquisite mixed-race daughter through Grand Central Station to make a train, or toward the foamy seashore beneath a magical sunset whose rays caught the highlights in their hair. Mothers and daughters always held hands and ran together— didn't they?—laughing private, female laughs at their own joint zaniness. And with a mixed-race child—a mixed-race girl—no one would question that they were mother and daughter, not in this day and age. Outsiders would simply imagine that the father looked like Lawrence.

It took some effort to convince Peter, the ever-practical planner, rational to a boring fault. They talked it over while straightening up the finished basement, which served as a playroom for the boys. Pete, gathering Duplo blocks, brought up the demographics of their town, the monochromatic public schools. Which, Catherine countered as she sorted dinosaurs from farm animals, were growing more diverse each year. But Pete pointed out that diversity didn't equal integration, especially when socioeconomics were factored in. The nonwhite children at Grayson's school tended to be the children of, well, the *help*. The nannies, the gardeners, those who lived in the housing projects on the west end of town. Pete asked Catherine to put herself in the shoes of a wealthy Black or mixed-race child who was caught between two worlds.

"It wouldn't be fair, Catherine." Pete dumped the Duplo blocks into their bin and dropped into a mint-green beanbag chair that said GRAYSON in large blue gingham letters.

Catherine resealed the dinosaur case and sank in behind him, straddling his hips, chin on one of his shoulders. "We can be trailblazers. We can change things." The town, she reminded Pete, was changing in any case. The international presence was on the rise. All over, you were beginning to hear new languages besides English and Spanish: Russian, Mandarin, Hindi.

"Somerville is becoming a melting pot," she told him, aware that this was a slight overstatement. "Why should our family be left out of the fun?"

Catherine can't remember now how it evolved, but this was the discussion that led to Pete's first run for office, town council, after which things had taken off. By the time Timothy joined them, Pete's political ambitions had blossomed. It was neither verbalized nor explicitly denied—simply understood that, for national office, having a Black child would be an indispensable asset.

Once they had completed home study—the process of gathering paperwork and references, of learning, in an awkward group setting with other white-parents-of-Black-kids-to-be, the meaning of bringing a child of color into a white family—they were placed in the pool to be matched with a birth mother. They were chosen quickly by a young woman who was white and married, already raising a child. She'd had a secret affair with a Black man, and her husband refused to raise the child in their home. It was going to be a girl.

Catherine and Pete were both thrilled initially, but as the due date got closer, Catherine felt a sense of foreboding. She began dreaming of her own lost baby girl, of the pretty, blue-gray face, the delicate white casket. Catherine began to ache inside, reliving the grief, preparing for more. Pete told her not to be ridiculous; this was happening. Their new Ella would be coming home in a matter of months.

But when the young woman delivered, the baby girl was the very image of her white husband, not the Black man with whom she'd cheated. Young husband and wife apologized to Catherine and Pete via the social workers at the agency. They brought their little girl home.

Following the disruption, Catherine went on medication: Lexapro, with a side of Xanax as needed. And, though it was contraindicated with the meds, her alcohol consumption ticked north. It was Pete who took the call from the agency notifying them of a boy who had been abandoned in the hospital, healthy, Black, and four days old. The birth mother, just sixteen, also Black—a straight-A student who had hidden the pregnancy, panicked at the notion of motherhood threatening her academic and career goals—had been found and was willing to sign the surrender once an appropriate family had been identified.

Pete said yes for both of them. On the way to the hospital, Catherine felt let down, depressed, full of misgivings. She had two boys; she didn't need a third.

"Honey, this baby needs a home," said Pete. "He needs us." But, as was so often the case with Pete since he'd entered politics, there was no soul in his words. "Anyway, we've come this far." So Timothy was technically Pete's idea, not Catherine's.

The last thing Catherine expected, after meeting the birth mother, who confirmed that the birth father too was Black—meaning that the boy would not be mixed, not a male version of her little ringlet-haired Ella—the very last thing, once the documents were signed and the nurse entered with the bassinet, where a tiny form squirmed in his maternity-ward-issued blanket, was Timothy.

He was placed in Catherine's arms. Immediately their eyes met, and Catherine gasped with recognition, her whole being resonating with the words: *It's you.* She realized she had always known this baby, been waiting for him all her life. Timothy stopped squirming and held her gaze, calmly, so calmly because he knew, and Catherine knew, that he was home. They both were.

Catherine's heart melted a bit more each time she gazed down at his dark brown face, at his eyes, sweet and pure, the nose, flawlessly round, and lips like a tiny bow. She was aware of Pete watching her as if he sensed it, as if he could hear it in the ring of her laughter when she played with the baby boy. Neither Pete nor the other boys would ever again come first for Catherine. She scarcely put Timothy down or took her eyes off the child for the first few years of his life.

Grayson, who was in first grade when Timothy arrived, sociable, already a budding athlete, adjusted easily. Barrett, an irritable preschooler, did not. Catherine's sister Victoria moved in to help out and provide support to the family. It was Victoria who noticed that Timothy differed from the other two—not just in appearance but in development. He spoke exceptionally early, in full, complex sentences. He was unable to be soothed by anyone but Catherine. And there were other things too: quirks, idiosyncrasies that predated the fascination with Mesozoic sea creatures.

Now Catherine circles the pond behind the farmhouse. With each of her footfalls, a frog squeaks and hops into the water like a slick-skinned, walnut-size Ziegfeld girl. The woods grow thick to her right—birches, firs, sugar maples. Catherine senses a presence watching her and turns in time to see something—a bobcat? a deer?—dash behind a tree. Catherine considers that she might be in danger but moves toward the border of the woods nevertheless. Something emerges gingerly from behind a thicket, a familiar shape. A crown of soft, wild curls, a child's face. It's a little girl in a thin yellow dress, staring right at her. Catherine stares back, then utters the word "hello."

The little girl runs, flees like a fox, and vanishes on the breeze. Catherine thinks of Jane Whittaker and suddenly recalls the name of the child spirit she loved. *Birdie*. It cannot possibly be.

Birdie

I run through the woods with the white lady chasing me, calling out, *Hello! Wait! Stop!* But I'm no fool and I'm too quick. I know, even if the boy called Timothy doesn't, what it is to be caught. It is the end, the very end of everything.

What I know, I know from being inside Mama, moving north through the country: woods and swamp, river and road. I know about traveling and hiding and waiting till dark. I know the stars and the sounds of screech owls.

What I don't know is *home*. What I don't know is *live*. Timothy asks if I *live* here or where do I *live*, and I just smile like a person does when there is no answer.

Home, says Timothy. *Home is where you belong.*

I say, *There's no such place for you or me. You'll see.*

I watch Timothy. They let him alone a lot. He carries a pail full of colorful things which he takes out of the pail and sets up in rows. They are funny animals—not cows or dogs or horses or pigs. He talks to them, sets them up and puts them back. Then does it again: sets up, puts back.

When Timothy does wrong, they don't hit him. He hits himself in the face and the head. Maybe they taught him to whup himself so they don't have to whup him. I watch the rest of them, the white man and lady and their yellow-headed boys. The lady is kind and gentle to Timothy. The man and the bigger boy seem kind too. Or they know how to pretend they aren't monsters. I know about that too: white people who will smile and seem good, and then show their real souls, turning away when the cat-o'-nine strikes, or when screaming mothers are taken from their babies. Still better to be around the white ones who pretend to be kind.

The younger yellow-headed boy has only wickedness in his eyes. He doesn't care about pretending. I watch him closer. I see him bother the animals Timothy sets up. Then Timothy hits himself again. I see Wicked Eyes hit Timothy too, put his hands on him, choke him. No one else sees. They think Timothy made the marks himself.

Timothy

My plastic reptiles aren't made to scale, but Mom said that I should forgive the toy company because it is probably the only one that Animal Planet could get to make prehistoric marine reptiles at all. There is a company in the United Kingdom that makes them too, but the faces on their prehistoric creatures are too cutesy and babyish and stupid looking. So I have to *make do*, which is what Dad says all the time.

When I first opened the box on Christmas, I was upset because I could see that the ophthalmosaurus, which is my favorite kind of ichthyosaur because of its wide eye sockets, was the same size as the elasmosaurus and the kronosaurus—which is all wrong because ophthalmosaurus was sixteen feet and kronosaurus was thirty-three feet and elasmosaurus grew up to fifty feet. Also, I was upset because those reptiles would never have been together because they all lived during different geologic time periods. Ophthalmosaurus lived during the late Jurassic and kronosaurus lived during the early Cretaceous and elasmosaurus existed during the late Cretaceous only. There was also a giant mosasaur in the box and a basilosaurus (which is a cetacean, not a reptile, even though the box only said PREHISTORIC MARINE REPTILES on it and didn't say anything about cetaceans) and a liopleurodon. They were the same size as the others. I knew that I was not supposed to be upset about a Christmas present and I was supposed to be excited, but I was upset and I couldn't help it because it was all wrong and I didn't think I would be able to play with them knowing that everything was wrong.

Dad sighed loudly in an exasperated way because he could tell I was upset and that I wasn't making do. So I explained what was wrong and tried to keep my voice calm and not cry and not hit myself. Then Mom said I could keep the reptiles apart from each other and play with them one at a time, since they could not have ever been together. I did not think that would be any fun at all and I was going to hit myself, but Grayson said he knew a way that I could play with them together.

Grayson said I could pretend that all my reptiles were time travelers and that they could communicate with each other across different time periods to warn each other about environmental changes that were coming up or about the evolution of other predators that could put their species at risk of extinction, which is what happened in real life. (People think it was all the asteroid's fault, but it was much more complicated than that.) Grayson is smart sometimes and a good brother. I liked his idea so much that I smiled really hard, and Dad was happy because he knew I was making do and not going to make any more fuss. And Mom hugged me and then she hugged Grayson because she was grateful to him for making me not be upset anymore, and then she hugged Dad because things turned out okay and he wasn't exasperated. The only one who wasn't getting hugged by Mom was Barrett, who didn't care because he got *Destiny* for his Xbox.

That was a really good idea that Grayson had. Now I mostly play Prehistoric Marine Reptile and Cetacean Time Travelers. But other times, I just lay the reptiles and the basilosaurus all side by side in order of which came first or which was the fastest or the biggest and I remind myself of all the facts about each of them.

Set Up is a quieter game than Time Travelers, so I am playing Set Up when I wake up the first morning at the Airbnb. I can't go on my iPad because there is such weak reception and I don't want to wake up Mom and Dad. I am downstairs in the birthing room, setting up my sea creatures in order of time, and it is very important that I do it right or it will be upsetting and not fun.

I don't hear Barrett's footsteps because he is only wearing his soccer socks and not shoes too. Since I don't hear him coming, I don't have time to protect my sea creatures from him messing them up, which he always tries to do. When Barrett kicks them, mosasaur and kronosaurus and basilosaurus go flying across the floor, and basilosaurus sticks partway into the grille in the floor. I scream and Barrett laughs and kicks the rest of them so they all go flying everywhere. I keep screaming and hitting myself and spinning around on the floor on my bottom trying to make myself feel okay. Now I can tell Barrett is worried, because he tries to make me be quiet so Mom and Dad won't come and put him in trouble for upsetting me.

But to make me be quiet, Barrett shakes me and yells, "Shut up! Shut up!" Which is the wrong way to make me be quiet. I scream louder and then I try to hit Barret instead of me. Barrett grabs at my hands to stop me. I fight and he fights back. I can smell cheese on him, which doesn't make sense because it is too early to eat cheese and get it on your hands. His smell makes me very, very, super agitated, and I kick and scream and try to hit him and me at the same time.

Birdie

Wicked Eyes has Timothy now. I can see them scrapping and battling and beating one another. Wicked Eyes is bigger and stronger. Timothy looks wild and scared. In his eyes I see the same look I saw in Mama's eyes right before the end. Though she was just a girl, she fought the white monsters when they tried to take us. She screamed loud and shrill, and the power in her voice spread to her body.

Mama did what she had to: took herself away before they could. She took one of them with her too. And now, I know what I know, but I never feel any of it. Not the breeze on my skin, not the earth between my toes, not the damp of dew, or the smell of honeysuckle. I see and I learn. I watch the people who come and go. I grow, I shrink, I change in the eyes of anyone who sees me. I can be anything anyone needs to see in me. But I never feel any of it.

I'm watching you, Wicked Eyes. I'm watching out for Timothy. No white monster is going to hurt him. Not while I'm here.

Catherine

Her eyes are open, taking in the lemonade sunrays through the curtains, along with the smells of potpourri and Pete's cologne. Catherine has moments like these, usually in the morning, occasionally with her evening glass (glasses) of cabernet, where she believes in the potential of her life. But now she hears a crash, imagines something large and expensive smashing, creating shards that might injure one of the boys.

Catherine jumps up. "Pete!" He's already moving.

Grayson, who heard the crash too, joins them in the hall and the three of them race downstairs to the birthing room, taking in the following scene: Timothy and Barrett, seated, frozen, a yard apart, staring at the wreckage of what was the largest in a collection of enormous yellowware bowls. Thick chunks of ceramic are scattered on the floor, mingling with Timothy's reptile collection.

"What happened? Is anyone hurt?"

"That thing flew at me!" Barrett's voice is high, panicked, as he points at a shelf across the room. "It barely missed my head!"

"What did?"

"The bowl! It came at me!"

Catherine looks at Timothy's wide eyes, now back at Barrett. "You were fighting, weren't you? Roughhousing. And you knocked it down."

"No! I said it *flew* at—"

"Bowls don't fly." Catherine kneels and crawls through the shards to check both boys for injuries: knees, shoulders, faces. They're both breathing hard, hearts racing.

"This is not our house." Pete, stern now. "There is no wrestling. No roughhousing—"

"We weren't! We didn't knock it down!" Barrett's voice breaks. "I swear it."

And Timothy says, "He isn't lying."

Timothy

I saw her do it. While Barrett was on top of me, trying to choke me to stop me from hitting him, I saw Birdie come out of the fireplace and stand watching us. I could see in her face that she was scared for me and scared of Barrett. She wanted to save me. The yellow bowl was so big and looked so heavy and Birdie is so small. When she lifted it, I was too surprised to speak, so I couldn't warn Barrett. She lifted it over her head and before I could tell her not to, she threw it at him. I pushed my brother as hard as I could so he would be out of the way and it would miss him. Then Birdie was gone, and it was both of us, sitting on the floor looking at the mess that we didn't make but were going to be blamed for.

When Mom and Dad and Grayson come and help us clean up the mess, Grayson finds every single one of my sea animals. I think that Barrett will be my friend now because I pushed him and saved him from getting hit by the bowl. I think, *Now Barrett will be grateful.* But when Mom is done washing our cuts, because we both hurt each other when we were fighting, Barrett goes in a room upstairs and slams the door. Dad yells at him again because slamming doors isn't being careful and something else might break.

Now I am alone in the birthing room, getting ready to play with my animals again while Mom cooks breakfast. I see Birdie watching me from the outside, with her face pressed up against the window. When she sees that I am looking back at her, she makes a motion with her hand that tells me, "Come here." So I go outside even though it is wet and dewy and I don't like dew. Birdie holds my hand and walks with me around the frog pond.

I ask her, "Why did you do it?"

And she says, "Why do you think I did?"

And I don't know what to say to that. I know she did it to save me and I'm glad about that part, but I don't want anyone to hurt Barrett except for me.

So I say, "Thank you," even though that is not the whole thing of what I mean.

Birdie

I know some things but not others. I don't know how it is or why it is that the man and lady treat Timothy like he is their own, just as kind to him as they are to the other two. Kinder it seems. When night was falling, the lady held Timothy in her lap along with a book with big, colorful pictures. She read some and let Timothy read some. I don't know if the lady will be in trouble for that. Timothy fell asleep in her arms, and she carried him to his bed and pulled the covers up to his chin and kissed his cheeks. I saw her soul, and it was not wicked.

I saw love in her eyes. She will not let him be sold.

Come morning, the man takes the boys, the two yellow-heads and Timothy, for a walk through the woods. When branches are low and cover the path, the man sweeps them out of the way, holds them high so all three boys can go under. I follow behind, watching Wicked Eyes carefully in case he gets too near to Timothy. I will not allow it.

When they come to a log, Timothy will not climb over with the others, so the man picks him up and carries him on his back like an infant. The man's hands are gentle but strong. The oldest boy is in the lead, while Wicked Eyes brings up the rear. Wicked Eyes picks up a stone and throws it at Timothy's back. He misses and tries again as they walk. He misses again. Wicked Eyes is frustrated, angry to keep missing. I know anger. Anger is how my father, the monster, came at my mama the night I was made. Anger makes a body determined. Now I pick up a stone and let it go. Wicked Eyes cries out in surprise more than pain. I chose a small stone and aimed it to nick his ear. Just a warning.

The man stops to tend to Wicked Eyes but doesn't put Timothy down. Timothy is special to them all. A favorite. A pet. I think he has been for rides in covered carriages.

Barrett

I'm still rubbing my ear when we turn back for the house. It doesn't hurt so much, but the feeling of something hitting it keeps going. It wasn't a branch swiping me or an acorn falling or something like that. Something in these woods wants to get me. It was like the trees saw me trying to hit Timothy with rocks and they tried to get me back. Dad wouldn't believe it, but Grayson might if I tell him later, alone, if he's not trying to act like a grown-up.

The house is so big I can see it now, coming through the spaces between the trees. Its red sides and black roof. How can a house so big not have any reception? It's dumb. Any kind of house like that, they should have enough money to have better internet connection. It's historic, Mom says. From the stupid nineteenth century, and it was a stop on this Underground Railroad thing. Black people took subways deep under the country to get away from slavery, which is kind of cool, but no reason not to have better internet.

When we get to a clearing, which turns out to be the start of the backyard, Dad shows us a thick wooden door in the side of a little hill.

"This was the root cellar," Dad says. Finally, he puts Timothy down because here there are no more logs or sharp branches or bugs that will freak him out.

"Who cares?" I say, to see if Grayson will laugh before he remembers that he is mature. He used to be on my side. Instead, Grayson gives me a look like I should have respect.

Dad ignores me and says, "The root cellar was where the runaway slaves were hidden before they could move on and escape to Canada."

I roll my eyes and make a sarcastic face. I say, *"Wow-ow-ee!"* to see if I will be in trouble. But Dad keeps ignoring me. Grayson looks at me and shakes his head like I am so bad he can't believe it.

"It's a very important part of history," Dad says.

"They risked everything for freedom," Grayson says, nodding and taking everything seriously. "The runaway slaves were really brave, and so were the people who helped them."

Grayson is looking at Timothy while he's saying it, but Timothy isn't paying attention. I bet he's counting by threes in his head or thinking about mosasaurs or something else crazy in his own weird brain. Dad bends down and hugs Timothy for no reason AT ALL.

"This is part of your history," Dad says to Timothy, who is not even looking at the stupid root cellar. Dad lifts the latch on the door and opens it. An old, dead smell comes out, and we can see gray stone stairs inside. It looks cold and buggy and scary. I am afraid Dad will make us go down there, but Timothy holds on to him and says, *"No! Too dark! Too dark!"*

For once I am grateful to Timothy for being a spoiled little freak. Dad shuts the root cellar door and says we should head back and see what Mom has for lunch.

While we cross the lawn, Grayson the Kiss-Butt asks Dad more questions about history. Since Dad isn't looking, I grab Timothy by the back of his shirt and before he can scream and get me in trouble, I say this in his ear:

"I will lock you in there. I will lock you in that root cellar." The fear in his eyes and the wet of his scared breath feels good to me.

Birdie

When the white man opens the door in the side of the hill, I can hear the souls in the cellar, the souls of Black folks weeping, moaning, lost in a fire that once burned down there. I remember some more things: I remember being in there, all the way inside, just before my time. I pushed and kicked and fought to come out. I wanted to be born in the light, to live in the light. The cellar was dark and cold, full of the sorrowful dead. I heard them then just like now. They would never make it farther north than where they were. So I fought and pushed with the last of my strength. I would not let myself be born in a cellar. But by the time they got Mama into the house, it was too late for me.

Barrett

In the middle of the night, I wake up because the wind is blowing through the open window. Outside, I can see the moon with creepy clouds floating in front of it. I wish I wasn't too scared to get up and close that window, even though Dad says it's important to let fresh air come in the room when you're sleeping. I don't like those creepy clouds at all. Grayson is breathing slowly in his sleep. I want to wake him up and make him close the window. Instead, I snuggle down further in the bed and pull the cover over my head, even though it smells weird.

But now I hear the sound of someone's footsteps nearby along with more breathing. I pull down the blanket and at first I think it's Timothy standing over me. It's not.

Who are you? I want to say, but I'm so scared that the words get stuck inside my throat. She is a girl, smaller than Timothy, with hollow eyes and hair all fluffed up, like the creepy clouds outside my window. She stands and stares at me but doesn't speak a word.

∽

In the morning, when we are having breakfast, I know what is going to happen if I tell everyone about the girl. They'll say she was a dream even though I know she was TOTALLY REAL. Still, I can't help it, so I tell.

Mom is the first one to say it, and she says it quickly. "Honey, you were dreaming. It was a dream, that's all." Her voice is rushed and high, and she gets up fast to get more coffee, like she does whenever she and Dad have a fight. When they fight, Mom drinks so much wine at night that she has to drink a LOT of coffee in the morning just to feel like herself.

Dad humors me and asks all kinds of questions about the girl.

"How old was she about?"

"Little but not so little."

"What did she look like?"

"She had puffy hair like clouds."

"What was she wearing?"

"A dress."

"Did she say anything?"

"No."

Dad asks more stuff but doesn't fool me into thinking he's taking it seriously.

Finally, Grayson says, "Barrett, stop. You're scaring Timothy."

And then everyone looks at Timothy—because for once in our lives, no one was paying attention to him. Timothy's eyes are superwide and scared. He's rocking like he does when he's about to get upset. Mom forgets about her coffee and rushes to crouch beside Timothy's chair. She clamps a firm hand on his shoulder because he likes that better than gentle stroking. Then Mom starts yelling at me.

"No more talk about this stuff, do you hear me, Barrett? No more talk about girls in yellow dresses with cloud hair! Enough!"

Me and Grayson look at Dad, who is looking weird at Mom like he's going to tell her to calm down. Instead, Dad copies her and says, "Enough, Barrett."

I glare at him and then I glare at Mom. I never said the girl's dress was yellow.

After breakfast, when we have cleared and Mom sends us up to get dressed, Timothy says, "Barrett, I believe you." He is the only one who does. That's worse than no one believing me. It makes me hate him even more.

Timothy

Barrett met Birdie. I am glad that she didn't talk to him, because that means that she is still my friend and not Barrett's. I am glad that she didn't try to hurt him again, but I am also glad that she didn't apologize for throwing the yellow bowl.

I get dressed fast so I can get back downstairs to set up my sea creatures before we go to a museum and a concert in town. I also want to be alone so Birdie can find me and I can ask her why she was looking at Barrett in the night.

My liopleurodon is missing. He is not in the container with the other animals. I dump them all out and count one at a time and then put them back and dump them out and count them three times. Then I look all over the room, because I only ever played with them here in the birthing room and did not take them anywhere. Liopleurodon is not in this room, which means that he is lost, as in *gone*. He cannot be gone, because that means that I would only have twenty-three sea creatures instead of twenty-four like I am supposed to.

I start screaming loud. "My liopleurodon is missing! My liopleurodon is gone!"

At first no one comes. Mom is in the shower and Dad must be on a call in the only part of the house that has good reception. Grayson must have on headphones. Barrett is the one who comes, saying, "Shut up! Shut *up*! I know where your stupid lilopoorodon is!"

And that makes me stop crying even though I am still breathing hard and snot is coming out of my nose and my brother said *lilopoorodon* instead of liopleurodon.

It is hard to talk because I'm crying. I say, "Wh-where . . . is . . . he?"

"I hid him." Barrett is smiling his meanest smile, and that makes me cry again. I punch him and punch myself.

Barrett grabs my hands and holds them tightly, saying "shut up, shut up" again.

"I'll tell you where he is if you just *shut up*."

So I shut up even though I am still angry and upset. Barrett tells me that he hid liopleurodon outside in the backyard. After that, I cannot shut up. I am super, extra upset, so I start screaming that I need my liopleurodon, and I know Mom must still be in the shower and Dad must still be on a call and Grayson must still have on headphones or someone would come and stop me from hitting myself. This time, Barrett takes my shoulder and holds on firmly like Mom does to calm me down. Even though it's Barrett and not Mom, the firm holding still works and I get calmer. Barrett copies Mom's voice that she uses when she wants me to stop being upset.

"Shh. It's okay. Shh." Which is not how Barrett acts or talks ever. But since I am surprised and since I like when he is nice to me, even when I'm crying, I keep calming down. When he sees that I will listen to him, Barrett says, "Good. As long as you stay calm, I will bring you to find it, okay?"

I say okay. So Barrett takes me outside into the backyard, which is much, much bigger than our backyard in Connecticut: it is more like a park with hills, and woods that make a fringe on the edge. Barrett brings me to the place where we were yesterday, where there is a patch of grass that dips down and there is the door to the root cellar.

Birdie

I see Wicked Eyes take Timothy across the field to find his toy. They stop when they get to the root cellar. Timothy is crying when I catch up to them. Neither boy can see me.

"You put him in there!" Timothy says this while tears stream down his cheeks. He is as scared as he should be. I've been in that cellar. I saw the terror in their eyes as flames ate their lives and their hope.

Wicked Eyes folds his arms and puffs out his chest and belly to make himself bigger. "If you want your lilopoorodon, you have to go in and get it."

"No!" Timothy says. "*Liopleurodon!* Say it right!" He pushes Wicked Eyes, which makes me scared. No matter how kind they all act, Timothy will get it for sure for putting hands on a white boy.

Sure enough, Wicked Eyes says, "I'll say it how I want." And hits him before I can stop him. Timothy falls down, blubbering hard, breathing too fast. He is trying to speak, but words don't come out because he can't catch his breath. He's going to faint. Maybe he is sickly and is going to die because of Wicked Eyes.

Timothy

I am on the ground crying because Barrett hit me and knocked me down. I can't breathe enough to make my voice call Mom or Dad or Grayson because I'm too upset. Everything is *bad, bad, bad!* And lio-pleurodon is still gone and I don't know what to do or how to get him and I hate Barrett, *hate him, hate him, hate him.*

Now Barrett opens the root cellar door and the cold mustiness seeps out a little and he says, "You really want your stupid dinosaur?"

"He's not a dinosaur, he's a marine rep—"

"Shut *up!*" Barrett yanks me by the front of my shirt right up to the open door so I can smell and feel the cold, scary dark of it. He is going to push me in, throw me down the stairs, and I will die and never see Mom or my sea creatures ever again. Finally, my voice comes out, shrill and shrieking while I am snatching at Barrett's fingers trying to make him let me go.

But now Birdie is here. Her eyes are big circles, and she is frowning with hating Barrett. She is holding up a big piece of branch, all ready to bring it right down on Barrett's head.

It is good that I have my voice back because I can shout at her "No!" and Barrett thinks I mean him, but Birdie knows I mean her. She keeps the branch in the air, not letting it down to hit my brother. But she doesn't throw it away either. Barrett can't see her because she's behind him. He doesn't know to be scared.

"Help!" I yell finally, calling for Mom and Dad but not Grayson because it's too long to say. One-syllable words are best to yell when you're scared. *"Help! Mom! Dad! No! No!"*

"Shut up!" Barrett keeps holding me, shaking me in the doorway over the top of the stone stairs that go down into darkness. Suddenly Barrett's eyes get big and his mouth opens.

Barrett

Timothy is on the ground and I've got him by his collar when the girl with the cloud hair comes out of nowhere. She's standing over us with this huge stick in her arms. Like last night, she takes my voice away. I open my mouth, but I can't scream.

Timothy

Barrett lets go and I run as fast as I can away from the root cellar toward the house, screaming for Mom, leaving Birdie and Barrett behind. Mom is coming out of the house looking scared. I smash into her and hug her tight.

Catherine

As Timothy barrels into her, Catherine sees it all over his head. The little girl, the ghostly image of Birdie, swinging a length of birch like a club. Striking Barrett, sending him back through the root cellar door. Catherine's feet stay rooted to the ground. She clutches Timothy to her chest.

Barrett

I am falling, tumbling backward through the root cellar door, down the stairs into the moldy, smelly, horrible darkness. I hit the bottom hard. I'm hurt bad at first. Then everything tingles, and then I can't tell what hurts, or even *if* it hurts. I am so scared, so scared. No one knows I'm here. Timothy might not tell because I was mean to him before.

Then the voices start. Low and high, scary voices, quick whispers, slow, quivery moans. I can't understand what they're saying, but they must be demons and monsters, filling my ears with their wailing. They are sad and hurt and scared like me. The voices come faster and faster and faster, like panicking.

There are flames lighting up the cellar, so I can see their shadows against the walls, flying all over, howling. The whole cellar is on fire and I can't move. Every part of me feels broken.

There was a story Mom read me a long time ago, or maybe it was a teacher who read it, about a kid who was bad all the time, so bad things kept happening to him. I think about the bad kid right now and I start crying because I know that kid is me. I will die right here. I can only move one hand. It's under me, against the pocket where I still have Timothy's dinosaur.

Catherine and Pete

Somerville, Connecticut, July 2015
"Catherine." Pete's edge-of-explosion voice breaks through her meditation. "Are you *trying* to fuck my campaign?"

Since Barrett's injury, they've been mostly separate: one home with Grayson and Timothy, the other at the hospital by their middle boy's bedside. Pete spent the night there but came home to prepare for a day full of meetings. Catherine will head back once she's gotten the other boys off to their respective day camps.

Pete is post-shower, still shirtless—enviable physique on display. There's a vein pulsing at his temple, jaw clenching. Catherine's eye travels from his face to the phone he's holding aloft. Anxiety rises in her throat, but she beats it back, maintaining the illusion of serenity.

"How exactly am I trying to fuck your campaign?"

"You reviewed the house without consulting me! Put this hocus-pocus bullshit on the internet where anyone can read it. This is just the sort of thing Paulson's people will seize on to make me look like an asshole."

"I had to warn people," Catherine says. "Nothing in the review identifies you."

"Except our profile photo."

"It's small. No one looks at those."

"Don't play dumb. You know how the press has been fixating on Barrett and his 'suspicious' accident at a Massachusetts Airbnb. And with this—" He shakes the phone. "With this wacko review you've written, we all look insane. Just because you can't face the truth about Timothy."

Catherine's pretense of composure dissolves. "Fuck you."

Pete sighs, softens his tone a notch. "I'm not saying Barrett didn't provoke him. I'm not saying it wasn't an accident. But to make up a story about some supernatural—"

"I saw it, Peter."

"Okay, Catherine." Full-on patronizing. "I know. We're all grieving. We're both anxious about the campaign and about Barrett, what his life—all our lives—will be like. All I'm saying is that Timothy is getting older. His issues may require more intervention than we thought."

Catherine turns away, whispers the thing she's said a hundred times over since they came home. "Timothy was in my arms when Barrett fell." She pushes past Pete en route to the kitchen. "*Boys!* Shoes on! Time to go!"

Pete watches Catherine grab lunch boxes and backpacks, then hustle Grayson and his tennis gear into her car. She returns for Timothy, whom she carries so he won't have to dodge the worms that came out in the rain overnight.

Before stepping into the vehicle herself, Catherine glances back at Pete, almost conciliatory. "I'm going to the hospital straight after drop-off."

"Okay."

"I'll text you my Airbnb password when I get there. You can take down the review yourself."

Pete opens his mouth. He wants to tell her that it will be too late. That his rival's campaign staff is too quick, too sharp. That the link will be all over social media. But he remembers the lost baby girls who should have been theirs. He remembers Catherine's face, each time her heart was broken. He remembers that Barrett—the Barrett that *was*, before the trip to Monterey—is lost forever too. Pete decides to let Catherine have these last hours, whatever the cost. He heads back inside.

The glove compartment housing Jane Whittaker's diaries is slightly ajar. Grayson must have knocked into it when he got into the passenger seat. Catherine slaps it shut. She considered leaving the diaries behind at Whittaker House with Post-its marking the pages about Birdie, a cryptic warning to future guests. Instead, Catherine left the warning review on the Airbnb site. She'll keep the diaries—evidence that there was a real ghost-girl who could have attacked Barrett. As if a centuries-old story by another crazy white lady might exonerate Timothy one day.

Barrett

Dr. Lilly wants them to talk to me all the time, just like before. Dr. Lilly says talking might reactivate my brain. It feels just as active as before, but the things I want to say can't get out.

When Dad comes, he talks to me in a weird, stiff voice, saying, "How are we doing, sport?" which he never called me in real life, even though I used to play soccer and now I don't. Then Dad tells me something about the weather and then he breaks off and sobs. I never saw Dad or any grown-up man cry before and at first it was strange, but now I am used to it.

When Grayson comes, he tells me about tennis and what he's learning in science camp. Mom brings my Harry Potter books and reads them to me but cries when she gets to the parts I like to talk about. I can still talk and ask questions inside my head but not aloud, so she doesn't know. None of them know anything I think anymore. When they're here I stare straight at them and don't even blink when they say, "Blink if you understand me."

When Mom and Dad come here together, they fight like always, only now they do it right in front of me because they think I can't understand. Dad says Timothy shouldn't be allowed to see me. He says it's too risky. Mom doesn't agree.

Now Timothy is the one who's bad, at least to Dad and Grayson, who think he pushed me. It's like it used to be for me. Me and Timothy are both sorry for each other, for how it is for us both now. Me like this and him hated by Grayson and Dad. Still, Mom won the fight with Dad, which means Timothy gets to see me.

Timothy is the only one who understands what I mean inside my mind. He is careful with the tubes when he climbs on my bed and puts his head next to my shoulder. He is always warm and has a good smell like mixed-berry juice boxes. His heart beats near my heart. I wait for the rhythms to match, and then I tell him things. I know if he repeats what I say to Mom or Dad, they won't believe him, any more than they believe about the girl.

But I tell him anyway.

6

TURPENTINE

The Damn Mountains Again

Brooklyn, October 2019
Michelle cuts short her walk along the Brooklyn waterfront, arriving back at work five minutes before her scheduled call with Timothy Rhodes's psychiatrist—a routine update to make sure she and the doctor are on the same page. Mentally replaying her last counseling session with Timothy, a sweet but anxious sixth grader who moved here recently from tony Somerville, Connecticut, Michelle goes through her mail, pulling out a new edition of *The Week*. She filters out everything about Trump and his treachery, pausing to take in a clip about a criminal case she's been following for the past year and a half. It's a double murder of a couple at an Airbnb—a gruesome stabbing—and the disappearance of the couple's baby. The police still have no suspect for the killing, but they've long speculated that the baby was taken by the Airbnb owner, a woman.

It would have been a crazy story in any case, just the kind of thing to stir Michelle's zest for intrigue, but this one had elements that made it compelling enough to share with her sister, Kaye. The wife was Black while her husband was white. They were from Park Slope, just like Kaye and *her* white husband. The two couples could have been friends.

The other thing was that this Airbnb was somewhere in the Berkshire Mountains, not far from the setting of what Michelle thinks of as the Horrible Thing That Happened When I Was Twelve. Besides Michelle's ex-girlfriend Dominique, Kaye is the only one who knows about the Horrible Thing. The sisters rarely mention it—Kaye's decision, not Michelle's—but between them, they refer to the site as "the Damn Mountains."

Berkshire County—with its lakes, its birches, its quaint-named towns: Stockbridge, Becket, Lenox, Monterey. Michelle can still smell the pines and grasses of the place, but also the acrid stench of turpentine from the art studio.

The Subject

Summer 1999

Michelle's sister Kaye was sixteen and going to work that summer as a mother's helper in Martha's Vineyard. Ma had worried before letting her go, wondering if she should trust Mr. Gifford, the father of that family, with her pretty, nubile firstborn. But Daddy reassured her. The Giffords were educators, employed by the city, required by law to have background checks. Besides, both Mr. and Mrs. Gifford came from old Black money, which Daddy revered. His eldest would spend the summer in a sprawling Oak Bluffs home, the pinnacle of safety and comfort.

It was Gordy's eighth summer, his last, the summer of surgeries that were only partly covered by insurance. There was no money to spend on day camp for Michelle. The only one with nothing to do, Michelle complained about it loudly, as if making a nuisance of herself would distract them from her little brother's illness, reducing its impact on their lives. Daddy, merciful and resourceful, found a way for his middle child to have a "real summer" after all.

A white artist friend—Daddy's old college roommate—lived in Egremont, Berkshire County, Massachusetts, with his family. It had been a few years since Daddy had taken Michelle and Kaye to visit, but they'd gone quite a few times when they were younger. "We're going up to the mountains," Daddy would say. Ma had stayed behind with Gordy, who was not permitted to travel except to Children's Hospital in Philadelphia.

The artist's mountain home boasted farm animals, massive trees, flowers, and other growing things you could pick and eat. Kaye and Michelle were allowed to go into the henhouse and search for eggs underneath the birds' warm bodies. The artist's daughters were older and took the city girls for rides on an elderly gray horse. These were the things that Michelle remembered when she agreed heartily to spend her twelve-year-old summer on the farm in Egremont. No one feared for Michelle's safety; the artist was a trusted old friend.

Though Ma wouldn't notice until later on, Michelle was tall for twelve—as tall as Kaye at sixteen and thicker, well into puberty, whereas her sister had been a late bloomer. Of course, Kaye knew about things that Michelle did not. Ma had talked with her firstborn about dating and sex and protection, as she would with Michelle in time. Not yet, though. Certainly not this summer, with Gordy's surgeries on the horizon.

So Michelle knew nothing when the artist's wife and youngest daughter, who still lived at home at nineteen, went to town for supplies while the artist and Michelle stayed alone at the farm. Michelle knew nothing when the artist told her he'd like her to sit for him so he could sketch her. She knew nothing when the sitting and sketching sessions became something that went on daily. Each morning, the wife and daughter would find something to do so the artist would not be distracted from his work, or from his young subject.

And Michelle knew nothing when the artist told her that the lighting in his studio required her to pull her top down and reveal her shoulders—only her shoulders. She knew nothing when he asked her to sit with her back arched this way so that the nibs of her breasts were visible through the fabric of her now stretched-out shirt.

Only when the artist began to pay her compliments—as no one had ever done before—did Michelle grow suspicious. In her family, Kaye was called the "pretty" one. Kaye had lighter skin, softer hair, and looked like Ma, while Michelle and Gordy favored their father. So when the artist said she was lovely, Michelle asked him why he was lying to her.

"I would not lie to you," the artist said, and reiterated, "You are a lovely young girl."

At this, Michelle's heart raced, not because she was flattered but because now he was lying about lying, and liars of any kind frightened her. And later on, when she asked to call her father, Michelle was told that she would have to wait. By this time it was pouring outside, a drumming, sheetlike country rain. She was told that the phone reception was down. She could call her father once the storm had passed.

When Michelle was finally able to call Daddy, the artist did not leave the room. He sat in a chair before a portrait he had done of his daughters when they were very small, their naked infant and toddler bodies rounded and pink, their dark eyes staring out of the picture frame under pale, tousled bangs. The artist watched Michelle as she spoke on the phone. His smile was benevolent, his hands clasped together.

"Is everything okay?" Daddy had known, somehow, that this was a time to ask only yes-or-no questions.

"No," Michelle said.

"Are you all right?"

"Yes," she said, though she was not certain.

Daddy heard the doubt in her voice. "Is there someone in the room with you?"

"Yes."

"Do you need to come home?"

"Yes."

But it was Tuesday, and Daddy wouldn't be able to come up until the weekend, when he was off from work. Ma couldn't come either; she had to bring Gordy to Philadelphia. Michelle told Daddy she understood. She promised to have fun and help with the animals on the farm. She caught the artist's eye and knew she could not mention the sketching sessions. Then Daddy asked to speak with the artist, his dear friend. Michelle handed her host the phone and went to help the wife and daughter with their chores. She could hear the artist laughing on the phone with Daddy. The sound of a man laughing with another man: deep, self-assured, and exclusive.

The following day, when the wife and daughter were preparing to leave, Michelle asked to come with them on their errands.

"Why not?" the wife said after a moment's pause, during which she had exchanged a look with the artist.

But the artist said it would be best if Michelle stay with him for just one last sketching session. He was making great headway, and she'd been a *dynamite* subject. Just a few more hours would be all he needed. Michelle did not know the words to protest, so the wife and daughter got in their Jeep and drove away.

As the sound of the Jeep's engine trailed off, Michelle found herself rooted to the ground, staring wide-eyed at the artist. This is the last thing she is clear about. The rest of the memory is in streaks and splashes. Running to hide in the henhouse, the artist's thin, blue-veined arms reaching for her, grabbing her, pulling her by the clothes and hair.

Being in the studio, pressed into the sofa, his breath and beard hot upon her face. Struggling, kicking over a pail filled with paintbrushes soaking in turpentine, the smell filling the room. His rough, calloused hand pressed against her mouth. Legs pulled apart, his other hand inside her. And then, and then . . .

It was too late when the Jeep returned. The artist's wife had for-gotten something. When Michelle heard the door, she ran from the studio, crying out, barreling into the woman. The wife took in the sight of Michelle's torn shirt, mussed hair, and tear-streaked face. She held Michelle close, engulfed the child in her soft, strong body.

"I'm taking you home." She said this over Michelle's head, looking at her husband as he worked at his zipper.

By then it really was too late. When she got home, Gordy's last weeks were upon them. Michelle sensed that there was no space, no air for her parents to manage anything else. Michelle only told Kaye, who offered her own comfort and sympathy but agreed that she should not tell Daddy or Ma. Kaye offered Michelle a hand to squeeze—as hard as she wanted, whenever she needed to—claiming the power to absorb and destroy Michelle's bad memories.

"Then tell yourself it didn't happen," Kaye instructed her. "And it *won't* have happened."

Michelle trusted Kaye. She did not detect the desperation, born of guilt, in her sister's tone. It would not occur to her for several years that Kaye's refusal to go to the Mountains was rooted in her knowledge of danger there. Kaye had saved herself, but left Michelle's fate to chance. Michelle would forgive her sister only after years of reflecting—tak-ing into consideration Kaye's youth that summer, along with the belief they'd both been raised on: that an unpretty child would not need protecting.

But at twelve, Michelle took Kaye's word as truth. She squeezed her sister's hand. She did not tell their parents. And yet, neither Daddy nor Ma ever spoke of the artist again, though the painting he had given the family as a gift was removed from the wall. Michelle would never learn about the phone call her mother received from the artist's wife one night, not long after Gordy's death. Michelle would not learn about the row between her parents where it was decided that the best thing to do was not mention the awful occurrence, but to let it fade in time. To let Michelle forget peacefully and move on.

Michelle's parents never knew *her* story of the Horrible Thing That Happened, or that the story lived alongside her, shaping her every moment—from her refusal to return to her formerly beloved dance classes, to the older boys whom she drew to her, whom she allowed to touch her, believing there was nothing left of herself to protect, to her grades in school, which dropped from As to Ds and Fs—until she met Calliope, who prescribed her journey back in time.

At a visit to the hair salon, Ma had found Calliope's business card, which promised "therapeutic mentoring for young women of color." Calliope had no license, no official credentials, just an intriguing card and a soothing voice on the telephone. Michelle was fifteen by then. Young enough for Ma to force her to go.

∽

Calliope wore a gold satin tunic with a colorful chiffon scarf around her neck. Lighter than Michelle but darker than Ma—an involuntary assessment Calliope herself would one day teach Michelle to outgrow— Calliope's salt-and-pepper sister locks hung to her waist.

Michelle had shrugged when Calliope asked what had brought her to her studio. Calliope used the word "studio" to help people relax, believing the term "office" to be sterile and off-putting. "Studio" did not relax Michelle. It opened something within her that she thought she'd locked shut.

"Your mind and body are in a state of disconnect," said Calliope. And waited. Michelle did not speak. Calliope tried, "Did someone touch you." It did not sound like a question, which made it easier to respond.

"Yes."

"How long ago?"

150

"I was twelve," said Michelle and cried for the first time since she had promised Kaye she would keep the Horrible Thing a secret.

"How many times?" Calliope said when it seemed that Michelle could respond.

"Once."

Then Calliope was silent, waiting for the story to come out. At first only pieces rose to the surface and then drifted back down. Calliope did not force Michelle to remember anything she was not ready to remember. They could begin reintegrating her *self* and her *psyche* without details.

One day, Calliope instructed Michelle to meet her at a dance studio in the Village. They descended a dusty staircase with a splintery banister and emerged in an enormous windowless chamber. It was full of women and girls of all colors and ages.

"This," said Calliope, "is where we dance."

People wore T-shirts, sweatpants, pajamas, and various flowy, drapey garments. The music, which reached them from speakers mounted on the ceiling, was more prayer than song. Accompanying the vocals were drums, pipes, and flutes. A small, sinewy white woman with a long gray braid and knotted bare feet stepped to the front of the room and sat. Everyone followed along, loosely mirroring the woman's movements—from the seated position on the floor, to standing poses, to slides, spins, and twirls—each body with its own random path across the space. Calliope danced too, first alongside Michelle, then away into the crowd. Michelle was tentative at first, keeping her eyes on the tiny instructor, swaying only gently in time to the beat until another girl—Black, younger and smaller than Michelle, but with movements full of exuberant commitment—slammed into her. As Michelle fought for her balance, the girl laughed, reaching for her. Michelle flinched. The girl stepped back but kept smiling.

"It's okay." The girl extended her arms toward Michelle more gently this time. Michelle fought her fear and allowed it. The girl moved closer and embraced her, swaying to the music now, wordlessly easing Michelle into the dance. The girl whispered, above the pipes and drums, "You are safe."

The phrase entered Michelle's being through her ear to spread throughout her body, mingling with her blood. And for the hour, she allowed herself to simply move, to feel herself in her body, connected to space, to the floor, to the air, to the other women and girls. The sensation became addictive, filling her up, reintegrating her along with Calliope's counsel.

As the years passed, dancing—the joy and freedom of it—wended its way back into Michelle's life and heart. But no matter how much time went by, no matter how she prayed or chanted, the dancing could not replace what the artist had taken from her.

Life Drawing

2012

For that, Calliope said, Michelle would need to return to the setting of her trauma. Michelle was twenty-six by this time, waiting tables in the Village, sharing an apartment in Harlem with four other women, considering what to do with her bachelor's degree in philosophy. It had been fourteen years since the Horrible Thing. Calliope's locks were now largely silver.

"I can't do that," Michelle said. "The farm has been sold. The artist died. His wife has moved to California."

It didn't matter, Calliope told her. Michelle must return to the Berkshires anyway. The environment was what mattered for reenactment. She must go back to the Mountains and find an artist to pose for. But this time Michelle would be in control of the circumstances. She would choose her own poses in the light of day.

Michelle did not understand. How, where, would she find such an artist?

Calliope said, "The details are up to you. What matters most is that you take back the narrative of the trauma. Take back the light and the rain. Reinhabit your body."

"How long will I need to be there for?"

"As long as it takes. I'll be here when you return."

So Michelle packed her bags, got on a bus, and found her way back to the quaint-named towns of Berkshire County.

∞

In time, she found a place to live in Great Barrington, with a group of grad students about her age who needed another roommate. She found a job waiting tables at a restaurant. And, some months after that, Michelle answered an ad from an art studio seeking a model for a life drawing class held at a library in Lee.

They needed her just once a week. Every Saturday she would wait in the hall in her white robe, tied at the waist, as the amateur artists— mostly ladies in their fifties and sixties, the occasional octogenarian— filed into the room and took their places at easels.

At this point the instructor would enter, then beckon to Michelle, who would square her shoulders, lift her chin, and stride toward her stool at the center of the room. Next, in a choreographed gesture, she would slip off her robe, swirl it around like a matador, drape it over the stool, and sit.

Michelle chose her own poses. Sometimes she would rest one hand on the opposite shoulder and cross one leg over the other. Sometimes she would place one hand on her knee and extend the other leg far behind her, arching her neck like a swan. And over the course of an hour, she would cycle through her poses, keeping her gaze calm, her breathing even, her heart rate slow.

When the class was over, she would rise, head high, and sweep her robe around herself. With a nod to the artists, she would glide across the room and out of the door, the picture of serenity.

It did not start out that way. The very first Saturday, Michelle was anything but serene as she sat there, all eyes on her naked body. She shut down, retreating into the back corner of her brain. It was the only way she could keep from shaking. When the instructor dismissed the class, Michelle fled the room, making eye contact with no one. In the hallway, she broke into a sobbing run. But turning a corner, Michelle found herself face-to-face with another young woman who opened her arms and held her.

"I gotcha." The woman breathed through her laughter, hair falling in smooth, dark waves around Michelle's cheeks. "I felt the same way the first time I posed."

She held Michelle by the shoulders now, looked into her face with bright black eyes. They were brown, actually, but the shadow effect created by the kohl she used made Dominique's eyes appear onyx. Her face was an upside-down teardrop, Josephine Baker teeth forming a wicked-child grin. Dominique wore a robe like Michelle's, one bare shoulder peering out. She was the model for the sculpting class that met at noon.

Dominique looked Michelle up and down. "*Shit*, you're hot."

And Michelle felt more exposed than she had minutes ago, sitting stark naked on the stool. It wasn't that she felt objectified by Dominique—women had objectified her before this. Instead, it was the fact that Michelle could feel herself becoming absorbed into Dominique's aura. There was a rift in the force field between them; Michelle could see through it, pass through it, only for this brief sliver of time. The choice was hers. As she equivocated, Dominique's smile faded, eyes growing full and wide.

"Sweet Jesus," Dominique said. "I'm sorry." She'd never experienced anything like the Horrible Thing. Yet Dominique could intuit enough from Michelle's downcast eyes and quivering shoulders.

Michelle sensed that Dominique understood something about her without being told. "It's okay," Michelle said. And returned the smile.

It was Dominique who taught her to stride into the library's art studio, head high, to swirl the robe like a matador, to arch her neck like a swan, one leg extended. But the power to be observed and reproduced in poses of her own design—that was Michelle's alone. And so, as Calliope had instructed, Michelle took back the narrative of the Horrible Thing. The dead artist's hold over her body and psyche was gradually whittled down to shavings.

All that remained—rich in the Lee art studio as it had been in the dead man's workspace—was the lingering odor of turpentine.

The Ancestor

Quebec, 1995

Grand-mère swore that it was true. Maman said nothing could be more preposterous. She would turn sideways, displaying her pointy nose, ribbon-thin lips, and ghost-white skin. Anyone could see that her genes were 100 percent European.

"The blood of *ma famille* is pure French," Maman was fond of declaring. "Of that I haven't the slightest doubt. Nor should you." She reminded Dominique that she must take everything Grand-mère said with a grain of salt. Grand-mère's marbles had been slipping away since long before Dominique was born. "The Black blood you have running through your veins comes only from your father, not from me."

Grand-mère insisted nonetheless. "It is not always visible to the eye, yet I am *indeed* Black. Descended from slaves who toiled endlessly in the hot sun of a plantation deep in the American South."

It was Grand-mère's favorite topic, for which she needed no prompt, no inquiry.

"Trace my roots and you will find a runaway slave." Dominique could recite the monologue along with her, imitating Grand-mère's voice, grown crackly from decades of cigarettes. "A midnight-colored ancestor fled the cotton fields alone on foot. He ran and hiked and swam. He bartered, begged, and clawed his lonely way into Canada. And here he set down roots, married a white Frenchwoman, and fathered generations of Canadians, each fairer than the last. But make no mistake, Black Africa lives within us!"

Maman would roll her eyes, muttering that Grand-mère was as white as she was. But Grand-mère would show Dominique and her brother JP newspaper clippings with photographs of the famous actor Sidney Poitier as proof.

"You can see the resemblance, can't you?" Grand-mère beamed with pride, holding the pictures of Poitier up beside her face. "It's obvious that we have a common ancestor."

There was no one else to verify the story of Dominique's maternal lineage. Grand-père had died before Dominique was born, and Maman was an only child. Therefore, it was Grand-mère's word against Maman's. And Maman never missed an opportunity to call Grand-mère's marbles into question.

Maman did not care for American Blacks. She believed that they were to blame for the high rates of crime in the States. Maman called American Blacks lazy, compared them to wild animals. Grand-mère on the other hand worshipped them: their musical talent, their athleticism, their age-defying skin.

Dominique and JP too were fascinated by American Blacks—Will Smith, Queen Latifah, *Prince!*—delighting in the possibility of being related to them. "African American" was much more thrilling than the heritage of their father, an ordinary first-generation transplant to Montreal. Baba had come from Nigeria to do his medical residency, had met Maman, a university student at the time, and decided to stay until she graduated. Baba was acceptable to Maman, despite his skin color. Because it was *not* skin color that bothered Maman so much about Black Americans. It was not what they looked like at all, but how they *were*, that she objected to. Native Africans like Baba were far more palatable to Maman: hardworking and upwardly mobile. Africans were willing to do whatever it took to overcome their baser, more primitive tendencies.

But by the time Dominique turned nine in 1997, her knowledge of American Blacks went far beyond Maman's stereotypes. The hottest African American television programs flooded daily across the US border into Dominique's playroom. And there was nothing primitive about the quick-witted, fashion-forward characters in Dominique's beloved shows: *Moesha, Sister, Sister,* and *Family Matters.* There was rap music as well, which thrilled Dominique, even when she could not understand the lyrics. Maman strictly forbade Dominique and JP from listening to rap music, which meant that rap was the only music they valued.

The year Dominique turned fifteen, Grand-mère used the very last of her marbles to exact a promise from her granddaughter. She must never, ever forget the story of their Midnight-Black Ancestor. Dominique promised. At which point Grand-mère's eyes took on a glaze through which the light of recognition ceased to shine.

This is everything Grand-mère told Dominique: The Ancestor had escaped from a plantation down south, just after the passage of the Fugitive Slave Act, which meant there would be no possibility of lasting liberty unless he crossed the border into Canada. At one point, he had slept at a farmhouse in Massachusetts—a stop on the Underground Railroad—where there had been a ghastly fire that the Ancestor had escaped as well. He then found his way north across the Canadian border, where he fell in with a colony of freed slaves in the Shrewsbury settlement. They spoke French; he did not.

That was all Grand-mère knew. It was no use trying to get more information out of Maman, who didn't believe a word of it anyway. So Dominique tucked the story away, unsure of what bearing it would have, or should have, on her own life. It wasn't until she was in her early twenties that JP had his DNA tested and learned that his ancestry was 62 percent African. Maman had clearly lied.

"The Ancestor was real!"

JP lifted Dominique into the air and swung her around. They both laughed. There had been no sign among the DNA results linking JP to Sidney Poitier, but evidence of the Ancestor was no longer in doubt.

Immediately, Dominique had her own ancestry tested and confirmed at 60 percent African. Third and fourth cousins were identified. Links between their digital family trees and her own revealed new names: Guidrys and Hutchinsons, Wilkersons and Johnsons, each of which came with "hints" about their stories. There were census records, marriage licenses, slave deeds, and finally links to arrest warrants seeking fugitive slaves.

Dominique descended into the United States and continued her search in earnest.

The Magic Ingredient

Massachusetts, 2012

The modeling for the library's sculpting class was a side gig for Dominique, as the life drawing job was for Michelle. They each had their reasons.

Dominique lived in the guestroom in the home of an elderly couple who sold antiques and custom-made jewelry. She had answered an ad and gotten herself hired as the woman's apprentice, helping to construct the lush silver creations the woman designed to hang from the ears or throats of well-heeled Berkshire weekenders.

"Their place is enormous," Dominique told Michelle, who had waited in the library's garden with a book until Dominique had finished posing. They had agreed after meeting in the hallway that they were not done with one another. When Dominique had changed into her sundress and sandals, they went for ice cream and then a long walk around a nameless pond.

Michelle was nothing if not the cautious type. She knew that a real friendship would take time. And yet, she sensed that with Dominique no one could stay true to type. The pull toward this dark-eyed Canadienne was intense, palpable. Michelle had never been so quick to smile as when Dominique confessed that her elderly hosts were away for the weekend.

"Convenient—no?" Dominique matched Michelle's grin, one feathery eyebrow raised.

On the drive in Michelle's newly purchased thirdhand VW, they talked ceaselessly, words spilling over one another. They shrieked with delight as they uttered similar phrases—about their reasons for and experiences of posing nude, about being young and brown in such an old, white corner of the world.

At the couple's home, they gorged on fresh berries from the old woman's garden, on aging brie from the fridge and stale crackers from an unmarked tin in the pantry. Over the next several hours, they drank three bottles from a case of malbec that the old man had in the garage. Michelle braided Dominique's hair and wove in flowers from the old woman's window boxes. She could not remember laughing as gustily as she did that night—at their spontaneity, their audacity, to partake of so much drink and food and space and time, to be paying for none of it.

In the downstairs bathroom was an enormous tub that they discovered to be a Jacuzzi. There were jets that vibrated and splashed and spurted. There was a nozzle with six different settings. Dominique and Michelle stripped naked and lathered themselves to pieces with bath bombs and salts and gels, high on wine, youth, their pheromones, and the richness they'd found in one another's embraces. It was not possible, Michelle knew, to fall in love over a matter of hours. And yet, and yet . . .

At daybreak Michelle opened her eyes to find the sun in the wrong place, its color off, its rays the wrong length. Then she understood: it was not daybreak but rather sunset. They had stayed up all night and slept the day away like a pair of girl vampires. Dominique's arm was slack over Michelle's belly; Dominique's smell rich in her nostrils, the flowers Michelle had bound into her new lover's hair wilted and scattered over the sheets. Their legs were entwined, hips touching. Dominique stirred, licked her ear, and Michelle released a roaring, joyful laugh. She was free, her mind and body integrated at long last. The magic ingredient she'd been awaiting had been Dominique all along.

The Seekers

2013–2014

"Where to this weekend?"

In the early months—once the stories of Gordy and Maman, the Artist and the Midnight-Black Ancestor had been shared—Michelle got a kick out of Dominique's quest, driving her along the country roads, learning about Underground Railroad safehouses, their secrets and histories. It was a thrill to see the makeshift gravestones and the rare, preserved trapdoors with rudimentary sleeping spaces beneath.

"Williamstown on Saturday," said Dominique. There were a few sites there. Other possibilities might pop up.

"You're like a mouse in a maze after cheese." Michelle loved Dominique all the more for her determination, no matter how often her leads wound up false.

Dominique liked the analogy and sniffed the air, making whiskers out of her fingers. "I'm getting close to finding out where he hid. I can *tell*."

Dominique had assumed it would be a no-brainer to find the Berkshire farmhouse whose fire the Midnight-Black Ancestor had escaped. She was mistaken. How many towns were there in Berkshire County? (Thirty-two, counting the cities of Pittsfield and North Adams.) How many safehouses had there been? They were *secrets*. No one knew! Maybe hundreds, once you counted the homes owned by Quakers, Shakers, *and* free Blacks. And, of that unknown number, how many had suffered fires? (Anyone's guess.)

If she couldn't comprehend Dominique's need to stick it to her long-dead Maman, Michelle supported her girlfriend's obsession nonetheless. They had both come to the Mountains to solve mysteries of their own identity. It was part of their bond.

But Facebook, as it so often does, ruined things.

$\curlyeqprec$

By the time Dominique and Michelle had been together one year and three months, they were subletting a little barn house in Stockbridge, near the Lion's Den restaurant where they both waited tables. On Saturdays, they both continued to pose for art classes at the library in Lee.

"We have a meetup in Becket on Sunday," Dominique told Michelle one Thursday as the latter was dropping the former off to work a morning shift. "It's at noon. Can you drive me?"

"We?"

The *we* turned out to be a band of others just as determined as Dominique to complete their ancestors' narratives by searching former safehouses. They had connected on Facebook and established a group called "the Seekers," numbers burgeoning in a matter of weeks, physical chapters forming all the way up the Eastern Seaboard. Anytime someone found information about a house or a well-traveled route on the Underground, they'd post it in case it had meaning for anyone else. They rejoiced in one another's breakthroughs and lamented each other's letdowns. Much as Michelle had been doing for Dominique all along.

"In other words," said Michelle, pulling up in front of the restaurant, "I'm not invited but you need me for a ride?"

"Bluntly put, but yes." Dominique shifted in her seat to face Michelle.

"Seriously?"

"What? You're not seeking *your* people." Dominique smiled, scooping her hair over one shoulder, playfully twirling the end. "It's just for the members."

"Fine." Michelle smiled back—not enough to hide the hurt, she didn't think, but Dominique missed it anyway.

"Great. Thanks." She brushed a kiss across Michelle's lips and hopped out of the car. Michelle wasn't working until lunch.

At home that evening, Dominique apologized—or made an after-the-fact concession, which was about as close as Dominique got to an actual apology.

"Hey," she said, plunking down next to Michelle, who was reading on the beanbag that served as a couch.

"Hey *what*?" Michelle lowered her tablet.

"Hey, you can come with me Sunday if you want."

"It's all right," Michelle said. Being asked along was good enough.

"You don't want to come? Or you *do*?" Dominique burrowed her head into Michelle's shoulder.

"No." Michelle warmed at the contact, the weight of Dominique's head against her. "You can have your Scooby-Doo ghost chasers all to yourself." She grinned as Dominique bopped her one with a throw pillow. Though Michelle had known from the start that Dominique did not believe in monogamy, in that moment the threat of sharing her with the Seekers had passed. Along with it had gone Michelle's grumpiness.

Still, she questioned the Seekers' methodology: reliance on the outcome of a Ouija board, séances held by candlelight in the dry, aged-wood libraries of these two-hundred-plus-year-old homes.

Each time Dominique invited her going forward, Michelle would quip, "Whose turn is it to bring the fire extinguisher?"

Dominique would roll her eyes. "You worry about so much shit. How do you get through the day? Live life!"

Another thing Michelle could not get with was the running naked through the woods, which the Seekers frequently did, calling the ancestors to join them and speak through them.

"It's just another method of contact," Dominique explained with a shrug.

"But *who* do you want to contact?" said Michelle. It was a question that had been on her mind since jump. "Your beloved 'Midnight-Black Ancestor' made it to Canada. Anyone sticking around here to turn up in a séance died before making it across the border."

Dominique looked for a moment as if she hadn't considered this, but recovered quickly. "I doubt he attempted the journey alone. He escaped a fire. Chances are, someone else didn't."

It was a good point. Michelle let it be. In any case, the Seekers really did seem to extract messages from beyond the grave. Nothing concrete, no *"It is I, your great-great-grandfather Jeremiah, who escaped from Kearneysville in 1852,"* but hints nonetheless, letting them know which libraries, which houses of records to check, and what addresses. The members would wake from trances with descriptions of locations on their lips, impulses to check barns or cellars. And when the group would investigate, someone would unearth a treasure—a name, a map, a letter. Two of the group members claimed they'd succeeded in contacting family members so far, and one swore he'd used the information gleaned at a séance to trace his lineage back to Africa.

Not that Michelle had the vaguest interest in taking part in such nonsense. She had no use for spirits or ghosts. Michelle had her own casual aspirations of locating her ancestors someday, but as she'd explained to Dominique with flirtatious snark, she did prefer internet searches to Ouija boards.

Dominique did not let up. "Everyone's dying to meet you."

"You talk about me with them?" Michelle didn't know why this gave her pause. Why shouldn't Dominique talk about her girlfriend? It should make Michelle feel good that she was on Dominique's mind when they were apart. "What did you tell them?"

"That you were skeptical of all this hocus-pocus bullshit." Dominique smiled, draping an arm around her. "Isn't that what you call it?"

"Yes," Michelle said.

"But you're curious."

"No."

"A little?"

"A very little."

"You're scared, though?"

"Maybe."

"I'll be right by your side. I'll hold your hand."

Michelle could not say no to Dominique.

Virgil and Penelope

Michelle was surprised that she and Dominique were the oldest people there. Everyone else was a student at one of the local universities. The house they used belonged to the white grandparents of Nerissa, one of the mixed girls. Scarce were the Berkshire homeowners eager to accommodate a group of young Black people summoning their ancestors' spirits. Nerissa's grandparents didn't know precisely what they did in the basement of the house or in the woods out back, but they loved Nerissa and trusted her. They were liberal to a fault and wouldn't let on if the group made them nervous for any reason.

The grandparents were not present on the night that Michelle caved at last and accompanied Dominique to the Seekers' gathering. Besides

Michelle, Dominique, and Nerissa, there was another girl, Ayana, plus three boys: Wesley, Antoine, and Giovanni.

The vibe among the group was familiar, warm, and chummy, with Dominique at the center of the humor and embraces. A joint went around, as did half sentences understood by maybe two members at a time, who would then pass a meaningful look between them. Hooking up was definitely happening among the crowd.

Wesley, though short and stocky, with a demi-goatee, was a world-class flirt. He kept grabbing the girls—Ayana, Nerissa, but Dominique most of all. Michelle, the darkest—the only one whose hair claimed true 4C coils—was invisible to him, which was fine, really. It was mutual. But the thing with him and Dominique gave Michelle a queasy feeling. She wasn't imagining it. When he spoke to Dominique, it was into her ear. Dominique cackled for him the way Michelle thought she cackled only for her. Being attached only to Dominique, Michelle felt her outsider status like a lead smock from the dentist—at once comforting and awkward. There was a way you had to *be* to fit in, relaxed, loose, open to hedonism, even as you got serious about contacting spirits.

Once people were a little high, a little out-there-in-the-spiritual-zone, it was time to get to the business everyone had come for. They dragged chairs into a wide circle in Nerissa's grandparents' basement and went about lighting candles—dozens of them: fat white ones, skinny purple and orange ones—and setting them out all over the floor. But the flames had to compete with the vents in the basement ceiling that, Nerissa explained, were painted fast in the open position.

Considering herself the only grown-up, with the questionable exception of Dominique, Michelle had to speak up. "Yeah. *That's* not safe." A candle listing toward a pile of dusty old newspapers.

No one could argue. The group went around extinguishing all similarly precarious flames, to the point where they were left with a single peach-scented pillar candle on a milk crate at the center of the circle of chairs.

It was a democratic séance in that no one led. They held hands and breathed together in unison. They recited incantations they'd lifted from YouTube videos. They called upon the ancestors to reach them, guide them, speak through them. Then they were silent, still clutching hands, eyes pressed shut, waiting in the candlelight's drafty dance.

All at once, Michelle felt Dominique stiffen and quake. Michelle opened her eyes as Dominique howled, *"Why have you called on me? What do you want?"*

Dominique whipped her head around, scanning everyone's alarmed faces. *"Why? Why? Why—"* Her next words tumbled out rapid-fire, slamming up against one another, unintelligible but for a few: "Devil!" "Bile!" "Lament!" and "Blood!" Her fingers dug into the hands of the members flanking her: Michelle on her right, Wesley on her left. Neither Michelle nor Wesley let go of her hands, even as Dominique jerked forward and rose. (It was a rule, Michelle had learned beforehand: no matter what happened during the séance, you *did not* drop hands.)

Dominique's body pitched violently from side to side while the others did all they could to avoid breaking the circle. Now she snapped her head toward Wesley. He was barely Michelle's height and Dominique was taller than them both, seeming all the larger for her possession by the anonymous spirit.

"Virgil!" Dominique cried out, face close to Wesley's, hair enfolding them both like a wild, wavy mist. "Is it you?"

"Um—no, ma'am, I'm Wesley," he said. "I'm living in the year 2014, contacting you for—"

"Virgil, *Virgil*! It *is* you! How I've searched!"

"Miss—ma'am," Wesley said. "Tell us your name. With whom are we—"

"*Virgil*!" Dominique's voice strained.

As she flung herself into him, Wesley writhed as if seized by electricity, calling, "Penelope?" Voice wavering and high. *"Penelope!"*

The candle flickered and snuffed them into darkness as Dominique's fingers slipped out of Michelle's grasp. Michelle was adrift, blind in the blackness, with no sign of Dominique, whose voice was obliterated by a chorus of shrieks. Someone banged into a wall or piece of furniture and cussed.

"Shut up, y'all!" a girl said. "I'm trying to find the damn light switch!"

Something crawled over Michelle's ankle—spider or centipede—making her start, then bump into someone's warm body. "Dom? Dominique?"

"It's Antoine." His baritone meant to soothe, his heavy-gentle hand on her arm meant to steady her. Michelle jerked back. "Sorry," he said. "My bad."

The lights switched on, blinding as the darkness. Nerissa stood at the foot of the stairs, one hand on the switch.

"Oh, they did *not*," she said. The others followed her gaze to the place on the floor where Wesley and Dominique were locked in a twisted embrace, Dominique's legs fastened around Wesley's hips. They quivered together, Dominique's head thrown back. Both their eyes rolled, revealing only the whites.

Michelle froze, unsure of what she was seeing. But the others sprang to action, closing in on the prone pair, chanting out a spell that they all clearly knew by heart. Of course they all knew the drill, Michelle realized, because this had happened before. Nerissa, Ayana, Antoine, and Giovanni took hands and encircled Dominique and Wesley, chanting, forming a knot that tightened as it swayed back and forth. Everyone knew but Michelle.

∽

"What was *that*?" Michelle asked Dominique in the car. It was the first they'd spoken since just before the séance. Even when the trance lifted and the other Seekers brought Dominique and Wesley water, rubbing their shoulders to make sure they were all right, Michelle had kept off to the side. The fact that no one was surprised by Dominique and Wesley landing in each other's arms as "Virgil" and "Penelope" made Michelle's heart pound with foreboding.

"What was *what*?" said Dominique, turning to glare at Michelle, as if she hadn't just made out with a man in front of her. Neither of them knew it yet, but it was the same look, the same tone Dominique would ultimately take when Michelle would arrive home from work to find Wesley in their bed.

"Nothing," said Michelle and kept on driving.

But two weeks later, the discovery of Wesley's naked behind in their bed confirmed that it was *not* nothing, that it had not *been* nothing for some time. Michelle, enraged and wounded, found what she could of Wesley's clothes, threw them at him, and threw him out.

By then, Dominique was angry too. Michelle had no right, she said, to feel betrayed.

"I told you how I feel about monogamy. There is nothing I have not been candid with you about."

༺༻

Things changed quickly after that. Michelle took on more shifts at the Lion's Den to distract herself from her breaking heart. Dominique was gone frequently. When Michelle found she could no longer bear waking up alone beside Dominique's empty half of the bed, she reached out to Calliope to say she might be done with the Berkshires.

"Have you accomplished what you set out to?"

Michelle considered it. In just under three years, she had replaced old pain with new. "Yes."

Shortly thereafter, she emailed her sister. Kaye said Michelle was welcome to stay with her family. Their Brooklyn brownstone had a guestroom Kaye used as an office, but she was flexible, happy to shift things around.

Michelle packed and left as Dominique watched from the beaded curtain at the front door, calling after her:

"*Tu reviendras!* You'll miss me!"

On the ride home, Michelle let the tears fall till it was too hard to drive. When she pulled the car over, she caught a glimpse of a road sign indicating that she was two miles from the town of Egremont. Just two miles and change, she thought, and the whole mess of this place would be behind her, Dominique or no Dominique. Michelle turned up the music, a 1970s funk mix that she'd made herself in a blue mood recently. She blew her nose, restarted the engine, and pushed on. As the Commodores sang "Sail On," Michelle felt the outer membrane of each pain—the artist family friend, Dominique, the bullshit ghosts—loosen and slip away. She passed through a storm whose end brought sunlight and hope. Michelle felt stronger. She was Brooklyn bound.

Lady Leanna

Brooklyn, June 2015

Michelle was living with Kaye's family in Brooklyn nearly a year when Dominique's name appeared on her phone.

"I have met the most incredible human being on earth!" Dominique said. Michelle's first response was a stab of jealousy. "She's at least eighty years old, six feet tall, and has posture better than anyone I know." Michelle exhaled, shoulders relaxing. Dominique continued, "Lady Leanna is a 'Seer, Medium, and Mistress of the Occult.'" She directed Michelle to a website. The home page was black with the word "Enter" in silver cursive.

Michelle clicked on the "About" page. Lady Leanna charged an arm and a leg for her services. All the Seekers had to pool their resources,

Dominique confessed. They chipped in twenty, fifteen, thirty dollars, whatever they could. On top of that, they were required to feed her: cookies, brownies, whatever anyone could make and transport. She preferred sweets, frankly. Sweets put her in the mindset to contact those who had passed to the other side. Southern sweets were best: sweet potato pie, pralines, coconut cakes.

Lady Leanna apparently knew all there was to know about safehouses on the Underground because her family—diehard abolitionists—had not only owned one right here in Berkshire County, Massachusetts, they were active station masters for over a century. Most of the safehouses were haunted, according to Lady Leanna. For as many escapees that passed through and moved successfully into freedom, there were also plenty who had succumbed to travelers' illnesses or taken their own lives upon being discovered, death being preferable to a return to bondage.

Interesting. Michelle could tell from the website that Lady Leanna was a charlatan, a scam artist, a caricature from a 1980s sitcom. Nevertheless, at least she might teach the Seekers how to run a proper séance without torching themselves in the process.

"You should come back," said Dominique. "It'll be worth it."

Michelle's heart raced for a moment as she debated. Then she heard, or imagined she heard, a male voice in the background and forced herself to remember how it had been. She told Dominique about her plans for graduate school and attempted to end the call right there.

"Wait," said Dominique. "There's something else I have to tell you." Her voice dropped at the end of the sentence, and Michelle detected the instant silencing of the male voice. Dominique had put some show or podcast on mute. The something else was serious. Not easy to explain, or Dominique would have done so before gushing about Lady Leanna.

"I'm listening," said Michelle.

"Wesley is gone," Dominique said.

"That's what you have to tell me?" Michelle felt rage brewing in the pit of her gut. "That's why you want me to come back? *Seriously?*"

"I have a son now."

Michelle almost dropped her phone. "A what?" She could not have heard correctly.

"Sidney. That's his name." The father was Wesley, Dominique explained, though he'd been awarded a Fulbright and fled to Oxford before she had revealed the pregnancy. "It's for the best. Wesley is a child himself. There's no way I'd want his help raising mine."

Michelle was speechless, unable to wrap her mind around the news that Dominique was a mother.

"I want yours, though."

"My what?" said Michelle.

"Help," said Dominique. And Michelle heard it for the first time. *Him* for the first time. The soft and shapeless gurgle in the newly formed throat. Baby song. It was real and close and powerful and sweet. Dominique clarified her request. "I want you to raise Sidney with me. I want us to be a family."

All her life, one thing Michelle had known was how to nurture. She never liked dolls or dollhouses, but from the time she was four and Gordy was born, she believed herself to be better at caring for him than anyone else. Her maternal streak was what made her apply to social-work schools. And, though she had never vocalized this, Michelle could not deny that while they were living together in Stockbridge, she had occasionally fantasized about a forever-life with Dominique that included children.

But since Dominique had shown her true nature in Technicolor, Michelle felt some relief in not being tied to her. Dominique was selfish and irresponsible. The last sort of person to be the parent of a child. And yet she was. Michelle decided she didn't want to know details, like how they were living, how Dominique was supporting them.

"I'll send you pictures," said Dominique.

"No, don't."

"Why not? You'll love him. You'll—"

"I said don't." Michelle bit her lip hard and hung up the phone.

Boy

Brooklyn, October 2019

Three months after that call with Dominique, Michelle began her master's program in social work. Two years after that, she took the job as a counselor at the Children's Empowerment School in Cobble Hill West, a private K–8 for kids with special learning needs and neurological differences.

Though Michelle loves all the kids she counsels, Timothy Rhodes is fast becoming her favorite. Eleven, lean, and loose limbed, Timothy was adopted as a newborn by a white family. On the autism spectrum like most of the Empowerment kids, Timothy has a look that reminds Michelle so much of her little brother Gordy it's uncanny. They have that in common, Michelle and Timothy: they've each lost a brother. Timothy's was in a coma for a while following an accident of some sort. The brother's death was a prelude to the messy divorce, the mother's relocation from Connecticut to Brooklyn Heights.

Timothy has an attachment to Michelle too. He told her she was the first "Black lady" he's ever really known. He knows he's allowed to come and sit on the beanbags outside her office when the pressure of class gets to be too much. If Michelle isn't running a group or with another student, Timothy can come in and talk if he wants, rest if he wants. Mostly, he reads old seafaring novels: *The Odyssey, Twenty Thousand Leagues under the Sea, Moby-Dick, The Sea Wolf.* He wants to be an oceanographer or marine biologist, he's told her.

Today, not two minutes after Michelle gets off the phone with his psychiatrist, Timothy appears before her desk, explaining that he's feeling agitated. Michelle has been working with him on identifying and naming his emotional states.

"Do you want to tell me about it?" Michelle says.

Timothy shakes his head and jams out his lower lip, looking enough like Gordy to make her heart ache. Then he spots the magazine Michelle has shoved to the side.

The Week is still open to the piece about the double murder. The photo of the Airbnb owner—the woman kidnapping suspect—is the same one that has appeared in papers since Memorial Day of 2018, when the bodies were discovered. There she stands, in front of the house, looking like any one of the hundreds of older white women Michelle met while living up there, posing for the life drawing class. Intelligent eyes, face pinched from thinking deep, self-important thoughts, mouth creased from smiling condescending smiles, mousy hair carelessly emerging from a headband in the aftermath of some kind of creative work—gardening, quilting, or pottery.

Timothy turns the magazine 180 degrees to get a better view, now places a finger on the woman's image.

"That's my friend," he says.

Michelle smiles. "You know her?" It's fascinating how some kids make connections between random occurrences and their own lives.

Timothy nods. "She was nice to me." He pulls the magazine closer. "But the house was bad. If we had never gone there, we'd still have my brother."

Michelle takes this as an opening to get Timothy talking. "Do you think about the house a lot?"

Timothy shrugs. A Gordy shrug.

"What about your brother?"

Another shrug. Michelle doesn't get much more out of Timothy that day, but soon he's calm enough to let her bring him back to class.

A few days later, Timothy stops by at the end of the school day with his mother. Unlike Timothy, his mother looks like the Connecticut of Michelle's imagination: white, blonde, expensively understated. But she's got a tired, *as-is* veneer, like Connecticut's country clubs and garden parties did a number on her.

Timothy's head is bent, hands before him as if in prayer. No—he's holding something precious. Michelle can see something pink poking through.

"It's good to see you, Ms. Leeds," says his mother, and Michelle responds in kind. Mom goes on. "Timothy has a gift for you. To thank you for making him feel safe here." There are tears in the woman's eyes as she tries, against the resistance of her Connecticut-battered cheeks, to smile. "It's really been a tumultuous few years." Timothy doesn't budge or raise his eyes. "It's okay, sweetie. Give Ms. Leeds your gift."

Timothy steps forward and places an object in the center of Michelle's desk: a whalelike creature made of clay, fired and glazed pink.

"It's beautiful," Michelle tells him, aware of emotion swelling in her chest. She picks up the tiny sculpture, smooth and still warm from Timothy's hand.

Timothy says something in a low voice that his mother encourages him to repeat.

"It's an ichthyosaur."

"He made it in ceramics class," says Mom, giving Timothy's shoulder a squeeze. Timothy whispers in her ear. Michelle can hear him asking to leave now.

Once they're gone, Michelle drops into her chair, stroking the ichthyosaur's side with a thumb. She weeps and weeps, unsure of what's opened this torrent of sorrow.

If she were to check her voice mail, it might clear things up. Michelle would receive the message from the Monterey police instructing her to contact them at once. She'd also learn that the Monterey police succeeded in reaching her sister Kaye, who left Michelle another voice mail: "Please call me; it's urgent." Not that Kaye's message would offer details. The subject is not something that can be left in a voice mail or written in a text but must be delivered voice to voice, if not face-to-face. In any case, Michelle neglects to check her phone.

The strange feeling stays with her throughout the workday, lasting through the faculty meeting, which does not end until nearly 5:00 p.m. Afterward, Michelle decides to take a long walk home rather than ride the subway, hoping the fresh autumn air will lift her malaise.

Michelle walks at a leisurely pace, unaware that she's been identified as the next of kin for a Dominique Sowande, who perished several days ago in a massive fire at a house on Beartown Mountain Road in Monterey—the very same Whittaker House where the double murder took place nearly eighteen months ago.

So it's with profound confusion that Michelle enters her sister's living room and finds her niece Billie reading a picture book to a very small round-cheeked boy. Michelle can see Dominique in the boy's eyes, his wild hair, the pout of his lips.

Billie looks up. "Hi, Aunt Michelle. This is Sidney."

7

THE STORY OF THE BIRTHING ROOM

1850

When the white lady tells her to hold the baby, to name it, so its little soul will go to Jesus, Clementine says, "No."

She can't bear to touch the child, to be its mother even for a second. Best to begin forgetting right away. But the white lady insists. They *will* pray. So Clementine's shaking arms receive the girl-baby, wrapped in a torn white sheet, streaked with blood. The baby's skin is blue-gray, but her features are even prettier than those of Missy Sylvia, who would be her half sister. At the white lady's urging, Clementine utters the hymn, the phrases distracting her from the lump of flesh in her arms, already cold. "Birdie," she says, naming the child after the cook in the big house.

It's a mistake to say the name out loud. The sound of her own voice, speaking of her own child, breaks Clementine apart.

2018

What should have been a three-hour drive from Park Slope, Brooklyn, to Monterey, Massachusetts—with hardly any traffic since they left early Friday morning, before Olivia's first nap—wound up taking five. Rob is annoyed but knows to keep his mouth shut, deferring to Galen in all things pertaining to Olivia and her innumerable needs. And Olivia, never having traveled such a great distance, needed to nurse not once, not twice, but thrice along the way.

Olivia finally fell asleep twenty minutes ago. Galen will stay with her in the car with the windows open for another forty minutes to make sure the baby's nap is sufficient. Rob can bring their things inside, Galen says, as long as he's careful not to slam the trunk.

Rob is careful not to slam the trunk, though there's a Rob in an alternate universe who does slam the trunk, slams it very hard indeed. Rob envies Alternate Universe Rob, who does not tiptoe around his wife, who expresses dissent, who gets laid occasionally, whose Galen, he imagines, did not lose herself post-childbirth. Rob is guardedly hopeful about this trip, however. He thought he saw light in Galen's eyes yesterday while they packed.

Galen had booked the trip—from Memorial Day weekend through the following Friday—before the baby was born. Unaware that she would require an extended maternity leave, she and Rob coordinated vacation time from the hospital where they both work—Galen as a psychologist and Rob as a heart surgeon. Rob wanted to spend a week at the beach, but Galen insisted upon an Airbnb in the Berkshires. An old red farmhouse that had been a stop on the Underground Railroad. There was a legend, Galen had read, that a freedom-seeking enslaved woman had died on the premises. Again, regarding Black history and culture, Rob defers to Galen. Before they married, they agreed to embrace *all* their heritage—Galen's African American along with Rob's Dutch and Scotch-Irish—for the sake of their future children.

Touting the house's amenities, Galen assured Rob that he could swim in a nearby lake, adding with a wicked grin, "and sun your pale ass all you want." What Rob really wants is a return to normalcy. How he misses that grin of hers.

Rob is halfway to the front door when he hears Galen's *"Psst."* As he turns, she blows him a kiss and mouths, *Thank you.* Rob smiles, thinking that there is no one in the world as beautiful as his wife.

When he lets himself into the house, Galen lowers the window of the car to take in the fresh country air, floral with a note of rotting wood. There's an antique wagon under a tree that someone has turned into a whimsical flower bed, full of petunias and geraniums. The front lawn is lush and full of wildflowers. Picturesque, but Galen will have to check the baby daily for ticks.

Olivia gurgles in her sleep and Galen shuts her own eyes, taking in birdsong against a whistling New England breeze. Spring murmurs of hope, after these dark winter months of wheeling the Bugaboo stroller along those cold, shop-lined streets of Park Slope, desperate for an inkling of new-mother joy. Sitting alone at pretty, nursing-friendly cafés with Olivia at her breast, just to be out of the house. Then feeling guilty for exposing the baby to germs, strange surfaces, the elements. Often, Galen would find herself forced to interact with another mother—usually white, always beaming, cheerful. Some days—after bundling Livi up and fastening the baby jogger's breathable plastic cover—she'd run through the streets of the Slope, the walkways of Prospect Park, losing hours, coming home numb. She'd nurse some more, then sit till Rob got back. With him, she could cry.

Light dims through her eyelids as clouds blanket the sun, revealing an image of the house in darkness. There's a flash of motion inside the windows, like flickering candlelight. She hears a piercing cry—a young woman's voice—sharp as glass shattering. Galen opens her eyes. The dream was real enough to be a memory. She's stepped into and out of some narrative of her brain's own making, now lost, even as the melancholy looms close by. Whimpers herald the end of the baby's nap. Galen stretches, steps out of the vehicle, and gathers her child.

"Hello!" An older graying blonde woman is walking toward the car, followed by Rob. "I'm Maxine. You—must be Galen."

They've spoken on the phone, but the family's Airbnb profile is a photograph of burly, russet-bearded, green-eyed Rob. That was Galen's idea. Not to hide behind her husband's whiteness but to break ground if necessary, to open doors that might otherwise remain shut. It follows that Maxine, the owner, had no clue Galen was Black. The older woman transitions from surprise to comprehension, then extends a hand, which Galen shakes.

"Oh! And this must be Olivia," Maxine says. "How precious!"

The tension fades as Maxine coos over the baby. Olivia *is* precious. Galen's ticket to acceptance with white mothers—old, young, and in-between. No one at the pretty, nursing-friendly cafés dares ask if cocoa-hued Galen is the barely-tan baby's nanny. Galen's regal posture, her Ivy League diction, her relaxed and styled hair, her designer activewear, the sizable diamond on her hand—these preempt such an error. But presenting impeccably—at all times—drains her. At home Galen implodes.

Rob pipes up, "Maxine's been showing me around. I told her you were the history buff." He takes Olivia from her and encourages Galen to enjoy the tour.

Maxine starts with the upstairs: the bedroom where Rob and Galen will sleep, the baby's room right across the hall, and an enormous, lemon-scented, modern master bathroom with a stone basin and matching shower. Downstairs is a living room with a plush green velvet sectional and mounted 77-inch television; an expansive kitchen with granite countertops and Sub-Zero everything else.

The rest of the ground floor has been preserved in its nineteenth-century glory. All is dark wood and wrought iron: a library with brimming shelves; a birthing room with a fireplace, a rocking chair, a spinning wheel, and a cradle. Galen gives the latter a push and it creaks pleasantly, as if remembering babes of yore. She smiles, imagining an old grandmother, one watchful eye on a sleeping infant, spinning by the fire. Quaint iron-handled tools hang from the mantelpiece: bellows, a poker, a wire brush, and a leather-handled knife. Galen wonders vaguely about the need for such a knife. To snip leaves off branches to make a clean burn? It's defunct now, judging from the bluntness of the blade. Her hand, as if of its own will, reaches for it, leaves it on its hook but strokes the leather.

"I'm interested in the history of this place," says Galen, now tracing the edge of the blade. "I've read that it was part of the Underground Railroad."

"Yes," says Maxine, smile brightening. "But the runaways weren't hidden here in the house. It was too close to the road."

Galen bristles at the word "runaway." As if her ancestors were teenagers giving their parents the slip. "The freedom seekers," she corrects Maxine. "I read that one died inside the house. Is that right?"

Maxine gasps. "Are you all right?"

"Why?"

"You've cut yourself. You're bleeding."

So I am, Galen notes, releasing the blade, letting it swing on its hook. "I didn't realize. It's fine." Strange. She felt nothing. Galen places her finger in her mouth to suck off the blood.

"I have Band-Aids in the kitchen."

"I'm fine," says Galen, unwilling to be cared for. "You were going to tell me about the freedom seeker who died?"

"She died right here in the birthing room." Maxine continues staring at Galen's finger. "That's all I know about her. But I can show you the root cellar where the rest hid if you like. Or, if you'd rather unpack now, I can point it out and you can take a peek at your leisure."

Galen nods. "I would like to get settled." She rocks the cradle again, enjoying the sound. With all the slick gadgets they have for babies these days, there's something about antique hand-crafted things.

1849

Durham Plantation, Craven County, North Carolina

Her mother's face and voice have faded over the years. All that remains is the memory of Mama's fingertips, round and firm, caressing Clementine's shoulders, rubbing her scalp between thick, well-crafted braids. Those fingers were warm when Clementine shivered at night, cool when the summer sun grew relentless. It's getting harder, but sometimes at night if she's left alone, Clementine will shut her eyes tightly, slow her breath, and bring back the memory of her mother's touch. There was a song Mama would sing to her, but that's gone as well.

They had lived together at the Crawford plantation in Thomasville, Georgia, where Mama was known as "Master's favorite." Clementine was five when the missus ordered her sale to another plantation in Wilkes County. It was Mama's punishment for being chosen. Clementine understands now that her caramel skin made her the living marker of Master Crawford's infamy. She was sold again at eleven, taken to the Durham plantation in North Carolina.

Here she works in the big house like her mother did, assisting Birdie, the old, mute cook. Durham is a widower, mean and harsh, feared by his children as well as by those he owns. He favors amputation as a punishment for his wayward property. He cut out Birdie's tongue as a penalty for gossip, sharing the secrets of the house with field hands who were purported to be planning a mutiny.

Since the age of fourteen, Clementine has been Master Durham's favorite, cursed like her mama. Clementine hears the whispers of the others who work in the big house. They hate her for being soiled by the master's fearsome touch. They resent the favors he bestows on her when the mood strikes him. Carriage rides. A new dress. A lighter workload, mostly attending to Sylvia, the master's youngest child and only daughter. Sylvia is just five years younger than Clementine herself. They are two motherless, lonely girls who—in another world, another day—might turn to one another for friendship. Instead, Sylvia is spoiled, demanding, and full of complaints. Always, Clementine is to blame for her misery.

Worst of all is the cost of the master's favoritism. His hands, his coarse mouth. The violent thrust of him in the darkness. The blows he delivers when she cries or bleeds or dares to turn away. The hatred in the eyes of the other house workers. Only Birdie shows Clementine kindness. The cook saves her soup, dries her tears, and offers a sympathetic glance, an occasional soft embrace. But Old Birdie has no words to cheer her.

∽

Bringing rations to the field hands' cookhouse is Clementine's responsibility. Every Saturday, just after dawn, she makes the journey from the big house kitchen door, past the garden, down a path through the low grass, and over a footbridge crossing the stream that divides the property. The cookhouse is at the near end of Slave Quarter Lane, where one row of old log cabins faces another of grand oak trees hanging heavy with Spanish moss.

The field hands accept the baskets Clementine brings—of cornmeal, molasses, flour, lard, peas, and meat, everything measured within the ounce—with a nod, an occasional grunt, but no word of acknowledgment, camaraderie being out of the question. But none of the field hands spit at her or glare at her the way the house women do. Clementine knows some of their names, faces, and stories. She's heard gossip around the house about plots to flee north foiled by slick drivers and other spies. She knows of Blind Zachariah, once caught reading, and Lame Joe, who got the hamstrings torn in both legs as a consequence for running. She knows Little Annie, two fingers cut off when she was caught pilfering food. Wintertime rations couldn't sustain

Annie's six sons. One by one, each boy was sold before he starved, leaving Annie cut by Durham in more ways than one.

By Clementine's sixteenth spring, she is with child, though her slight build and the way she ties her apron conceal the fact from others in the big house. One early Saturday, after dropping off provisions at the cookhouse, Clementine is startled to find Little Annie blocking her path, arms akimbo. Annie is built like a young boy and barely comes up to Clementine's nose. Clementine wonders whether the trousers she wears belonged to one of the sons who got sold. Annie is deep black, purple black, with sloping, hooded eyes and tiny braids peeking out from under her headscarf. She holds out her three-fingered hand, a tiny cotton pouch resting in her palm.

"Here," says Annie, raspy voice just above a whisper. "Take it."

"What is it?"

"Nettle leaf." Annie drops the pouch in Clementine's basket. "For you. For the baby."

Clementine has told no one since she began counting too many days since her last blood. "How did you know?"

"I have a sense about such things," says Annie. "Your walk is different." Clementine is flattered to think that anyone has noticed her at all, let alone picked up a change in her walk. Annie tells her to drink the leaves in boiling water. "It's what I did." She drops her eyes and moves on down the path.

It happens again the following week, the week after that, and the next: Annie has something new for her, some herbal preparation to assist with her condition. Clementine finds herself looking forward to the encounters, the closest thing to a friendship she's ever had. On the fifth week, Clementine empties her basket at the cookhouse, then makes her way in the direction of home slowly as usual, giving Annie a chance to catch up with her. Before Annie can appear, strong arms grab Clementine from behind, nearly knocking the wind out of her. A hand covers Clementine's mouth, preventing her from crying out.

Day is just breaking as she's dragged behind the slave quarters, all the way to the end of the row, into a storm-battered old shed where no one lives. Clementine hears men's breathing, men's voices. Terror quickens her heart.

"Don't hurt her!" Clementine recognizes Little Annie's gravelly voice and relaxes. "Let her be."

Once released, Clementine turns around, eyes adjusting to take in the images of two men, field hands, judging from their worn clothes and postures. Annie stands between them.

"What do you want?" Clementine says.

"Your help," says Annie. "We mean to run."

2018

Galen watches Rob's powerful back and shoulders emerge from the water, then vanish again, arms pumping in rhythm, commemorating his glory days on the Princeton swim team. They were lucky to arrive in good time and good enough weather for a swim their first day. About fifty yards from the shore, Rob pulls himself up onto the anchored raft and waves at her, wet hair haloed in sunshine. Galen waves back, then shifts the beach umbrella to make sure the slumbering Olivia is safe from the sun's afternoon rays. Rob dives back in. In no time he's hovering over her, dripping lake water, grinning his wide, freckled grin.

"You should take a dip," he says. "I'll watch Livi."

"Too cold."

"Bracing," Rob corrects her.

"Really." Galen casts a skeptical eye out over the lake, glistening onyx in the afternoon light. She rises and slips off her blue-and-white caftan, treating Rob to a gander of her mostly-returned-to-pre-baby physique in its lavender bikini. She glances at the baby and steps toward the water's edge, toes mingling with tiny pebbles and lakeweed in the icy brew.

Galen shivers but goes forth. Rob used to tease her about being an indoor city girl. Then, when the despair set in after Olivia's birth, he stopped teasing altogether, treating her gingerly, always on guard. She can sense his longing for the old Galen, who was quicker with a biting comeback than tears. To show that she's still here, Galen flashes a smile back at him and squares her shoulders. She takes a running dive, ignores the chill, and swims all the way out to a tiny island about fifty feet past the raft.

The surface is more marsh than land. In the center is a gray-barked cypress tree that begins with one thick trunk and branches into two separate entities. Galen walks around the tree in search of a spot where the ground is more solid. All at once, she sees a shape whip past, then disappear into the lake with a splash. An animal, she thinks: a beaver or opossum. Galen approaches the spot where it vanished, where the water is shaded and murky. She hears Rob call.

"I'm fine!" Galen calls back. "Just checking something out!"

On the far side of the island, there's an ancient, half-rotted rowboat washed partly ashore. Water laps erratically at its base. Something is alive down there. Venturing closer, Galen peers under the rowboat's raised hull, eyes adjusting to register a woman's head and neck. Galen masters her racing heart and leans closer. The woman is submerged up to her shoulders, wearing a full cloak that floats around her. She has tiny dripping braids that stand out from her head. The sun glints off the water, illuminating the woman's dark brown face, the fire in her eyes. The woman raises one hand, revealing the stumps of two fingers.

Galen's brain fires as if she knows this woman. Not her name, but *her*. The memory is incomplete—nothing specific like a classmate from grad school—but there's recognition nonetheless. Galen fights the compulsion to join the woman with the three-fingered hand, to huddle beside her in the shadowy pool. She blinks, and the woman is gone.

Galen scrambles to the place where the boat drops into the water. She peers underneath again, then wades out, searching the weeds.

"Gay!" Rob's voice. "What's happening?"

Unable to make a shred of sense out of what she saw or didn't see, Galen steps around the tree to show Rob that she's in one piece. A handful of clouds circle the sun. *It must have been a trick of the light,* she thinks, *an optical illusion.* Though Galen can still see the face of the woman, her identity just out of reach.

"You're shaking." Rob has a towel ready when Galen makes it back to shore. She takes the baby but cannot lose the image of the woman's eyes gazing from the shallows.

"Are you okay?" Rob repeats.

"Just cold."

Rob cannot know.

1849

Little Annie and the two men—Caleb, thickset and powerful with a vigilant gaze, and Josiah, younger, bolder, quicker with a smile—require things for their journey that only Clementine can procure. Information first and foremost. Clementine promises to share whatever she learns from the Durhams' dinner table conversations, from the whispers of the other house workers, pertaining to the conditions and potential risks for runaways in North Carolina and the neighboring states. They also need physical items: A pot of grease from the stables that Annie will mix with herbs to disguise their scent and throw off the dogs. A knife for protection. Rope—Clementine doesn't know what for. Closer to the actual time of flight, they'll require food—some dried meat, a loaf of bread or biscuits—until they can get someplace that will provide a meal. And, with hope and luck, Clementine will secure a compass. There's a silver one that the master keeps on his writing desk. She can picture it sitting there, but she knows there's no way to take it without him noticing. He'd know right away it was she who'd done the stealing. No one else comes in his room. Just her. To clean, and when he wants her there.

"I'll do my best," Clementine tells her new friends. But are they friends? Soon Annie and Caleb and Josiah will be gone from this place, and Clementine will be left alone with the silence of Birdie, the sneers of the other house workers. And her baby, which won't be hers at all. It will belong to Master Durham to do with as he pleases. Clementine shudders, imagining herself growing big, then pushing the child into a cold and dreadful life that hates its mother, will hate it too. Another dread is that the baby could come out white, which would be worse. On the Madsen plantation, there were whispers about a high yellow boy raised in the big house, believing the master's barren wife was his mama. His own mother, who worked in the house, was his nanny, nursed and cared for him till he was grown. She took his truth to her grave.

1850

Clementine gathers the things they need slowly. Now that her condition is no longer a secret, Birdie has given her old clothes that bag and sag, easier to conceal things. She finds a rope in the cellar and hides it under her apron. Saturday morning, Clementine tucks it under the rations in her basket. Each week, she delivers something the three need for their journey. Mostly it's Little Annie who receives the supplies, squirreling everything away beneath the floorboards of the shed.

On one occasion, however, it's Josiah who meets Clementine outside the cookhouse.

"Annie's seeing to one of the hands who got bit by a snake," Josiah tells her. "She sent me to meet you." He gives her a smile and a slight bow of his head. Strange that she feared him at first, the day they pulled her into the shed. Now she knows him by his good nature, though once when she spied him wading shirtless in the stream, either cooling himself or catching a fish, she could see the deep lash marks on his back.

It's news Clementine has for him today, gleaned from listening to the house workers talk about a brand-new law. As she explains that it's going to be harder now, more dangerous for anyone trying to make it to Canada, Josiah's gaze rests on hers in a way that hastens her pulse, sets a shyness creeping over her.

"It's not good news," Josiah agrees, "but I'm grateful for the warning."

He offers to carry her basket and walk her to the big house. Clementine gives a light nod, surrenders her empty basket, and accepts his arm noticing, as they walk, the curious eyes of young children peering at them through cabin doorways. Josiah's legs are long, but he measures his strides to match Clementine's. She can feel herself blushing, until she remembers his lash marks. Durham wouldn't like to see her on anyone's arm. And the master has spies—the overseers, even some of the house women—to watch over his living possessions when he can't assert control directly.

"You'd best let me go on alone from here," Clementine tells Josiah as they cross the footbridge, the kitchen garden coming into view. The path here is neatly tended. No cover of trees or shrubs.

Josiah bows again and hands Clementine back her basket. She thanks him and hurries on.

∽

On the following Saturdays, it's Annie who meets her at the cookhouse. Clementine wonders whether something about herself put Josiah off, or if he's keeping his distance for fear of the master. Either way, she concludes, it's for the best.

Mostly, Annie, Caleb, and Josiah need intelligence on the master's plans. When he's traveling, things relax on the plantation. Everyone exhales the breath they hold in his watchful, brutal presence. His sons Thomas and George are lazy young men, spoiled like their little sister Sylvia. They take everything for granted, including human property. Best to run when Master Durham is gone.

With business at hand, there is less conversation with Annie. No more talk about how Clementine is getting on as the baby grows inside her. Clementine senses Annie's gratitude, but companionship—such as it was—fades. She is useful to Annie, to Caleb and Josiah, nothing more. Just as she is useful to Sylvia, to Master Durham.

On laundry day, while Sylvia is busy with lessons, Clementine stokes the fire to keep the water hot, as her fellow house workers, Phibby and Hanna, wash the sheets, speculating about the upcoming cornhusking celebration at the neighboring Collins plantation. Master Durham will be in Raleigh, leaving Thomas and George in charge.

"Master Tom—he'll let us go for sure," says Phibby, nodding agreement with herself. "He says we work best when we get our time for enjoyment."

"His daddy doesn't subscribe to that," says Hanna, eyes downcast, a glow in her high cheekbones. It's common knowledge around the big house that she's sweet on one of the Collinses' stable hands.

"His daddy doesn't need to know." Phibby chuckles, giving Hanna a playful swat. "You'll get to see your sweet Ronnie. Don't you worry."

Clementine has a flash image of Josiah. What would it mean to think of him that way—as her *sweet Josiah*? She shakes herself. He's going to be gone soon. No sense in thinking about him like that.

Now Phibby is explaining to Hanna how it's all going to unfold. Master Thomas and Master George and Missy Sylvia will drive their carriage to dine as guests of the Collinses. The slaves from the Durham plantation will make the brief pilgrimage to the Collins property on foot while the four overseers ride alongside, keeping watch over the lot. There will be music, food, whisky—pleasures rarely enjoyed in the daily life of a Durham slave. Best of all will be the husking contest. Anyone who finds a red husk will win a prize.

Clementine listens to their talk, takes in every detail she can. Little Annie and the men will want to hear about this. Most likely, they'll run the night of the husking.

Though Clementine is right beside them, neither Phibby nor Hanna pays her any mind. When she first came in with the wood, Phibby eyed her belly with a grunt but said nothing, didn't offer to lighten her load or tell her not to carry so much at a time. Now Phibby leans away when Clementine adds to the fire, pulling her skirts clear of the grating.

The women go on chatting as Clementine stokes the fire. Hanna never looks her in the eye, never speaks to her—not even to ask for more wood or a sturdier paddle. *As if it's a sickness she can catch,* Clementine thinks. *And why,* she wonders, *did the master choose me instead of Hanna, who's just as light, just as slim, with hair as long?* Hanna would be as much of a prize sitting in the back of the master's carriage underneath a parasol. Clementine shudders, remembering how—before she started to show—she was trotted out like a thing, stared at, groped, breathed on by the master's old men friends. *A li'l-Negro princess.* How they'd laugh, pinch, and poke. How still she had to remain, taking it all, lest she get whupped at home.

"You're lucky," Clementine says aloud to Hanna, stabbing at the flame. Hanna raises her wide brown eyes.

"What'd you say?"

"I said you're lucky it's *me* instead of you. You *know* you are."

Clementine doesn't wait for Hanna's response but sweeps out of the room to see if Sylvia's tutor is still working with the girl. Perhaps she'll listen in, snatch a small piece of learning.

༄

Late at night, Clementine is in the tiny room she shares with Birdie, downstairs off the kitchen. Her eyes are open, staring through the window at the moon. It's harder to sleep now that there's a baby inside her, growing toward the miserable life outside. If it's a girl—to be raped, pawed, and fouled. If it's a boy—to be beaten, sold, or otherwise taken from her.

Now Clementine hears a familiar thumping in the hall outside, a crash and a clatter as Master Durham—drunk and stumbling—upsets the order of the kitchen. Clementine smells his breath before he's inside the room. Birdie stirs but can't do anything to stop what's coming. A minute later, he's upon Clementine. By the light of the moon, she can see the veins in his neck throbbing. The angry set of his jaw. The force of his rage. He's lost at cards. Gotten swindled or cheated. In any case, she'll bear the brunt. He can feel her dread, her revulsion. He shakes her, slaps her face, then tears her robe. In no time he's inside her, the terrible thrusting, the beastlike grunts. Clementine bites her own arm to keep from crying audibly. He finishes, slaps her again, and stumbles off.

Clouds drift in front of the moon and Clementine rests her hands on her belly, praying for the baby to stay as small as it is, to die inside her.

2018

Dinner is over. They grilled the fish and vegetables they'd bought on the way up. Olivia is playing quietly on her mat while her parents have a drink on the enclosed sunporch. Citronella candles keep a check on the mosquitos that find their way through the aged screen. The backyard is a sprawling meadow, flanked by gardens near the house, woods at the farthest end. As the shadows lengthen, frogs sing from their perches encircling the pond. Rob touches his Sam Adams to Galen's glass of sauvignon blanc. She's not supposed to drink on the meds, but one can't hurt.

"Happy summer."

"Happy summer," she replies. "It's beautiful, right?"

Rob doesn't take his eyes off hers. "Right." He dares to slip a suggestive toe under the hem of Galen's filmy sundress. She reenacts a giggle, like the old days, and gives his foot a half-hearted swat.

"Later," she says. "*If* Livi sleeps tonight."

"*Big* if." Rob takes back his wandering toe. Bringing up the topic of their sex life usually backfires. Galen gets flustered, defensive, explaining how the meds kill her libido, how self-conscious she feels about sex while she's lactating. Rob always says he understands. Though vis-à-vis nursing, there seems to be no end in sight, even though Olivia is beginning to eat solid food. In any case, Rob is banking his good behavior, hoping that one day, very soon, Galen will be done with the meds, lactation will end, and he'll reap the rewards in hours upon lost hours of connubial bliss. If only Galen would lay off the skimpy dresses for the time being.

Rob says, "Did Maxine give you the full tour?" Changing the subject, giving her space.

"Everything but the root cellar."

"It was kind of creepy," says Rob. "Dark. I can't imagine having to hide in there." He takes a swig of beer and looks out at the garden. Trying not to think about sex.

"I want to go," Galen says, rising abruptly.

"Yeah?" Rob beams up at her, incredulous. "Really? Now?" By *go*, he assumes she's thinking what he's thinking.

"Now," she says, pulling him to stand. "I want to see the root cellar. You put Livi in the Björn and I'll go find some flashlights."

So, Galen is not thinking what Rob is thinking. Not by a long shot. Awash in disappointment—that Galen's unexpected enthusiasm centers around checking out the root cellar rather than, well, *him*—Rob drains his beer.

"Let's wait till morning," he says. "It's too buggy now. What if Livi gets bitten?"

Not even their baby's welfare can dissuade her. "I've got netting in with my hiking stuff." Galen gulps the remainder of her wine and dashes into the house.

Five minutes later, the family is crossing the dusky meadow with lanterns—Rob, wearing Olivia, mosquito netting stretched over the infant carrier. The root cellar is partway across the property, near the point where meadow meets woods. Rob's lantern illuminates a wooden door wedged into the side of a hillock. As he lifts the latch and creaks open the door, a complex, earthy smell rushes out. Galen raises her lantern over the mouth of the cellar, making out a narrow stone stairway.

"You stay out here with her," she tells Rob, and begins descending the steps. The beams from her lantern bounce against the gray stone wall. Moisture and age have rotted away most of the shelving that once housed carrots, turnips, and sweet potatoes that sustained the inhabitants of the house through long Massachusetts winters. She sees the unmistakable imprints of Rob's sneakers on the dirt floor, leftover from his tour. Galen follows them down the corridor till the ceiling slopes too low for Rob to stand. She proceeds around a bend as Rob calls her name.

"I'm fine!" Galen calls back, heading deeper inside. The shelves look sturdier back here. One holds a mortar and pestle; another supports a collection of tin canisters. Galen imagines the escapees holing up down here, nibbling seeds and roots to survive. As she reaches out to touch a ceramic urn, her lantern blinks. No good to be this far from the doorway without light to find her way back.

"Rob? I'm coming back! My battery is low!"

The only response is a gust of wind and a dull thud. "Rob?"

With the light she's got left, Galen makes her way back along the passage, around the bend to the stairs, only to find the door shut.

"Rob!" She dashes up the steps to find that it's latched. Calling her husband's name, Galen pounds and pounds at the heavy wood structure in vain. Meanwhile, the lantern flickers recklessly, now dies out. Galen panics in the pitch darkness, knocking, calling, kicking the door. In desperation, she backs up, meaning to throw herself at the door, but stumbles, sliding backward down the stairs. Galen scrapes her knees, tears her dress, but catches herself with her hands to avoid serious injury. On the bottom step Galen sits in near shock, registering the silence, complete but for her own breath and heartbeat.

Now she hears, *"Hush."* An implausible sound, uncannily like a whisper. It can't be, Galen tells herself. It *cannot* be a voice, just a chance breeze that got trapped inside somehow—never mind the scientific impossibility of such a thing.

"Hush." Again. Galen shuts her eyes, aware that fear is playing tricks on her, re-creating what she's spent so much time reading, imagining, and wondering about: The people who made the journey north. What they were like. How it must have felt to hide here, to wait fugitive, praying for a clear sky, a bright moon, and stars to travel by unmolested. Who were they?

"Be still."

"Who's there?" Galen cries out.

"Hush." The whisper again. *"Hush. Be still. You'll get us killed!"* More voices coming faster, blending together. *"Hush. Be still."*

Galen covers her ears and buries her face in her knees. But a sharp pain seizes her abdomen. She grabs her belly, distended and hard, like when she was pregnant with Olivia. Possibly the fish was bad. Or the vegetables. How crazy is this? She's so frightened that she whimpers, shaking herself. *No. No. No.* But how insanely real it seems.

Galen quiets her mind, forcing herself to be present, aware only of the sensations of her body, like in yoga class. Slowing her breath, being mindful of the pressure of the stone stair against her body, her thin dress with just a jean jacket thrown over it, the sudden cold. The pain, the fierce bloating. She recites the simplest meditation mantra she knows: *I am breathing in, I am breathing out. I am breathing in, I am breathing out.* Galen notices her thoughts, lets them pass by without judgment. But oh—the pain! And the voices. She hears them still: *Hush. Hush.* "I am breathing *in*," she tells herself emphatically. "I am breathing *out.*"

Yes, breathe. That's it, baby, that's it. Nice and slow. Breathe in and out. You're gonna make it. Gonna be okay. Hands, small, rough, but still soothing on her forehead, her arms, her taut, tight belly. The rough, whispered voice. Breathing in and out along with her. *You're gonna be okay.* The panic eases, if not the pain. Galen relaxes, accepts the touch of the hands, reclines with her head in the other's lap, eyes still closed. "I am breathing in . . ."

How many minutes, how many hours go by?

"Galen? *Gay?*" Rob is shaking her gently. "Honey, what's going on? You're scaring me."

He pulls her up from the cellar floor, accidentally swinging Olivia sideways in her carrier.

"What happened?" Galen says, rubbing a scraped knee. "Where *were* you?"

"Right there by the door." He shifts the baby back into position. "Where else would I be?"

Behind him she can see the stairway, the open door, and a glimpse of treetops against sky, nightfall not quite complete. Galen realizes: It's she who has gone. She who has returned. With scarcely a minute lapsed.

"You okay, hon?" Rob says. "Did you fall or something? Are you hurt?"

"I'm fine," she replies. "My lantern died. It freaked me out."

"Understandable." Rob puts an arm around her as they mount the stairs. "It's a little too spooky down here. Even with a working lantern."

Back in the house, Galen nurses Olivia once more before bed. When the baby is settled in her crib, Galen crosses the hall, kisses Rob goodnight, and allows sleep to consume her. She dreams of heads in the water, three-fingered hands, and whispers in the cold darkness.

1850

Cornhusking Day draws to a close with the Durham slaves meandering home, overseers leading the way and bringing up the rear on horseback to make sure everyone is accounted for. But the riders are drunk, and it's dark between the torches they hold aloft. No one notices Annie and Caleb slip into the woods, where Josiah has likely gone on ahead. Only Clementine knows their secret, which she promised to keep or die. But now she fears for their lives more than for her own. For their sake, she hopes never to see them again.

At the celebration, she danced with Josiah. He grinned at her and said how well she moved despite being with child. Clementine's heart leaped as she noticed how wide his smile was, how his eyes sparkled as he laughed and spun her around. Josiah clapped his hands in time to the wild music of the fiddle, and Clementine felt she couldn't bear to see him go.

He read her thoughts. Glancing around for eavesdroppers, Josiah leaned in close.

"You could join us."

Clementine's eyes widened for a moment. But hands on her belly, she shook her head. "Not like this."

"But you could," he said. "You're young and strong and—so am I." His soft brown eyes held hers.

"I can't," she protested. How could she?

"I'll be with you," said Josiah. "I'll help you keep up. I promise."

Clementine opened her mouth but had no rejoinder. No one, no one, had ever promised her anything before. Then, a horde of other men, splashing corn liquor from their cups, surrounded Josiah, absorbed him with their noisy guffaws, and pulled him away. It seemed all in fun at the time, though it was strange that the men came from Collins's plantation, not Durham's. Clementine did not see Josiah after that.

As the festivities wound down, Clementine was called into the kitchen to help the house women clean up. She glanced through the window, hoping Josiah might be searching for her, perhaps meaning to coax her away, perhaps to say goodbye. But all she saw, besides people gathering, beginning their farewells, was Master George and two of the overseers inspecting a pair of powerful gray horses while Master Collins looked on. No sign of Josiah.

And now, walking home, Clementine doesn't join in the singing of the others, just tries to relive the dancing, Josiah's hands—one holding hers, the other at her waist. Clementine stores the image in her heart to give her peace when things get bad.

"Girl." A male voice close by. *"Girl!"*

Clementine turns to stare into the ghostly face of Thomas Durham. Just four years Clementine's senior at twenty, he is lean and towering. Master Tom's waistcoat is askew, ascot untied and hanging. "I'm talking to you—hear? You *mind* me, now."

His words slur with liquor. Clementine takes in his unsteady gait, considers bolting out of his reach, weighs the risk of retaliation. But Master Tom is in sounder shape than she thought. He grabs her arm and pulls her toward him, claps a hand over her mouth, and yanks her into the dark woods.

He's powerful, strong as his father if not stronger. Liquor whets his rage the same way. Obscured by the gloom and trees, they stumble along, Clementine wincing, whimpering under Thomas's thick palm. At last, he pushes her back up against a broad, solid oak, tears her dress open, and forces his way in. Clementine shudders with fear and disgust, presses her eyes shut as she does with his father, praying for it to end.

The whoop of a screech owl pierces the air. But Clementine knows it's no owl. She feels them out there—Josiah, with his soft eyes and wide smile, Annie with her firm but kind directives, anxious, watchful Caleb—calling to one another with their secret signal. And Clementine does what she's never done in her life. *Fights.* She opens her lips against

Master Tom's stinking hand, separates her teeth, and clamps them down hard on the bone of his thumb. Thomas howls in agony but doesn't let her go. Clementine keeps biting down, even as he forces his other hand against her throat, pressing the air out of her.

They struggle together and fall, Tom on top of Clementine, one hand still around her slender neck. She panics, reaching breathlessly behind her for a branch or something to beat him back with. Her hand finds a stone, cool and broad, embedded in the ground. Clementine utters another prayer and the earth gives way. One-handed, with the borrowed strength of a guardian angel, Clementine brings the stone up as hard as she can to meet Tom's head with a crack. He releases her, falling back, unconscious. Clementine stares at him, unable to move till her gaze lands upon a slim, gleaming silver chain, dangling from his pocket. Clementine pulls out Master Durham's compass and runs as fast as she can without a backward glance.

She follows the cries of the "screech owl" till she comes upon the meeting place: an abandoned boathouse by the swamp. She drags herself inside.

"I'm coming too." But as her eyes adjust to the darkness, she takes in only the figures of Little Annie and Caleb.

"Josiah?"

Caleb shakes his head.

"Sold," says Little Annie.

"What—*how?*" Clementine is aghast as the others relate how no one but Master Durham, his sons, and Master Collins knew about the secret trade planned for after the cornhusking. Two of Collins's best horses in exchange for Josiah. Clementine reels, unable to catch her breath. Caleb helps her to a pile of logs set up as a makeshift bench.

"No!" she says, tears coming down like a babe's—tears of shame and fright left from her struggle with Master Tom, tears for Josiah, the loss of hope's spark. "It can't be. It can't!" She holds her face, sobbing until Little Annie silences her with a shocking blow, knobs of her missing fingers making blunt impact with Clementine's cheek.

"You hush your mouth, girl, or we're all done for. Are you with us? Or do we leave you right here?"

"With you." For what else can Clementine say?

Little Annie looks at her own hand, then studies Clementine's face in a shard of moonlight coming through what was once a window.

"I hadn't meant to do that," Little Annie says. "I know you were sweet on him. And no one knows better than me what it's like to lose someone you love to the trade. I learned sometimes the body's pain dulls the heart's."

Clementine takes this in, chastened. What was Josiah to her compared with the yearning Annie must feel for her boys?

"There's no sense crying for Josiah," Caleb adds, tone gruff, but softer than Annie's. "Could have been any of us. The plan is we go, no matter what."

Clementine swallows her grief, and they go.

☙

They walk all night and all the next day, counting on the Durham brothers and all the overseers to be too hungover to notice their absence till late. Fortune had Missy Sylvia spending the night at the Collinses' home or the girl would have known Clementine was missing right away. Still, they reckon it's Sylvia who sounds the alarm. Sylvia whom they've got to thank when the dogs come. Annie's salve is powerful, though; it throws off the beasts. The three fugitives sink low into the swamp till the sound of barking subsides.

☙

For three days, relying on luck and prayer, they manage to put distance between themselves and the Durham place. When the bread runs out, they hunt for roots and berries. They travel by night, checking Master

Durham's compass in the moonlight, following the stars. They keep tight by the swamp, hiding by day. Where the ground is steep and roots make traps for untrained feet, Caleb will offer Clementine a strong arm for support, a hand to guide her. When the terrain is flat and Clementine struggles to keep up, she whistles, like Caleb has taught her: a wordless command to slow the pace.

"How do you feel?" Annie asks each day when they stop to rest. Her voice is always harder than the words. The answer expected, "Fine," is the one Clementine gives.

"You *stay* fine," says Annie. "That baby's going to be born free."

Clementine nods, though after all the wishing she's done, the praying for the baby to die, she wonders whether Annie's demand is too great a shift for her mind to make. Clementine never thought about running for the baby's sake. She's been running for herself, away from the man who put it inside her. Besides, caring about Josiah, then losing him forever, taught Clementine the risks of letting yourself dream. But—*born free*. Her own child. Such a notion!

On the fourth day, Little Annie says, "Before long, we'll find us a swamp town where they'll take us in for a spell."

Leading the way deeper into the mossy wet, Caleb explains that there are colonies of Blacks and Indians living free, hidden in dwellings around the swamp. Clementine can't imagine how folks could settle this close to plantations without being caught. But on the fifth day, they come upon one such establishment in a remote spot concealed by a thick curtain of mist. The inhabitants, various shades of black and brown, speaking dialects Clementine hasn't heard before, give them food, shelter, several days' rest, and the courage to move on. They continue along their way, relying on members of other such colonies to sustain them, to guide the three of them north, beyond the reaches of the swamp.

In exchange for the silver compass, a free colored man in Norfolk helps them gain passage on the Boston-bound cargo ship where he is employed. Massachusetts is a free state, the sailor tells them, but with no papers, they'll be returned if caught.

"Meantime, you all stay below in the hold."

None of them has been on a ship before. They keep silent and out of sight, as best they can, among the sacks and barrels, the rats and other vermin. But the lurching, pitching, and rocking echo inside Clementine's gut. Again and again, the free colored crewman smuggles her up to the deck, where she heaves the contents of her stomach, mostly bile, over the side. Each time, Clementine fears that the baby might make its exit along with the matter she expels. But the child clings fast inside her, hardy and stalwart. And for the first time, Clementine thinks of the baby as a person with a will. A heart. Some kind of sense.

"You hold on now," she tells her baby. "We're moving like that, see? Because we're on a boat. Just hold on and we'll be all right."

And the baby answers, moving inside her. Just a kick and a shift. But it's enough to assure Clementine that she's two lives now, not one.

Clementine can't guess how many days pass before the ship finally docks. She and her companions remain belowdecks till the colored sailor introduces them to a white man whom he calls "Conductor Dodd." The latter apologizes before chaining Caleb's wrists. They'll travel by carriage, Dodd explains. If they run up across catchers, the ruse will be that they're headed north for construction labor. The women will be hidden under the boards of the carriage compartment in blankets.

After a day's journey, something goes wrong. From their hiding places, Clementine and Annie hear shots that spook the horses. The carriage picks up speed, then goes rolling, reeling, and over on its side. Clementine's arms cover her head, then her belly, as she's bounced and flung inside the compartment. *Hold on, Baby, please, please hold on.* Now the carriage is still, but here come more shots and the shouts of men. Then silence.

"Annie?"

"Hush up!" Annie whispers close by her elbow. Then adds in a sharp hiss, "You keep *still*!"

Their hearts pound like drums; breath comes in short pants. But they keep still. They make no sound. Only the baby moves, twists, and kicks, to Clementine's great relief. She speaks silently to reassure it. *We'll be all right,* though she has no reason to believe her own words. Hours later, Annie forces open the compartment to find the black of night and a sliver of moon. No house nearby, just the road with woods on either side.

"Come on." Little Annie pulls Clementine by the sleeve, and the two emerge to find the carriage resting in a gully, smashed up. One horse lying on its side, dead. Conductor Dodd, same state. Caleb is gone.

It's just the two of them now. Clementine finds her eyes dry, no tears for Caleb. It's only survival now. For herself, her child. She and Little Annie make the next leg of their journey on foot together, hiding in the woods and in abandoned sheds. Dusk finds them in the garden of a church, where they're spotted by an old white man in a black wide-brimmed hat.

"Make haste," he hisses at them, beckoning. He provides a meal, rest for one night, and advice. In the morning, the man directs them to a pond where they're to wait for a boatman.

"Take heed," he tells them. "Pattyrollers are everywhere."

It's midday when they find the body of water, more bog than pond. A half-sunken rowboat offers refuge during their vigil. They lie inside, feet at either end, heads side by side, gazing up at a blue sky where clouds dance a reel before a golden sun. Clementine swats at a fly and lets her cloak slip to the base of the boat, enjoying the breeze.

"One of my boys made it free," comes Annie's voice.

"He did?" Clementine says, hoping for a story. She's overheard plenty of gossip, but with Birdie her only companion in the big house, no one tells Clementine stories. "Where is he now?"

"Don't know for sure. It was my firstborn, Louis. My handsome boy, black as ink. He got sold to a place in Virginia, but last I heard he'd run. Never heard about Louis getting caught, so I believe he made it all the way to Canada."

"But you don't know?"

"I do know," says Annie. "I *do*."

But Clementine knows, from the way Little Annie's voice drops even deeper than normal, that it's not a real story at all—just a hope Annie keeps alive inside her. Clementine wonders if her own mother has made a story of her too.

Thinking of Mama, Clementine dares to lift her head out of the boat to look out over the glistening water. What swells inside her is hope of her own—for something good: a life for herself and this free-born baby. The thought emboldens her to reach one hand into the water. As her fingers touch the surface, a surge of tingling energy compels Clementine to dive in. She swims, deliciously free, pumping her unencumbered arms and legs, the water caressing her belly, which feels strangely light and childless. After a bit, she pauses, treading water, looking out ahead at the shore, where a red-bearded white man stands holding an infant. Is it her baby? In a white man's arms? Clementine doesn't know him, though his face is calm, almost pleasant. She is curiously unafraid.

But the reverie ends and Clementine finds herself back with Annie, big with child again, one hand still reaching into the water. Her weight against Annie's unbalances the boat and tips them over. Annie's startled cry, their scrambling and splashing, gain the attention of a dog, whose barking brings on the shouts of men.

"Get down!" Annie gulps air and submerges herself. Clementine follows suit and there they crouch, in the shallows beneath the upturned boat, sneaking breaths, shivering, occasionally listening, waiting for evidence that they've escaped discovery.

2018

The thing about being reached for, reached for by Rob, is how *claimed* it makes Galen feel lately. Before the baby, she didn't mind. Their grabbing, touching, and holding one another was balanced, mutual. And while she loves him still and finds him as beautiful as always, it exasperates Galen that Rob never gives her the space or opportunity to reach for him. No sooner does she set down the baby than she meets his hungry, craving eyes, followed soon after by his reaching arms. Male arms, white arms, collecting their due.

Galen rarely thought of him that way before—as *white*. He was only Rob, representative of nothing but himself. Their commonalities—their shared wit, aesthetic, values—outweighed their contrasting skin tones. But Olivia's arrival, along with the baby's fair skin, hair, and light eyes, changed something in Galen. Wherever she goes with her child and husband, she feels the weight of other people's scrutiny and unuttered questions. If she were one of her patients, Galen would force herself to examine her feelings about this. Instead, she amasses them in a cloud of undefined anguish. Medication barely takes the edge off. Galen thought it would be easier here, away from busy, prying Brooklyn. But this house, with its past, makes it worse. All she can think of when she looks at Rob is that his forbears owned hers.

"Are you okay?" Rob's constant query.

"I'm fine," she tells him. "I just need some tea." Galen gets out of bed as quietly as she can, avoiding a loose floorboard that might resonate and wake the baby. Livi is in her crib across the hall, but the baby monitor is on.

"I'll be up soon," Galen tells Rob before he can offer to join her.

In pitch darkness, she feels her way downstairs to the kitchen, makes her tea, and takes it to the birthing room, where she settles in the rocking chair. She shuts her eyes and rocks, inhaling the mingling aromas of chamomile and old, smoky wood. Time lives here in this space. History, death, memory—they're all contained in this preserved section of the house. Galen considers herself: an affluent Black woman psychologist married to a white cardiothoracic surgeon, vacationing in the very spot where an enslaved woman died for freedom. *And yet,* Galen wonders, *how is my marriage—my family—anything but a point along the historic continuum that began with white masters and the Black women they owned? Raped?*

The thoughts shock Galen. How could she compare Rob—for even an instant—with enslavers who raped their human property? How could she consider her own privileged circumstances in the same breath with that of the woman who died here?

And—*what's that sound?* Galen's ears toy with her. *There it is again.* The same piercing cry she heard while napping in the car with Olivia. It becomes a wailing, growing louder, louder. Alarmed, Galen discovers the source of the sound: her own throat. One hand flies to her neck as she rises, teacup shattering on the floor, eyes dancing past the tools on the mantel: poker, bellows, brush, and knife. Reflected in the darkened window just beyond the hearth, Galen can make out the swollen postpartum form of a young girl wrapped in bloodstained sheets, arms raised, fending off a threat. In empathy Galen's own arms stretch forth to beat it back—whatever it is—adrenaline surging, eyes refocusing, or else playing tricks on her. For the young girl flailing, fighting for what's left of her life—it is not a girl. It is a woman. It is herself.

1850

Clementine lies on the dank earth of the root cellar floor, head in Annie's lap. They waited all day and half the night for the boatman, who brought them to the big house just a mile up the road. The white lady, Mrs. Whittaker, who barely looked older than Clementine herself, gave them hot stew, dry clothes, and brought them here to the root cellar, where they've been ever since, waiting till it's time to move on.

The root cellar is a strange place. Like a carved-out pit in the earth with just a kerosene lamp to light their days. But the light won't stay lit. Every time it flickers and fails, Clementine has a feeling of being watched. Mrs. Whittaker brings them food and lets them empty the chamber pot, but they stay within the depths most of the time. The oddest thing about the cellar is that it whispers. Quick, urgent hissing sounds, too soft, too fast to decode.

"Spirits," Annie declares after the first night. "Same as in the cabins back at Durham's. Full of the spirits of folks that passed over the years."

"But people didn't live out their lives in here," says Clementine, "just passed through."

"Some folks must have got left behind and died inside."

When Clementine's eyes widen, Annie reassures her. "I don't reckon the spirits mean us any harm or they'd have done it by now." She closes her eyes, listening, then nods. "They have a story to tell. Just like us."

Annie walks around the cellar, here and there pressing her ear to the walls, listening, trying to comprehend the discourse of the spirits. But Clementine, who cannot make out any words, wonders whether the whispers are spirits at all or rather caused by the tiny, agile paws of field mice burrowing in the earth. Better a mouse, she thinks, keeping herself calm.

After several days in the cellar, Clementine wakes with a start and a stab of pain. Each time it hits, she bites her lip to keep from crying out until she can hold in the sound no longer. The tightening grips her innards, too strong for silence.

"Hush!" Annie says. "Be still. It'll pass." She places gentle hands on Clementine's belly to soothe her, but the girl howls again.

"Hush now!"

"I'm sorry. I can't stop it."

"Baby's coming." Annie knows too well. "I'm going to fetch the lady."

"It's not safe," says Clementine. A day earlier, Mrs. Whittaker, eyes full of concern, showed them a poster with their names and descriptions—promising a reward for their return. Clementine cries out once more and Annie insists: she'll go ask Mrs. Whittaker for help, at least for hot water and towels. So Annie climbs the stairs, slips through the door she's wedged open with the bit of rope, leaving Clementine frightened and alone with her pain and the headstrong baby who would not wait, just *could not* wait, until they were all the way to Canada.

Annie returns to the cellar with Mrs. Whittaker, who tells Clementine it's not sanitary. "The slave hunters are everywhere," Mrs. Whittaker says, "but we have no choice. We'll take the risk."

Which is how Clementine finds herself on the bed in the birthing room by the fire. It takes longer than she would have thought. And the pain, the pain! Mrs. Whittaker gives her a wooden spoon to bite down on to mute her screaming. By the time she delivers, Little Annie has disappeared. Gone, Clementine imagines, to find her child. *And now,* she thinks, *here is mine.*

But Clementine shudders as she stares into the blue-lidded face of the child who looks like Missy Sylvia, but prettier. The intrepid child who kicked and shifted and held on so fiercely throughout their journey. The child who dared Clementine to believe in a free life.

She prays as Mrs. Whittaker bids her, but chokes on the meaningless words. Clementine names the lifeless child "Birdie" after the cook, then hands her over and turns toward the wall. She feels a scream coming up from within her chest, erupting into the tiny room, shaking the very frame of the house.

"Hush!" says Mrs. Whittaker, tears in her own eyes. "None of that, now. You mustn't make such a noise!"

How long Clementine's howling goes on, she doesn't know. She keeps her eyes shut and floats on the sound, willing her body to dissolve into the mist of her grief and wild thoughts. Her cries make a song of trouble, and trouble's what trouble begets. The noise draws the catchers, who have traced her from the Durham plantation, following the lead of the stolen silver compass. First comes the pounding of horse hooves on the road, thundering closer, closer. Then, the smashing of the door, followed by the loud, deep voices of men, hateful words and cusses. Next come big, broad, heavy hands on her body. Hands like Master Durham's, Master Tom's, white men's hands, pulling, grabbing, taking their prize. She sees his green eyes widen as he rips her clothes from her body, her body from her heart.

Clementine loses sight of Mrs. Whittaker, of her cold, little girl-baby, Birdie. Bitterness absorbs every notion of the future that she's dared to entertain, every scrap of hope.

2018

Finding himself alone in bed at 3:15 a.m., Rob makes his way downstairs to find Galen asleep in the birthing room rocking chair, a shattered teacup on the floor beside her. *We'll deal with that in the morning*, Rob thinks. Gently, he lifts his wife, meaning to carry her back up to bed.

1850

There is nothing inside Clementine but hate, nothing outside her but the man's green eyes and cruel, broad white hands that are the cause of every evil in this world. Rage makes Clementine stronger than she's ever been—her small brown hands invincible. She fights even harder than she fought with Thomas in the woods, wrests a leather-handled knife from the man's belt.

2018

Panicked and desperate, she screams, eyes wide, pushing at the white man's chest with one hand. The other flails madly, reaching for something with which to defend herself.

"*Galen!* What are you doing? It's me!" But her screaming drowns out his words as the leather-handled knife from the mantel swings forth, finding her grip.

1850

Clementine meets his green gaze with fury in her own. The dagger is one with her arm, driven by her will and refusal to be taken again.

With a final howl, Clementine buries the blade into a soft target, allowing the warm blood to spill. Clementine laughs aloud, knowing she'll never have to mind another white man. She makes her own choice: gripping the knife with both hands, she turns it inward, and sets herself free.

2018

Early the next morning, Maxine arrives with extra bath towels. Upon entering, she hears a creaking sound from the birthing room and discovers little Olivia, sleeping peacefully in the antique cradle, which is rocking smoothly from side to side. Maxine steps closer, looks past the cradle, spots the tipped-over spinning wheel. And there they are.

1850

The most painful story Jane Whittaker will write in her diary is that of the young Negro girl who gave birth in the house, the babe whom Jane herself delivered. How the pattyrollers arrived just as they were naming the child who was born blue and cold. How the young girl fought, desperate to keep herself from bondage, how she slew the man who would subdue her and drag her home, how she then died by her own hand. Jane will be confused about the details, will write several versions of the truths her memory conjures.

Jane was just twenty-two herself. She was left alone to protect the fugitives passing through the root cellar while her father-in-law and husband traveled on business. Jane had recently been ailing, recovering from a fever that her own child, a little girl called Henrietta, did not survive.

The only charges in the root cellar were two small females, so there was little to fear. But the younger one was with child, which Jane had not known. The baby's time came just as the slave catchers were surveying the area.

Jane knew she would not be spared, so she hid herself and the stillborn infant in a secret compartment inside the pantry. It was hot and close inside. Jane kept her breath shallow and silent. As the violence transpired in the birthing room, she prayed—for herself, for the young mother, and for the soul of this poor babe, pressed against her chest.

In the version of the memory that Jane will always favor, the Lord heard her and delivered a miracle. The infant grew warm, sputtered, and began wailing. Jane discovered her breasts were magically full and aching at the sound of the baby's cries. With haste, she allowed the babe to suck, silencing her, saving them both.

In the morning, Jane ventured out of the compartment with the child, Birdie, in her arms. The bodies of the Negro girl and the young white man lay in a grisly heap on the birthing room floor beside the overturned spinning wheel. Jane averted her eyes as she prayed for the Lord to rest their souls, then placed the infant in the cradle to sleep. Blue no longer, the child appeared to Jane rose-cheeked and fair as her own lost Henrietta. Jane sat and rocked the cradle, determined to keep her safe.

8

FLY AWAY

Little Annie

Whittaker House, October 2019

The high yellow girl called Dominique Sowande takes in my words, eyes growing into black pools when I tell her about the nine sets of bones left behind from the fire.

"One escaped," she says.

"Just one of the ten," I say. "I've always held it was Louis, my oldest."

"Your son's name was Louis?" There's a tremor in the yellow girl's voice when she repeats his name, like she's come right up on the thing she's looking for. "He could have made it to Canada."

When Dominique tells me that's her home, I have to think about the word and what it means. Canada was once a story to me, a dream, a hymn. When I got there, it was a real place with a promise of dignity. Didn't look too different from parts of Massachusetts—woodland with lakes and rivers and farmhouses. But it felt strange and uncertain to have all that: a place to live free, to earn a living, to breathe the air knowing it belonged to me.

"You made it all the way to Canada and then came back?" Her eyes flash in the candlelight.

"I went back for my other children," I tell her. "And to help with the Underground. I learned the quiet skills you needed. I learned the coded talk of 'fleece' and 'freight,' of 'tracks' and 'trails.' I learned to be invisible."

That is when I heard that my youngest child, my last baby boy, Silas, was alive and on the run. I had no idea where to find him, but as there were plenty of others to guide and lead into Canada, I thought I may as well start with the station I knew best.

I didn't need the stars that time. Clementine's spirit pulled me back to the root cellar in the clearing. Others I met along the tracks had told me there were three waiting inside. I'd have had plenty of time if I hadn't looked inside the house itself, hoping like a child or a fool that Clementine would still be there, still big with child after all that time. I tell the yellow girl how the wind picked up as I crept across the grass and looked in the windows. That's what caused my delay.

I felt my friend before I saw her. Clementine whispered through my body and put her cold hands on my cheeks and shoulders. She said "Annie," and I knew her voice from all those months we traveled together. I knew her smell and the rhythm of her breath. Hadn't I been there in the cellar alongside her, cradling her head in my lap? Hadn't I made her breathe, thinking I could help her keep that baby safe?

Clementine asked me why I came back. I was scared to speak to her because, while I always did believe in spirits and ghosts, while I'd listened to their voices all my life, I never saw one up close. Not until that night, when I became one myself. But when she asked again, I answered: "To see you." Which was God's own truth, even though I didn't know it before that moment.

Clementine took my hand and washed away the purpose that brought me there. She showed me the little girl who died inside her the night we parted for good. Clementine named her Birdie for the cook back in the big house in North Carolina. That pretty angel at her mama's side looked past me and floated right through my bones. What I felt right then was a fearsome brew of peace and sorrow. I knew that it was my last night, that I would never save another Negro. Not the three inside the cellar, not my own Silas.

I had the cellar door opened when they got to me. The pattyrollers meant to take me—not kill me—sell me back down south with the others. As one held me against the open root cellar door, the other looked me over and said my size and my missing fingers meant they wouldn't get much of a price. While they talked it over, I signaled for the three inside to go, to run and hope for the best. Then I made like a madwoman, hollering, biting, kicking the white men, hoping to distract them from the runners.

The one whose hands weren't on me fired his gun. It was fast, and if there was pain, I didn't last long enough to feel it much. Quick as rain, my old friend came and wrapped herself around me. My eyes rose high up into the night sky, and I saw them pack two Negro men into a wagon. Don't know what happened to the third. I always think about him and hope he got away. Maybe it was my Silas. What that would mean.

Now the yellow girl asks, "Can you see me?"

"Get closer to the light. Now I can."

"Do you know me?"

"No."

"Please look closer. *Please.* I told you my ancestor escaped from here. Could he have been one of your boys?"

It's that needing, pleading sound in her voice that makes me look. Really look hard. Oh, now. I just don't know. Maybe. The hope I've been keeping alive all this time comes from nothing but a picture my mind made up. The truth is, I wouldn't know their faces anyway, besides the beauty, besides the blackness. Louis was nine when they took him from me, Silas, not even four. It's been too long to remember what they looked like.

But then I hear a small voice say, "Mama." I see him now, tugging on Dominique's arm. He says "Mama" once more, but she chastises him for disturbing the ceremony, telling him go play on his *eye pad*.

"Mama, I'm scared."

I tell him, "Hush now, baby. It's all right." I rise out of this body and go to him. His eyes open wide in fright. He calls louder for his mama, and I see he's not mine. His mama is the yellow girl, but I believe there's something about him—the eyes, the forehead—that came from me. When I reach for his face, the boy jerks away, upsetting the candles on the windowsill. One catches the curtains, which light right up.

So this time, I'm here when the fire starts. The first thing I do is save the little boy who's not my son but just might be my own great-great-great-grandbaby. I take his hand, cover him with my soul, and pull him free. I mean to save his mama next, but when I turn back to the house, it's too late. She's gone the way of the rest.

And hopping through the flames, laughing, tossing the embers around like pine cones, is a little girl. The fire can't touch her shining smile, or her wild cloud of hair.

~♉~

The flames grow, leaping, popping, swallowing the place they called Whittaker House, its stories, its secrets from recent days and long ago. It consumes the traces of blood, the remnants of skin, of clothing and cast-off possessions of guests who have come and gone. All of it slowly, thoroughly burns to the ground.

And here's what else is true. The day after that fire—the property's second, the complete fire—a woman historian from the Monterey Historical Center, her fire inspector husband, and his real estate agent brother all come to take a look at the ruined farmhouse that still belongs to the Whittaker family.

Someone suggests that the fire got started for the sake of an insurance policy, but someone else argues that there's no one around to collect. Maxine Whittaker, the most recent inhabitant, who turned the place into an Airbnb, has been all over the news lately, suspected to be on the lam somewhere—with a stolen baby, a disguise, and an alias. Maxine's late husband, Claude L. Whittaker, has an estranged daughter, an expat living in Osaka with her husband and children. The house is officially owned by the daughter's cousins—the Brothers Burke, founding partners of an entertainment law firm in Los Angeles. Between them they are childless but for a single heir—Kaye Ayesha Leeds—who knows neither her biological father nor the fact that the property would one day be passed down to her.

And the Burke brothers' mother, an octogenarian by the name of Leigh-Ann Whittaker-Burke, the only family member left in Massachusetts, is equally inaccessible. A resident of the Birches Assisted Living and Memory Care Facility in Lenox, Leigh-Ann suffers from dementia. She believes herself to be a psychic and seer, calls herself Lady Leanna, Mistress of the Occult, and has a bad habit of escaping at night. Once she disappeared for a week and was discovered walking barefoot through a cemetery in Salem.

A call to the Birches reveals that Leigh-Ann's bed was found empty again the morning after the fire. No one has seen her since. And when the remains of the fire get processed, the victims identified, Mrs. Whittaker-Burke is among them. There is also a Giovanni Bates, an Ayana Chesterfield, a Nerissa Miller, and a Dominique Sowande—members of the Seekers, a group of African-descended young people known to hold séances to contact fugitive ancestors. But one of the bodies puzzles the medical examiner. The texture of its bones does not match the rest. It is later determined by a forensic anthropologist that the bones, including two fingers that are nothing but stumps, are over two centuries old. The Seekers, says the anthropologist, must have exhumed that body from a nearby burial site.

Well, I can't say anything about that.

But our truth is this. We are done with our unanswered prayers and wishes and questions. I—Little Eight-Fingered Annie—Clementine and Birdie, the nameless ones who died in the first fire, all the others whose spirits have inhabited the place. We are done, forever done, with the ache of *Almost*.

I am finished with the pain of missing my children. For I can believe it now: it was my Louis who stole away north by the light of the Drinking Gourd, who escaped the catchers here in the Berkshire Mountains, and fathered generations, leading to the yellow girl with the undone hair, and finally, to her little boy—the one I saved, to whom I leave my dreams. I am finished with the riddles and the rage. Ready to leave this world and move on to the next.

So follow me. Let us float with these embers riding on the wind. Grab your baby, take my hand, and away we'll fly.

AUTHOR'S NOTE

Whittaker House is based on a real former Underground Railroad safe-house in Monterey, Massachusetts, that belonged to my father-in-law, Gary Rosenberg, and my stepmother-in-law, Linda Waxman. They bought the house a few years before my husband and I got married. We spent countless weekends up there, especially once my children were born. It was "the country" to all of us, the site of cookouts and family gatherings and endless make-believe games that my children and their cousins played in the dark, creepy nooks of the "old" sections of the house.

The root cellar, once a refuge for African Americans who'd escaped enslavement, lies—as it does in this novel—in the center of the property, its wooden door embedded in a hillock. There was one nineteenth-century formerly enslaved woman who had made her way into the main house. She'd expired there, allegedly leaving her spirit to haunt the premises. My stepmother-in-law shared this story with me, igniting the spark that would one day become *Embers on the Wind*. Who had that woman been? Why did she come into the house, when it was so close to the road, so dangerous? How had she died? I would never stop thinking about her, inventing possibilities.

As the only Black woman in the family, possibly the only Black adult to visit this New England farmhouse since the days of the

Underground, I had this hope that the spirit would be happy to see me—her descendent, her sister, many times removed.

Late, late at night, when all was silent, safe for shy spirits, I would dare myself to venture downstairs to the unrenovated section of the house, which smelled of old wood, of life and books and long-extinguished fires in the hearth. I walked those creaky floorboards, silently calling to the ghost.

Like Galen in "The Story of the Birthing Room," I wondered: Did I stir the spirit's curiosity as she stirred mine? After two centuries of white people creeping about, making coffee and pies and pots of chowder, what would she think of a free Black woman, a member of this white family who sits at the table, swims, and hikes with the others? Who reads, writes, takes in whatever entertainment the others do?

What would the spirit think of other Black women like me—who appear to live easily in the white world? Educated alongside white people, working in white spaces, meeting white friends for intimate coffee chats? We know the protocols of whiteness better than white people. Many of us deliver what the white world asks of us—politeness, clear diction, fit bodies, straightened hair—with little effort. Have we arrived? Is our brand of freedom what the enslaved woman had sought? Or are we merely clinging to survival as she once did?

But no, I told myself. Thanks to the resilience of all the formerly enslaved who fought and gained freedom, I have some power. Over my destiny. Over my voice. So, I wondered, could my words heal the spirit woman's soul? Could my story provide her peace? After all, what she'd sought for herself came true for me.

Almost.

ACKNOWLEDGMENTS

I would like to thank my agent, Dr. Uwe Stender of Triada US, for being a champion of this book and for believing unflinchingly in my talent long before *Embers on the Wind* was anything but a notion. I would like to thank my brilliant, supportive, and super-insightful editors Selena James and Michelle Flythe, both of whom saw my book through fresh eyes, understood my vision, and inspired me to strengthen the links between the stories and develop the characters in ways I had not thought of. I would also like to thank the entire team at Little A.

Thank you to my beta readers, LaToya Jordan, Kelly Tsai, and of course, my friend and "Blewish Sistah," TaRessa Stovall, who has seen me through my writing journey for nearly twenty years. Thank you to Cavarly Garrett and Emily Rothenberg for more early reads. Thank you to Audrey Rosenberg for her limitless support, friendship, and insights.

Thank you to Gary Rosenberg and Linda Waxman for their loving support, for the years in the place that evolved in my imagination to become Whittaker House, for telling me about the root cellar and the lady ghost.

Thank you to Wilma and Steve Rifkin for talking things through, for cheering me on, for hearing me out far into the night. Much love to you both.

Thank you to Portia Poindexter, who suffered through the novels I tried to write back when we were in seventh and eighth grade, to Helaine Worrell and Erika Gaynor, who have tolerated my endless ramblings for too many decades to count. You three are my sisters, who know me inside and out and believe in me even when I question myself.

Thank you to Cate and Evan Baily for encouraging me from the beginning of my adult novel-writing aspirations. Thank you to Amy Baily for her guidance and support. Thank you to Karen Dulberg Rousso, my brilliant friend, for being there to talk about Every. Single. Thing.

I would also like to thank my wonderful Debut 2022 authors' group and the Women's Fiction Writers Association for letting me vent and offering guidance throughout this process. Thank you to Diane T. Wakefield and Jamara Wakefield for their insights on Dorchester in the 1980s.

Regarding my research for Timothy's fascination with prehistoric marine reptiles, I want to acknowledge the online reference site Thoughtco.com as well as National Geographic's online *Sea Monsters Education* series.

Thank you to Bill Shunn, the *Piltdown Review*'s editor, who loved "The Story of the Birthing Room," a very, very early version of which won second prize in that journal's 2018 Winter-Spring Fiction Contest. Thank you to *Literary Mama*'s Felicity Landa and Colleen Kearney Rich, who published an early version of "The Coffee Shop" and nominated it for a Pushcart Prize.

Thank you to the Spirit of the House on Beartown Mountain Road for living dormant in my writer's brain for all these years, waiting for the right moment to emerge. Thank you for letting me imagine you all kinds of ways before I came up with Clementine—named for my paternal great-grandmother, Clementine Guidry, who was born in Louisiana in 1860.

In terms of my research on the era of enslavement, I owe much thanks to a variety of sources, including the wonderful work *Slavery's Descendants: Shared Legacies of Race and Reconciliation*, edited by

Dionne Ford and Jill Strauss, and *The Long Walk to Freedom: Runaway Slave Narratives*, edited by Devon W. Carbado and Donald Weise. Also, collections of slave narratives from the National Humanities Center, *Essence Live*'s brief film "Were Slaves Really 'Well-Fed'?" hosted by Dana Blair, the digital archives found on PBS's Black Culture Connection site, and the digital archives of the Canadian Encyclopedia.

I would also like to honor my great-grandparents, George Williamson, who was born enslaved in North Carolina in 1844, and Mary Williamson, née Mosby, born enslaved in Louisiana in 1846. Both lived to see Emancipation, to marry and raise five children, the youngest of whom was my grandfather, Moses Williamson, who supported his family through the Great Depression by working as a Pullman porter. Moses and my grandmother, Albertina Williamson, née Hutchinson, had seven children, the youngest being my father.

The generations of my father's family were widely spaced. My grandfather Moses's parents were in their forties when he was born; my grandfather was near fifty when my father was born. Dad was in his forties when I was born, meaning that none of us ever had the good fortune of meeting our grandparents. Nevertheless, pieces of them all live on in me and whisper in the pages of this book.

Thank you to my son, Theo Rosenberg, for his early reads and input on the "action" scenes. Thank you to my daughter, Zoe Rosenberg, my Girl with the Cloud Hair, my muse and inspiration, for challenging me to think everything through from all angles.

Most of all, thank you to my husband, Jonathan Rosenberg—my rock, my first reader, my re-reader, my *if-you're-awake-can-you-just-quickly-look-at-this-one-thing-before-you-fall-asleep* reader, my true love, who, when the kids were little, went out of his way to give me writing time even when I didn't ask, who makes me laugh every day even when I'm stressed and overreacting to life's big, small, and medium-size hurdles.

Last of all, I want to acknowledge my parents, Mel and Lorraine Williamson, who loved and supported me from my birth until their deaths. From an early age, they instilled in me a love of books and creativity and cheered for just about every mark I put on paper. To them I owe everything. Mom, Dad, wherever you are, I love you, I thank you, and I regret only that you did not live to read this book. I hope it would make you proud.

QUESTIONS FOR DISCUSSION

1. In *Embers on the Wind*, the notion of "*Almost*" means coming right up to the threshold of freedom only to be foiled by circumstance. The cellar spirits, who perished in the first fire, made it "*Almost*" all the way to Canada, "were on the verge of hope," when their dreams were dashed by flames. More than two centuries later, Kaye and Galen are both affluent, educated, successful Black women. Would you say that they have attained the freedom sought by the cellar spirits? Does the fact that both women have white husbands and inhabit largely white spaces have an impact on their brand of freedom? How do you think the thread of *Almost* still touches the lives of Black women in the twenty-first century?

2. A tragic theme in this book is the separation of mothers and children. Some examples are Little Annie, whose six sons are sold away during the age of enslavement; Pam, whose infant daughter, Ayesha Kaye, is stolen by social workers in 1984; and Baby Olivia, who is abducted in 2018 following the death of her parents. What do you think about this historic breaking of Black familial family

bonds? In what ways do you think this legacy affects Black parents today?

3. Conversely, adoption—formal and informal—is presented in this book as the flip side to the coin of parent-child separation. While Kaye's adoption has been kept secret, Timothy's is visible and discussed in his family. What do you think the impact of race is on these two adoptive families? How do you imagine Michelle—who becomes a school social worker many years after caring for her sickly brother, Gordy—will take to adoptive motherhood, given that Sidney is the progeny of Dominique and Wesley?

4. Catherine, the only white mother in the book, appears to have more parenting challenges than Kaye, given Barrett's anger, Timothy's autism, and her own resentment of Peter. While what we see of Kaye's homelife seems happier than Catherine's, do you recognize any freedoms and liberties Catherine might have that Kaye lacks?

5. Are there ways in which affluence does or does not shield Kaye from racism?

6. Regarding Michelle's 1999 assault at the hands of Mr. Iler: Do you think Kaye was responsible? Should she have alerted her parents to Mr. Iler's voyeuristic behavior? What do you think about the therapist Calliope's unconventional prescription for healing Michelle's trauma: to dance and reclaim her body and then return to the Mountains to reclaim the narrative?

7. There are a variety of sexual and romantic relationships depicted in the novel, including the tender courting of Clementine by Josiah; Pam's experimentation with the oldest Burke son; Catherine's flashback of seducing Lawrence Reeves, the Black lacrosse player; Rob's passive longing for Galen, who has lost her sex drive due to postpartum depression; and Michelle and Dominique's heady "girl-vampire" romance. Do you think the author is deliberately offering up these pairings as antidotes or counter-tropes to the traumatic image of enslaver-enslaved sexual violence?

8. What do you think about the acknowledgment of colorism in the book? For Clementine, being light skinned earns her privileges but also puts her in harm's way. Although she gets an easier workload and rides in covered carriages, she is the constant victim of the master's sexual violence. Later, Kaye is known as the "pretty" sister for having light skin. Ma sees Kaye, but not her darker younger sister Michelle, as deserving of protection. Little Annie, whose boys were all "midnight black," is reluctant to trust Dominique due to her "high yellow" skin tone. What impact if any has colorism had on your life or the lives of your friends and family?

9. For both Kaye in "The Obelisk" and Dominique in "Turpentine," DNA tests hold profound discoveries about their biological origins and degree of African ancestry. Have you or anyone you know had your DNA tested? Did the results surprise you? Did they impact your sense of identity in any way?

10. In "A Gift from the Earthbound," Leigh-Ann tells Maxine, "Earthbound spirits are earthbound for specific reasons. Something is incomplete for them in this world." All the supernatural elements—Kaye's visions in the Obelisk, Lady Leanna's summoning, the Seekers' séances—are aimed at solving something incomplete, usually discovering a connection to one's familial origins. Birdie is the book's most mystical character. As the spirit of a stillborn child, she not only shapeshifts to appear different ages, she is also the only ghost who freely communicates with a modern character without being summoned. What do you think Birdie offers the characters she meets? What is incomplete for her?

11. *Embers on the Wind*'s central, silent main character is Whittaker House, a former stop on the Underground Railroad. The farmhouse bears witness to the three time periods shown in the book: the mid-nineteenth century, following the reestablishment of the second Fugitive Slave Act; the 1980s, when Laura Ashley décor was all the rage; and the current twenty-first century Airbnb era. With each subsequent age, the Black people who visit are granted increasing access to its space. While Clementine only sees the insides of the root cellar and the birthing room, Pam is allowed into the kitchen and later into one of the upstairs bedrooms. By the twenty-first century, Timothy and later Galen have free range of the house and its grounds. How do the Black characters in the book differ in their perception of the house? Think about the houses and buildings you have visited in your life. How does your perception of these places depend on their history and their current context?

ABOUT THE AUTHOR

Photo © 2021 Michael Stahl

Lisa Williamson Rosenberg is a writer, former ballet dancer, and psychotherapist specializing in depression, complex trauma, and racial identity. Lisa's essays have appeared in Longreads, Narratively, Mamalode, the *Defenders Online*, and *The Common*. Her fiction has been published in the *Piltdown Review* and in *Literary Mama*, where Lisa received a Pushcart nomination. A born-and-raised New Yorker and a mother of two college students, Lisa now lives in Montclair, New Jersey, with her husband and dog. For more information, visit www.lisawrosenberg.com.

Made in the USA
Monee, IL
22 August 2022

12231985R10142